I0685881

THE FIRE'S SOUL

BOOK THREE OF THE CRYSTAL MYTHOS TRILOGY

AUSTEN RODGERS

Copyright © 2020 by Austen Rodgers
www.austenrodgers.com
Illustration and Cover Design by Jeff Brown
Edited by Bodie Dykstra
Interior Images by Stacy Sheppard

First Edition: October 2020
ISBN 978-1-950278-07-7 (paperback)
ISBN 978-1-950278-06-0 (ebook)
ISBN 978-1-950-278-08-4 (audiobook)
Published by Hypercube Press
www.hypercubepress.com

HYPERCUBE **PRESS**
SCIENCE FICTION AND FANTASY

CONTENTS

PROLOGUE

L
ike the sharp crack of a whip, she was there. Life flooded her veins, and joy seemed to radiate from the atmosphere. There was a sort of harmony in her connection to the things around her: the living plants and creatures, the static of energy in the air, and the very fiber of this reality. It was peaceful. Almost everything she could possibly have wanted was in the courtyard with her, but just one thing was missing, and she couldn't quite put her finger on it.

Cobblestone paths snaked through flower gardens and precisely shaped bushes, tall and green. A yellow sun lit the blue sky, its heat warping the air atop the clay-shingled roofs that loomed over the hedge wall. Where was she? She didn't know, and it didn't matter. This was right where she was supposed to be, and something deep inside told her that this place was where everyone started.

The goddess rose to her feet, soaked in the warm air with her chin high, and set down a path through the garden. The blue gown floated around in the breeze, tickling her bare ankles with each step. She liked the color of it. There was a reason she wore it and a reason she had arrived there in the courtyard; she just had to find it for herself. To be among the sun, the air, and the plants was beautiful, but this place wasn't *just* for her. It belonged to others, too.

The weaving cobblestone paths did not confuse her; a sense led her through it even though it was her first time here. She exited through the flowered archway and stepped onto the narrow street outside the garden. The yellow stone buildings loomed over her, and the road stretched on before her. She passed the wooden doors and shuttered windows of hollow, empty apartments, so many of them without so much as an alleyway or an intersection. All was quiet but for the padding of her feet. Soon the streets would be packed, the homes occupied and brimming with others like her. She knew she was just one of the first.

The air opened up around her as she stepped out before a gatehouse where thick sandstone walls came together. Other roads joined there, too, coming from other gardens and places even farther beyond the city. At her approach, the gatehouse winches rattled and spun, lifting the portcullis off the ground. Heavy iron-banded doors swung open with a groan, and a man stepped out.

The hair on his head and face was black, and his smile formed warm creases under his eyes. The pull was irresistible; there was nothing she could do but reach out and embrace him in a long hug. They took hands and twirled through the doors under the gatehouse and into the courtyard beyond. Betwixt marble statues of men and women and sun-soaked benches, they danced until the sweetness of their laughter filled the empty courtyard. He was a companion. A brother or maybe a lover.

We were meant for this.

"Have you chosen a name yet?" His voice was smooth and comforting.

She furrowed her brow. What was her name to be? The thought that she might need one had not occurred to her until now, and the seemingly endless number of possibilities only worsened her uncertainty. There was a name that was just for her, if only she could remember it.

Seeming to sense her frustration, he smiled and squeezed her tighter, his white teeth glimmering in the light. His adoration of her was apparent, and he was handsome. Their compatibility was, dare she think, perfect. "That's all right," he said. "Your name will come to you. I call myself Abzu."

He pulled her by the arm and took her through the courtyard to the base of the temple. Earthen stairs of a brownish yellow zigged and zagged up the face of that multileveled ziggurat. They briefly paused on a flat landing to catch their breath, where a dark doorway set into the bricks seemed to hide mysterious secrets beyond it. But the interior of the temple was not their goal. They left the dark archway behind them and pushed on to the top.

A belvedere of marble pillars and ornamental balustrade enclosed this level's parapet. In the center, there was a deep well that brought up its water from the core of the world. She placed her hands on the bricks, looked down, and watched the shimmering glow deep beneath the water's surface, and she knew the well's importance at once.

"That's where we come from," she said as she realized it.

Abzu leaned against the well next to her, the wind blowing his black hair. "It is. Father, who was once one, is now many. He's done it for us. For our joy. We're very lucky."

She smiled, knowing it was true.

"So have you thought of your name yet? I want to know it."

"No," she said. "I'm sorry." And she walked past the well and placed her hands on the railing, which was warm from the sunlight. From the ziggurat's pinnacle, she could see out over the homes that seemed to stretch for miles in every direction and could spot the garden she had come from, as well as others like it. But beyond the city's fringes, the water of a crystal-blue sea shimmered. At once, she yearned to be a part of it, to swim underneath its lapping waves of foam and among the coral-forested floors.

A shout filled her ear as something whizzed past her head. A long, black, and blurry thing that scared her so much she dropped to her knees and clutched the side of her head, slamming her eyelids shut in terror. Then there was laughter far off and growing quieter. A warm hand on her shoulder. When she looked, Abzu was there, lifting her to her feet and taking her chin into his hand with such tenderness she could not help but follow along in hopes he would console her with a kiss.

He said, "Don't be afraid. Look."

The black blur wasn't very big anymore, and it wasn't mysterious or frightening at all. The thing that had flown past her head was a person, arms stretched as he soared through the air. As he flew, he yipped and cheered until he disappeared between the rows of houses below.

"He's new, too," Abzu said. "We are all trying to find our place. Our others."

"Why?"

"Because Father thought it was best that we love each other, communicate with one another, and be joyous."

"But *he* didn't love me," she said, pointing to where the

man had just been flying. "I could feel no love like I do for you. He laughed when he scared me, and I was not joyous."

"I do not think it was his intention to frighten you so, but that is free will. You cannot control others' feelings. If you could force someone to love you as I do, it would mean nothing to have it."

She didn't like that answer. It was wrong. If everyone loved her like Abzu did, she would be happy. And Father wanted them all to be full of joy. He *made* them to be full of joy.

Abzu produced a golden mirror from behind his back. It was small, and she wasn't sure how he'd been hiding it, but the moment she took the fragile thing into her hands, it didn't matter. In the reflection, she could see her black eyebrows and her long hair, which trailed down to her hips. Her sharp, angled nose was there, her lips and her jaw. She was all there, in that reflection, but so was the watcher.

In the deep cosmos of her pupils, there was a twinkle of another's eyes that was not her own. How long had the watcher been there with her, watching the goddess's every move, feeling her every emotion and thinking her every thought? The goddess was not sure.

The watcher was all anger and fury yet so enveloped in sorrow and regret, the goddess knew. She was a woman with blonde hair and green eyes so full of tears and terror. She thrashed as she cried, and the horror on the watcher's face was a sign that this was not the first thing she had seen.

Was the watcher from the past or the future? The goddess wasn't sure of much, but she knew the other's presence didn't matter to her now, for all she could do was watch from inside herself.

"So what is your name?" Abzu asked again, his voice deep and warming.

The watcher disappeared from the pools in her eyes. She lowered the mirror and forgot about her immediately like the woman had never even been there in the first place. The goddess smiled and said, "My name is Ti'amat."

CHAPTER ONE

Unlike how the worlds began, Angela exploded *into* her body. Too many sensations flooded her all at once; air clapped against her eardrums, light seared her eyes, and her flesh, as she slipped back into it, was crushed with what felt like the weight of a thousand boulders. The bed lurched underneath her, filled her belly with the sensation of falling as she gasped for air.

Ejected from the weylines, she found that her time walking in the goddess's skin was complete. Everything was spinning and spinning. Her mind, and the world around her.

Wind howled through a crack in the wall where rays of light broke through, highlighting the specks of floating dust in the air. The room was decrepit and dirty, so foreign she did not realize it had been her own until moments passed. Clothes had been ripped from the dresser and tossed onto the closet floor. There were so many that the door could not close. In place of the bedroom window was a misshapen fireplace of red clay bricks that had been shoddily thrown together with no mortar. The fire was nothing but coal and wispy strands of smoke now, but since when had all this been changed?

Every bit of the brain in her skull was an inferno of blistering pain. Swirling memories smothered her from every angle, flashing through her mind like lightning. They were like a deck of cards, shuffled and out of order, making even her most recent memories hazy and mixed with others that were not her own.

Images and feelings blended together. Some were unrecognizable and foreign; there were places in her mind that she had never been to, people and faces she had never met, but they seemed real. Those sleeping visions had not been dreams; she had truly been there, not in this body, but in *hers*.

She clutched the blanket over her, soaking in the little warmth it trapped. Not all those memories swimming in her head were her own. And as she thought and separated the ones that were her own from those that were *hers*, she remembered what had happened. She remembered the Nephilim she had fought over Dingir and the strange corruption that seemed to eat away at the creature from the inside out. The black energy that pounded the air and melted through flesh and scale. She remembered Udug and the darkness inside him. The hand she had taken, the pitch-black void in Donny's eyes and the words he had said: "Just touch my skin and I'll show you everything from Vi'dinor and even worlds earlier."

Angela remembered whose neck her sword had bitten into.

Where is Neti?

A rush of terror gripped her from the inside out, spurring her into motion. She threw the blankets off, failed to find her footing, and fell off the side of the bed, only to vomit thick, coagulated yellow bile onto the hardwood. Her head pounded like never before. Muscles ached when they shouldn't have, but she wiped her mouth on the back of her hand and swayed as she tried to rise to her feet again.

The mortar in the wall had crumbled and separated between the slabs of sandstone, and she watched the crack grow larger as the familiar sensation of falling returned. She stumbled, caught herself on the dresser. The black-hilted sword with a square, golden guard rattled to the floor next to her. Teshub's sword. She hadn't noticed it leaning against the furniture.

As she bent to pick it up, the metal platform beneath her home flexed downward, then came back up again as it bobbed in the wind. That was not typical. Haunted by the memories and dreaming visions that kept hitting her mind, she was begging to feel sick again, but she had to move, had to discover what happened after she had taken that hand.

Clutching the sword tightly, Angela pushed herself through the bedroom door and out into the living areas of her home. It was in a sorry state when the Nephilim had come, but now it was worse. A decrepit, dim and dirty shell of what it used to be when she and Michael lived there. Waste and trash were stuffed into corners. Cracks in the walls let frost and snow trickle in, while the crumbling ceiling dropped piles of stone where it was the weakest.

But the red embers in the fireplace meant that someone had been looking after it. And recently. Scattered throughout the mess, there were other signs of life. Underneath the kitchen window, a book had been laid open on the table to hold its page. She made her way across the creaking floor and gently touched the kettle and mug next to it with the back of her hand. Not warm, but not as cold as the air around her, either. Someone had been living with her, and she hoped against hope that it was Neti.

With a trembling hand, Angela walked to the front door, grabbed the doorknob, and turned it. As she pushed the door open, a chilling blast of wind tore through her clothes and sank its claws into her skin. From the unusual cold and the sight of what was left of Dingir, she lost her breath.

Sections of the golden roadway outside her home had been ripped free from the platform and fallen into the sky below the city. Thick walls of frost and ice clung to the faces of tall apartment buildings and homes up and down the street, the dangling icicles fatter and thicker than trees. Out of the seventeen homes she could see from her patio, only hers had a narrow path cleared of snow. There was so much snow piled on the road in front of her home and in the air that there was nothing to see but white. Not a single person was out in that storm.

Does anyone still live in Dingir? Where is everyone?

Angela braced herself and stepped forward. Down the steps and out the front gate, she went as quickly as she could. If there was anyone to find, they would be at the Ascendancy in the center of town. The air was cold and scentless as it whipped wave after wave of blinding snow across what was left of the street. Already, her skin and toes were growing numb, and the path in front of her was being buried before her eyes. She turned off the street and into an alley, getting out of the wind's path that went long-ways down her street.

Before she reached the street on the other side of the block, she came to an open section of missing metal plates. Through the hole, she could see the blue and cloudy sky beneath the city, the rusted pipes smiling up at her like a mouth with rotten teeth. Ice crusted the outer edges of the hole, threatening to throw off her balance if she tried to jump across. She thought about it until the platform beneath her feet bobbed and the buildings around her groaned as metal rubbed against metal. Clutching herself, she turned back. It was clear; Dingir was crumbling and abandoned. The fact that she had woken up in her home maybe just a few short months before it fell from decay was frightening.

As cold as it was, the only way to the Ascendancy was through the snowy streets. She debated heading back home and getting better clothes. Whoever had laid her in bed had dressed her well, but thick woolen socks were not enough to stave off the bitter bite of soaked socks in the snow. Still, she couldn't will herself to head that way. Not with the memory replaying over and over in her head. She had to know if Neti was dead.

With a deep breath, she rushed from the building's cover and out into the whistling wind again. Head down, she charged down the block. In places, the snow reached the middle of her thigh, but she pressed on and plowed through it. When her bones began to freeze and her muscles tightened, she reached for her souls' energy, as she probably should have at first, but felt that something was different.

In the core of the Anunnaki soul was a speck of black. Touching it only made it bigger, more apparent, more alive, and when she realized what the mark she now bore was, terror raced through her. Like a hook, the black was buried deep and anchored so tightly to her soul that she could not rip it free. A tendril of oozing darkness throbbed, led away from her soul, and connected her to a goddess she did not want to think about. Not now. She had to focus on one thing at a time or else her head might combust.

At her command, energy and warmth surged through

her, and she regained her speed, dashing through the drifts and down the streets until the white steeple of the Ascendancy loomed over her. Most of the ornamental brass spikes on the roof's edges were still there, and even a few stained-glass windows remained intact, but the place where she had served her people was nothing like what it had been.

Before she reached the door, ice underneath the snow caught her off guard. Her foot slipped out from under her, twisting her ankle. She fell, and her weight slammed into the ground. Everything was cold. Everything hurt. Freezing white flakes clung to her as she rose and cursed into the air.

There was naught but the sound of the wind. Like the rest of Dingir, the Ascendancy seemed like a desolate ruin, empty and abandoned, but she clenched her jaw and limped for the oak double doors, and they swung open.

Two men dressed in scraps of leather armor and thick animal hides stepped out into the cold. They winced and shielded their faces against the weather, and their eyes grew wide when they noticed her trudging closer. Beyond the bearded, dirty men and the open door, the inside was dimly lit with flickering firelight. Broken chairs thrown into a pile confirmed the worst; the Ascendancy was nothing like it was before, but gods, it looked *warm*. The strangers rushed to her, scooped her up by the arms, and began to help her walk. Tarnished and rusting tether guns hung beneath the folds of their furs, swaying as they pulled her inside.

Soldiers, she thought. *So some form of the Ascendancy still exists.*

One slammed the doors shut while the other settled Angela onto the cold floor and covered her with his cloak. She shivered, catching her breath and listening to them speak.

"It's her, isn't it?"

"Who else could it be?"

"I don't know. Give me a break."

"It has to be her. I can't believe it. She's awake."

"What should we do?"

With quivering lips, Angela lifted her head and spoke, her breath fogging in the air. "T-Take me to Neti. W-W-Where is he?"

What little color was in the soldiers' faces seemed to drain all at once. "The Dalkhu boy?" one of them asked. "The one who fought with you and the others against the Nephilim?"

She could only nod and clutch the cloak tighter around her.

The soldier struggled to find his words as he fingered his beard, but finally, he said, "I-I can take you to him."

The other man turned to him with a strange look in his eyes, like he was asking his cohort if he was certain, then shrugged.

Angela pulled a little more heat from her souls, then lifted herself from the ground, yet still her knees wobbled. The soldiers helped her stand, pulled her back toward the door they had just entered. Angela sighed. They were going outside into the freezing cold again. Confused, she looked up at their ragged features and asked, "You have your shifters. Can't you just take me through the veils? I-I'm not able to take us myself. Otherwise—"

"We can't." the first soldier said, shaking his head. "City's got no crystals left. We go on foot."

Another pang of terror rippled through her. Things were adding up, pointing to the fear she swallowed and the thoughts she was hiding from herself in the back of her mind. Those thoughts were dire, and she could not believe them until she saw everything for herself. She was not ready to accept them.

The door swung open, and they stepped out into the bitter cold, then traversed the mounds of snow that smothered what used to be the front lawn of the Ascendancy. There had always been the occasional snowfall in Dingir, but Angela couldn't remember ever seeing so much frost, ice, and precipitation.

The soldiers did their best to support her injured ankle and keep her moving forward. She let them lead her and focused more on sorting out the swirl of thoughts and memories in her head than the ground right in front of her. She was thankful that their bodies helped block some of the wind.

Where they were going wasn't far, just across the lawn and the road in front, but it still felt like she'd been freezing for ages before they entered the enclosed courtyard of an apartment complex. Behind those stone walls, most of the wind was staved off and the snow was kept clear except for the water crystals that clung to the branches of potted pines and firs. There were dozens and dozens of them, rows resting against walls and on benches. The soldiers urged her forward, then stopped before one. There, on the outside of the pot, the old symbol for "Dalkhu" and "boy" had been pressed into the clay next to his name. Angela dropped to her knees.

It was true—she had killed Neti.

Tears stung her eyes. Her memories were no lie. As she had moved to slash her sword at Udug and the goddess that possessed him, Neti had teleported between them and took the blow to make Angela believe that the goddess was real and that she really did have the power to take over a soul entirely. Neti's eyes had been black. Black like Udug's, black like the weylines, and black like the hook that was now attached to her soul. She'd opened Neti's throat with her sword.

Angela found herself clutching the frozen pot, shaking and heaving as her crying slowed. Something was coming, she knew. On the horizon, a storm was forming. Brooding and coming closer. It was more than just a hunch, far deeper and more certain. Nothing would be the same again.

A soldier grabbed her by the arm, tried to pull her onto her feet and away from Neti's cremated remains, but Angela would not go. She shook, kicked his shin until he was driven back. She dove, grabbed the pot with both arms, and *pushed* with her souls. With all the swirling pain and the memories mixing with the dreams in her skull, traveling through the space between worlds was a challenge. Staring directly at the pot in her arms—the source of her grief—as she went did not help one bit.

Over and over, she thought, *I killed him... I killed him.*

When she finally got a hold of herself and her will grew strong enough, she slipped back out from the endless halls of empty space and staggered onto the dirt underneath a bush. Branches and thorns clawed at her skin as she fought to regain her footing and stand. The garden that rested on the sinkhole floor was not as she remembered it.

What used to be their home was now fully overgrown; hazel bushes and fir trees reached up to her chest, as well as roses and acacias, while vines clung to the sinkhole's gray stone walls that rose up around her. It was warm. *Summer* warm, and humid. It was just a few weeks ago that this place was naught but ash from the Nephilim's attack, but if she'd been sleeping long enough for winter to pass and wild seeds and saplings to grow up to her chest, *years* had passed.

Angela swallowed the thought, burying it deep inside until she could deal with it. Hoping to find a shovel, she searched the three old chambers that she, Teshub, and Neti had slept in. There were still rotting scraps of burnt wood, fabric, trash, and now animal feces, but everything of value was gone. Even the chest that had survived the fire, stuffed underneath her bed frame, was now missing entirely. Looted by humans, most likely. So she took to digging out a hole in the sinkhole garden by hand, right next to where they had buried Teshub.

As more and more dirt packed underneath her nails, she reassured herself that this place was where Neti's body belonged. For the Dalkhu, it was custom for a councilman's family to be buried with him in the crypts beneath the Kissum. Neti's father rested down in those caverns, but his dad, Teshub, the one who raised him, would be right next to him in the sinkhole they had shared. That was where he belonged.

When the hole she had dug was large enough, Angela placed the entire pot inside and used a rock to break the hardened clay. Dirt and ash spilled out as she picked out the pieces of pottery, leaving nothing but him and the small tree he fed. After filling the hole with dirt, she rose and took a step back to look down at it, hoping the tree wouldn't die from the sudden change in climate.

Tears dribbled down her cheeks when she told him she was sorry. With an iron grip, she clutched the piece of pottery that bore his name, treasuring the memento. And then something stirred inside her. A looming presence grew more and more clear until, like a viper's strike, she was there in a flash.

"Touching." It was a mother's voice, soft and gentle.

Equal parts terror and fury raged through Angela's

blood. Even without turning her head, she knew who was now in the sinkhole with her. The aura was all too familiar; she'd spent eons feeling her presence and hearing her voice as she watched events of other worlds unfold through her eyes. Angela wanted to believe it was all a spinning, dizzy dream that clogged her mind now, but she remembered enough from those dreams to know, without a doubt, that Ti'amat was as real as a goddess could be.

As Angela spun to face her, she noticed that everything around her had stilled. Her heart yet raced, but the wind no longer pushed the tops of the plants around her. There were no more birds chirping and no hot and humid breeze against her skin.

When they first encountered one another, Ti'amat had come to Angela in Udug's gray-haired body, then jumped into Donny's when the former died, but she wasn't sure if what was in front of her now was a real body or an illusion. Like Angela had seen in her dreams, Ti'amat stood before her in a tall, elegant body, and she was, in fact, a woman. Long black hair reached down to her hips. Thin, high cheekbones and crow's feet gave her an air of age and wisdom, but she still retained a venomous beauty.

"You're awake," the goddess said, sweet and warm. "I didn't realize that taking you out of your body would take such a toll on you."

"Why are you doing this?" Angela blurted. Tears began to roll down her face again as anxiety and dizziness returned to her. She was in the presence of a *goddess*. The blackness in her chest was smothering, nauseating. "Taking hold of people like this is wrong. It's worse than wrong. It's *sick*. And why show me all these terrible memories I can't make sense of?"

"So you, Angela, may understand why you must let go

of everything you cherish and give me the revenge I so desire. If you fight the path I lay before you, it will only hurt you more. I will get what I want: Antum beneath my foot."

"I don't understand, you stupid—"

As Ti'amat waved her hand, Angela's mouth closed against her will. The desire to shut up had come from *inside* her, from the rot in her soul. Fear bubbled in Angela's gut. She reached for her mouth and tried to pry it open and speak, but she couldn't overpower the urge to keep quiet. Even her breathing had ceased and her lungs began to burn for air. No part of her body would do as she demanded. It was like she was frozen, doomed to stare out of her skull until she passed out or died.

The goddess's expression was filled with annoyance; she glared with those gray eyes, long and hard, like she wanted Angela to understand that *she* was in control and she would not stand for interruptions. Ti'amat stepped closer and said, "We're connected now." With her finger, she poked Angela in the sternum. "A single touch is all it takes to form a bridge between me and another soul. I could possess you like I did Udug and Donny, spy through your or their eyes, anytime I want, but I won't. I swear it from this day forth, I will not inhabit your body. Not fully, anyway, and I'll only be with you or your friends when I come to visit and speak with you. Now…" Ti'amat leaned closer, ran a finger along Angela's jaw, slow and tender like there was not an ounce of cruelty in her. "Behave."

Suddenly, the weight lifted, and Angela could breathe again. She gulped and gasped, reached for her throat. That was the very power Ti'amat had used to control Neti and make him move to catch Angela's blade in his neck, and the fact that the goddess had used it against her made her blood boil.

How dare she extend her evil grip to me. It is a mockery, a coward's weapon. It is her fault Neti died, not my own!

"You killed Neti," Angela snarled. "Destroyed my home. You think I'll just bend my knee and do what you want?" She spat near the goddess's feet. "I won't give you the satisfaction of revenge, even if it kills me."

The goddess tipped up her head and laughed. "Oh, I'll have my revenge. I could just take what I want, but I know I would carry on unfulfilled for eternities thereafter. I need a challenge. A fair fight. When every crystal shard is accounted for and you let Antum out of that soul of yours, we'll settle things. I'll split you both into so many pieces you'll blow away in a light breeze. Like dust." She smiled, her teeth as white as pearls, then turned away.

Deep inside, Angela could feel the blackness in her soul, the hook that tied her to Ti'amat. How much control did she really have over her own body? Would speaking again irritate the goddess? Could she strike her down now?

Are my own thoughts even mine?

There was only one way to find out. Angela asked, "W-Who is Antum? You mentioned her before, like I was her, but I'm not—"

Without turning to face her, Ti'amat raised a hand to cut her off. Angela stopped speaking at once, assuredly of her own will this time. "Rest first," the goddess said. "In time, you'll learn more about your soul than you could ever dream of." Her thin lips flexed into a smile over her shoulder, toxic beauty and charm irradiating. "After Antum and I have settled our dispute, I'll be free to do what I will with these worlds. Maybe pull them all back together again, rebirth my lost and beloved world of Vi'dinor..." The goddess disappeared without a sound, leaving Angela with nothing but a haunting chill running down her spine.

The wind resumed, blowing the tops of the saplings and shrubs in the garden around her. Birds began chirping, and all at once, the air was hot and humid again.

There was only one explanation to the strangeness that had occurred: the goddess hadn't actually been there, in the flesh, with her. Her silent vanishing trick wasn't teleportation. There was no way she could have silenced the deafening slap of air that accompanied slipping between the veils, and nothing could explain how time seemed to freeze. It must have been a vision. An illusion conjured from her connection to the goddess, the black hook inside her own soul.

Angela wanted to get rid of it more than anything, and that meant she had to find a way to kill a goddess.

CHAPTER TWO

The frozen wind sunk into Angela's bones as she imagined the snow crystals cutting tiny, spiderweb slashes into her cheeks. The cold burned, and she pushed through the battered doors and stepped into what was left of the Ascendancy. The air was a little warmer inside; a fireplace had been installed at the end of the lobby where the front desk used to be, the fire inside crackling and burning scrap timber and books. The yellow bulbs that hung from the ceiling and fixed to the walls were now dead and useless, while candles scattered around the edges of the room and stretching down the halls helped illuminate and define the edges of the space.

Mounds of fur in the corners of the room moved. Soldiers, at first rising quickly to their feet, hesitated and relaxed when they seemed to realize it was she who had entered. It was the same two Uri Gallus as before, and they looked her up and down with concern but didn't ask her where she'd gone with Neti's remains. She was glad they seemed to know better.

Softly, Angela asked, "Is Sarosha around?"

The two soldiers glanced at one another, making her worry that something had happened to the Grand, but one stepped forward and said, "She is. I'll take you to her." He motioned with his hands, and she followed him into the hollow halls of the Uri Gallu wing.

It was not long before the soldier stopped at a wooden door with a corroded brass plaque that read *Ja'noel Yishren, Grand Uri Gallu*. "Here," he said and stepped to the side.

Angela took a deep breath, turned the knob, and stepped inside. It was brighter and warmer inside the office than in the rest of the Ascendancy. Dozens of candles filled the room with dancing shadows. The big desk she'd expected to be there in the center of the office was gone. A smaller one had been pushed against the far wall, under the stained-glass window, and a dresser rested in the corner next to it. There was a cot on one side of the room and a few chairs on the other, shriveled figures wrapped in furs on both.

"Angela!" It was a man's voice, one that seemed so familiar and friendly yet so far off that she couldn't remember who was shrouded in those animal pelts. He rose from his chair and moved in to hug her faster than she could recognize him. His blond hair had reached his shoulders again, and this smile was a little happier than she remembered his last one being.

"Donny?" she asked.

He nodded. A twinkle in his eye told her that he was happy to see her, and they stared at one another for a long moment, analyzing and dissecting expressions in the hope of glimpsing the time the other had experienced. It was a great relief to see that his eyes were icy blue again, unlike the pitch black they had been when she had seen him last and taken his hand. Ti'amat was not here.

"So," another voice said, "you've woken up—finally." It was a harsh tone, a ragged voice that could be none other than Sarosha's. The thin woman rose from her cot to reach Angela's level, but unlike Donny, she did not have any warmness to her. Underneath her hood, her cheeks were gaunt, eyes sunken, cold, and distant like she was little more than a skeleton with skin.

Angela scratched the back of her head as Donny rushed to the dresser, pulled out a deer's pelt, and handed it to her. She threw it over her shoulders and said, "Yeah, I'm here. But something tells me I've missed a lot."

Sarosha's laugh almost seemed like a sneer. "You can say that again. Things have changed, and not for the better."

"How much time has passed?"

Sarosha's bottom lip quivered as though she was on the verge of crying as she said, "Four years."

Angela's jaw dropped. She could not believe that she had been sleeping for four years, yet when she thought of the frozen wastes outside, the ripped metal platforms, and the ruined homes all throughout Dingir, she knew better. It had to be true. She asked, "It only took four years for the city to come to *this*?"

"The winds have changed," Sarosha said in a defensive tone. "Ever since the day you fell asleep, it's been cold and harsh out there. The city fell into a decline like none other. People fled to Earth, and those of us who stayed are trapped. Well, most of the remaining public, anyways. We estimate around 150 people still live in the city, but there's no easy way to go and check every home with the weather like it is."

Angela bit her lip. It was even worse than she had thought. Her suspicions before were spot on; Dingir practically *was* abandoned. She said, "The Uri Gallu out there had said something about not having any more crystals…"

"Well," Donny interjected, "that's not entirely true. As far as the public is concerned, including the Uri Gallus out there, Dingir is completely out, but the Bui'dus have all the remaining crystals for safekeeping. Some of every color. We had to confiscate them from the soldiers to keep them from leaving, but that turned the situation more dire. They took offense and left faster, and now there's only a handful in Dingir, but we aren't completely trapped."

"So there's still time…" Angela said, grateful.

"Still time for what?" Sarosha asked, crossing her arms.

"Ti'amat is still collecting herself, the crystal pieces that house her power. As long as we still have some shards, we have time to find a way to kill her."

Sarosha lifted her head and laughed. "So Ti'amat is a *her* and you think you can kill her? I've always admired your tenacity, but you're insane. Do you not remember what happened? That beam of energy that slew a Nephilim we could barely scratch? The once-thought-dead councilman with blackened eyes? The bolt I put in his head, only for him to jump into—" Sarosha cut herself off as she motioned to Donny.

His eyes fell to the floor. He fiddled with his fingers. Somehow, he must have felt guilty about it. He was hiding something. Probably had been for a long time. Just the look on his face told her as much. Before Angela could console him, Sarosha continued. "Ti'amat said she was a god, and I believe it because, to us, she is. We do not compare. The best we—no, *you*—can do is fulfill the promise you made to me to find Ja'noel, and we will flee and hope for the best. Go to Earth. Scatter like roaches and hide at the slightest scent of her."

Angela rattled her brain, tried to think of the best way she could convince her that this was not the end. "Ti'amat has plans, Sarosha. She wants to rebuild the world before this one, Vi'dinor. She told me herself it was her 'beloved world,' and if she does that, there will be nothing of the worlds that we know. They'll be swallowed, destroyed. There's no avoiding this. And I'm sorry, but that means I've got way bigger things to worry about than finding Ja'noel. He will have to wait."

Sarosha tried to rebuke but stumbled over her tongue and failed to find the right words.

Angela ignored her, turned to Donny, and asked, "How long was Ti'amat with you before the day she took you over?"

Donny swallowed and kept looking at his hands. "What do you mean?"

"Ti'amat has to touch you, physically, before she can make a connection to your soul and possess your body. When did she touch you?"

A long breath escaped him, and finally he raised his gaze to hers. There were tears in his eyes, like he felt he had betrayed her. "When I was locked down in the cells, while you and Neti were hiding from the Nephilim, a man came and placed his hands on mine. Ti'amat knew I was your friend, and so she started spreading her influence to everyone she could. I... I'm sorry. I didn't know what was happening to me, and I wanted to tell you, but—"

Angela winced at the mention of Neti but held herself together and cut Donny off with a wave of her hand. "But you couldn't. I know. She wouldn't let you. Don't hold it against yourself. Ti'amat has been tying herself to those of us with souls for years. That goddess is a plague."

Donny relaxed a little. "You know, I thought Ti'amat

was just an entity—the Anchor Crystal—that inhabits people, not a goddess."

"She is all of that. When I took your—*Ti'amat's*—hand, she pulled me out of my body and into the weylines. In that sea of black, she showed me bits and pieces of her own memories so I could understand why she's here and doing all this."

Angela's head hurt as her mind instinctively dove into all those ancient memories implanted inside her. She rubbed her temples. There had to be some answers somewhere in the deep recesses of her mind. "These memories in my head are such a convoluted mess I can't make sense of it all. But a long time ago, in countless worlds before, Ti'amat was a goddess given life through the dissolution of what they called the All-Father. And that's how she came to me just today, as a woman, and she's bent on believing that I'm someone named Antum. I'm still trying to wrap my head around it all, but it's clear that if we don't do *something*, Ti'amat will destroy what's left of Dingir and Earth and Kur."

Sarosha sighed. Her gaze wandered to the glowing stained-glass window, where she stared and thought in silence for a moment. It must have been heart-wrenching to hear that finding the man she loved was a low priority, but it was true. Now she just stood there, stuck in depression. The Grand had lost her initiative, her courage.

Sarosha sighed, turned to face the others with a wet glimmer in her eyes. "I've done everything I could to save this place. I begged, on literal hands and knees, for craftsmen and traders and hunters and soldiers to stay. I sent squads to camps on Earth to try and bring back men and supplies and ended up losing them to the call of freedom. I've done desperate acts I'm ashamed of, just for favors. Just to keep everything from falling apart. I watched this city die because you just wouldn't wake up. More and more people stopped listening to me. I *need* Ja'noel to hold this all together because I don't have the strength to do it. So when I say that you are going to fulfill your promise and find him, you are going to *do* it."

Guilt tugged at Angela's heart, even though she had no control over how long she'd slept. She felt sorry for Sarosha because the raw emotion in her voice reminded her how she had felt about Michael. He had been her glue, and so had Neti, in a different way. That boy was irritating and compulsive, but he had been a voice of reason when she needed to hear it and a source of laughter when she was down.

The innate need in her to be strong and protect her friends and family had always pushed her forward, but now the number of those people was dwindling, and she knew she had to hold on to them tightly or risk losing them forever. They would live on in her memory, she swore.

"Yeah," Angela said. "I know what I promised." She did not say that she'd fulfill her promise, but she did not say she wouldn't. That had been intentional. Sarosha's green eyes were piercing as she tried to read her like a book, and for the moment, she seemed to understand. The Grand waved her hand toward the door, then turned away. "Leave me. Both of you."

Angela was the first out the door, Donny following closely behind her. Once they were out in the hall and the door was closed behind them, Angela muttered a curse, her breath fog in the hallway. "If I could go about this differently, I would. Sarosha needs to get off her high horse and get with the facts."

Donny placed a hand on her shoulder, pulled her to a

stop, and made her face him and stare into his ice-blue eyes. "You can't be mad at her," he said. "A part of her probably doesn't want to believe that you've woken up. These last four years you've been asleep, we've all tried to forget what happened. Tried to stop worrying about what's going to happen. Block out the pain. But now you're awake, and we can't. We all know something is coming. Some more than others." He smiled thinly like he was trying to cheer her up, but it was not a real enough smile to do that.

Donny always meant well, and to everyone. She didn't think she'd ever seen him pissed or vengeful, and now he was trying to smooth over the roughness between her and Sarosha. She recognized that, but how could she focus on finding Ja'noel when the idea of a being so powerful loomed over her? Let alone how she was still going through the steps of grief over Neti. She had to remind herself that even though it was her blade that had sunk into his neck, his death was Ti'amat's fault, not her own. She had to remind herself to be angry with the goddess and to not be disappointed with herself.

Angela let out a frustrated sigh and leaned her back against the cold stone wall. "I thought that if I could keep myself free from Dingir and Kur, I could get a taste of real peace, do the humans some justice, but all I did was get myself twisted up in the same old conflict. Pushed the wrong people too far, created enemies, and made myself an outsider to the people who shaped me into who I am. I created a stalemate based on fear. But now, all I want is for everyone to be safe and away from all of this. Away from what's coming. You, Sarosha, the soldiers, Toth and the Dalkhu. Just for once, no wars, no fighting. Just peace for all."

Donny shrugged. "You're a soldier, Angela. You know that's not how things work. The things we love take fighting for, whether or not we're ready to give it our all. Maybe we should search for Ja'noel together, huh?" His eyes sparkled with hope.

She didn't have the heart to turn him down right now. "Sure, Donny. I'd like that, but I don't even know where to begin."

A feminine voice from somewhere down the hall said, "That's easy." It was a rough, hard voice that cut through the silence, and it was not Sarosha's. The stranger's silhouette stepped forward and put her hands on her hips. The flickering candlelight revealed a sharp, angled jaw and exhausted golden eyes. Her hair matched the brown color of her leather armor, which was heavily worn with scuffs and marks, and around her waist she wore a belt with a tarnished brass buckle, a tether gun, and a shifter. She said, "Start where he was last seen. For that, you'll have to go to Earth and find the old Etlus that disbanded from the camp he was last seen at."

Angela wasn't one to shy away under pressure, but this woman's stare made her feel uncomfortable. "Who are you?" she asked.

"Meet me in the record room tomorrow morning," the woman said. "I'll gather the others. It'll take some convincing, but I think we can prove to them that your fight is in Dingir's best interest. Then it's just a matter of motivating them."

"Motivating who to do what?" Angela asked, stumped.

The woman's white teeth flashed in a smile before she turned away and stepped around the corner, disappearing without another word and leaving Angela confused.

"Who was that?" she asked Donny, hands in the air.

"That was Jezreal. She's a rough woman, but she means well. She was one of the soldiers you were actually supposed to train. One of the Bui'dus Ja'noel formed."

Angela remembered that Sarosha had said something about the Bui'dus, but only now did the name of the independent soldiers mean anything to her. She was supposed to teach them how to use their souls, teleport between worlds without shifters, and cast spells, if she could. But they hadn't expected Ti'amat, and they hadn't expected Angela to fall asleep for as long as she had. Considering Jezreal had been wearing a shifter at her waist, Angela figured they hadn't learned how to travel between the worlds by themselves, but she hoped beyond logic that they had. She would need all the help she could get if she was going to kill a goddess.

CHAPTER THREE

Waves slapped the surface of the water above her. Bubbles gurgled and twirled upward as they escaped her mouth, shimmering in the rays of light. The sounds of fish and other creatures filled the sea with other noises, but over it all, she heard someone calling her name. A man's voice. Abzu, and he was standing on the beach outside the city where she was born.

What does he want? she wondered just before the answer came to her. *He has brought me the last piece…*

With a twist of her body, she pointed her nose toward him and began to slip through the currents. He was far away, but it wouldn't take her long to reach him. In this long, serpentine form, she could cross oceans with little effort. Her tongue could taste those who touched her briny waters, and her eyes caught more light through the sea's blue haze. This was a form she would keep forever, but she knew this swim was likely the last she would have in this world.

Mulki was crumbling. Dying. Above, the sky was splitting, rupturing to expose pockets of gaping unreality. Earth shuddered and moved. Below, she could feel the tremors beating like a drum in the deep sea. The nether abyss of darkness reeked of chaos like it had once long before her time, and its waters were connected to everything.

Abzu would not admit it, but no drop of water began unsalted. Ti'amat was sure of it. The oceans far outsized his freshwater springs. Rivers poured and fed and refilled the seas—she would give him that much—but most of his water had evaporated from hers in the first place, then dumped onto land. That made his water borrowed. All of it was destined to return to her and the seas she commanded, and without her and her water, none could survive. She relished that fact.

As the seabed rose beneath her and she neared the beach, Ti'amat's long body dissolved and the arms and legs that Abzu was familiar with developed again. With dignity and grace, she walked up the shore, the waves lapping at her calves. It had been some time since she last felt sand between her toes and even longer since Abzu had seen her in a shape like his own. She could tell by the tears welling in his eyes that he now remembered why he'd loved her then and why he feared her now.

The black hair atop his head was sheen, but his face had taken a splash of dried red color. He was dressed in colorful robes lined with gold and silver that sparkled in the sunlight, but they were torn and damp with blood. Curled into a ball at his feet was a blond-haired boy with cuts along his face and forearms.

Ti'amat, smiling as she approached, said, "You've brought him. I'm happy. We might survive this yet."

Abzu took in a deep breath, steeling himself. They had not seen things the same way for some time. His approach to the other unruly gods was weak, while hers had been stern, and the arguments they had did not stall her actions. She had watched the twinkle of love in his eyes fade as he became more distant. Once, she had been upset and ashamed that he was afraid of her, but now that he had no choice but to side with her if he wanted to live in any regard, spirit or body, she reveled in her power over him.

"I did bring him," he admitted sourly. "So, go on. Eat him, you wretch." He clenched his fists and turned his back, the red sash around his waist blowing behind him.

"Why does this upset you so? Bringing him shows you are wise. Self-preservation is not a sin. Do not hold it against yourself. I've told you before: their souls live on in me, as you and the others will. If not the mother and father who created so many, who could best shelter their souls through this strife and peril?"

Abzu glanced over his shoulder, eyes hard, but he did not speak.

Ti'amat, smiling, resumed. "This is the only way we will survive. You know as well as I that the fresh water and the salt water *must* be together."

It was a stretch of the truth. Alone, she was the ruler of the seas. She did not need him to live on past this world, only his power to birth new life in the next. Again, Abzu looked away, choosing not to say anything rather than argue. The time for fighting had come and gone, and now was the time for exodus. The defeat in his eyes was palpable.

The boy at his feet finally looked out from beyond his slashed arms with soft, purple eyes. His blood had stained the sand a pinkish color. Ti'amat waved her hand upward, motioning to him, and he rose to his feet slowly. His knees wobbled, and he stood no taller than her waist, but he was no boy. His appearance meant nothing. He was a god as old and mature as she was. One of the first.

"Show me," she commanded, and the boy raised a shaking hand. When he opened his palm, translucent threads spiraled upward from his skin, dancing in a circular motion until they weaved together and solidified into a jagged crystal the size of an apple.

"How obedient. Marduk and his rebels can cleave their portions of this world all they want. They can cannibalize Mulki and create their own haven—I won't stop it— because he fails to understand that once those gods are separated from one another, they won't stand a chance." She sighed and crossed her arms. "But first, we must survive this damned world's undoing, and then we will rebuild. Do you understand what's about to happen?"

The boy clenched the crystal and raised his gaze to meet hers. He glistened in sweat and sea spray, lip quivering as he said, "I do."

Ti'amat tried to hide a smile but couldn't. She bowed her head, her black hair dangling past her stomach. With her feet in the water, she drew upon the power in the abyss of chaos. As her sea eyes returned to her, her vision grew cloudy and the smell of the blood on his arms filled her nostrils with salt. Scales emerged from beneath the soft skin of her neck, and she stretched a still-forming maw forward to take him between her teeth at once. Quickly, she swallowed, and the heat of his body warmed her throat on the way down—but what warmed her more was the boy's soul melding with hers.

Within moments, at her command, crystals sprouted from the pores in her hands, pricking her like tiny pins. If she could smile in this form, she would have. When the world splintered, smashed, and exploded, her souls would survive, anchored in crystal. Already, her bones began to stiffen as the boy's power took its hold. He was not the first god Ti'amat had consumed, and he would not be the last. With her mind, she reached outward and touched Abzu, who still faced the city, and asked, *Are you ready, Father?*

ANGELA SAT UPRIGHT AND REACHED FOR HER THROAT, unsure if what she'd just swallowed was spit or if the sensation was a result of Ti'amat's planted memory. It had felt so normal. So real. The ocean breeze on her arms, the sand under her feet, the way her neck had stretched...

Slapping her cheeks cleared the chilling thought from her mind and the sleep from her body. What replaced the waking fatigue was the touch of a cold breeze rolling through the crack in her bedroom wall. Even though Sarosha had offered her a bed inside the Ascendancy, a part of her could not leave her house behind until it fell into the sky below the city, as risky as that was. There were too many memories here to abandon this place.

As she threw the blankets off and stood, a voice behind her made her heart lurch into her throat. A woman's voice. "I don't know for certain how everything began, so I only accept the things I learned myself: that the first of us were exceptionally different than the others we birthed after."

Terror sank its claws into Angela's chest. She swallowed, knowing the voice like the back of her hand. For what felt like eons, she had said things she hadn't meant to in that very voice. She spoke it in her dreams and in her waking nightmares like flashbacks. With a deep breath, she turned to face Ti'amat.

Gods... She is beautiful...

The goddess's black hair draped over her like it had just been trimmed and combed. Lines of makeup formed wings that sprouted from the corners of her eyes. Angela had seen things with those eyes in memories and dreams. Even *did* things with those hands when she hadn't wanted to. Steeling herself, Angela asked, "What do you want?"

Ti'amat's eyes hardened. "Your mind and soul wander while you sleep. I felt you stirring. Knew what it was you were dreaming of. In that world—the first world, Mulki—a handful of us were given life by a father we never knew. Some gods tried to investigate the core of that world and learn its secrets. A few claimed that our father was just an entropic cloud of cosmic energy or a sea, as I like to think, but the truth that was unanimously agreed upon is that he was a contemplative entity that, upon creating us, abandoned us, and none of us really understood why or where he had come from. In the end, all that mattered was our gifts and the gifts our children bore."

She allowed her eyes to drift toward the floor for a moment, considering something. Angela dared not interrupt.

"While there were a handful of others there with us in the beginning, Abzu and I were the first," she said. "And we loved one another for quite some time. We partnered, created countless other gods by sharing our souls and our bodies with one another. It was beautiful. But each of us was different. One could grant the spark of a new soul while others could form different kinds of matter from nothing. We figured that our father wanted us to work together and create beautiful things through teamwork and form community and bonds with one another, but I believe we were brought into existence not only to create but to give order and purpose to the lesser things we created.

"Some of our children were more rebellious than the others, but their treachery spread to the others in time. They began tearing Mulki apart just to spite us first ones, and once I started consuming them, gaining their souls, things only got worse and I could not stop. Abzu and I killed hundreds in order to gain their abilities." Ti'amat sighed for a long moment, like it hurt for her to say it, but Angela had spent enough time in her mind to know better. The goddess did not feel regret. It was theatrics to her. A means of manipulating Angela into giving her what she wanted.

Ti'amat moved around the room, her sandals slapping against the wooden floor to add to the cheap illusion that she was really there, then sat at the foot of the bed not a few feet from her. She looked deeply into Angela's eyes as though she would find something there, then said, "You see, crystals are very special, regardless of color or kind. They are the vessels of spiritual energy—and far more durable than any fleshy body. Crystalizing myself was a sacrifice that had to be made to ensure my own survival, and it worked. Time and time again, I was crushed and broken into a thousand different pieces, but that only meant a thousand different seeds were planted."

"Angela?" The bedroom door swung open, creaking on its hinges. Donny stood in the hallway with a look of concern about him. He was wrapped in furs and holding a steaming mug.

The foot of the bed was empty, and Ti'amat was gone, vanished from the room, and in her absence, Angela realized the feeling that had gripped her soul had disappeared as well. She was herself again, and she was alone but for Donny. Her shoulders slunk as the tension and anxiety in her chest released all at once.

"I-I…" Donny stuttered. "I-I'm sorry if I'm intruding,

but I knocked and you didn't answer, and I wanted to be sure you—"

"I'm fine."

"But… But your eyes… You were just sitting there with black eyes. Are you all right? Was it her?"

For a moment, Angela thought and worked it out in her mind, taking in deep breaths and letting them out slowly. That was the second time Ti'amat had visited her in real time. The first time had been in the sinkhole, and if what Donny had described was accurate, that meant two things. Time did not cease flowing during these visions and she had not heard his knocking, which meant that Angela was unconscious and unaware of what was really happening around her. She had been completely under Ti'amat's influence. Her eyes had gone black, and it reminded her of the first time she'd met the goddess in Udug's body and then in Donny's. Angela was now just as tied to her as them. Helpless.

"Yeah," Angela said. "The black eyes come with her visits. That's how you know she's there, listening. But let's try not to get too caught up in that." She rose, faked her best smile, and squeezed past Donny on her way out of the bedroom. He didn't say a word, only looked down at the extra mug in his hand.

The padded bench in the living room was covered with upthrown blankets and pelts. A tea kettle, still steaming, rested on the kitchen counter, and light filtered through the boarded window above the table where a deck of cards and a book lay.

She'd agreed to let Donny continue to live with her in her home, as he had been living there for the last four years. After she had fallen asleep from that fateful first encounter with Ti'amat, he moved in to become her caretaker until she awoke again. Many of his belongings were moved into her home before the freezing cold had settled over Dingir and before the city truly began its rapid decay.

He had moved his writing desk in and placed it on the opposite side of the fireplace, but gauging by the thick layer of dust, she guessed he hadn't sat there in ages. His book collection made hers look bigger, and besides, having someone around to keep her from falling too far into hopelessness was probably for the better; the lack of privacy with him occupying the front of her house was a small price to pay. If only he hadn't let it get so cluttered and messy, Angela wished.

Offering her the warm mug, Donny said, "I'm glad you're all right now. Here."

Angela pushed it back with a weak smile. "Thanks, but I'll pass. I'm heading out."

He looked offended. "Already?"

"Yeah."

She scoured the entryway closet and threw on a heavy coat, but before she opened the front door, she paused and looked back. Donny sat himself down at the small kitchen table under the window, his back to her. He sighed, sipped his tea, and flipped a card.

The guilt of leaving him behind was too much to bear. "I'll see you later," she said.

He lifted an arm in a distant wave, not looking over his shoulder or saying goodbye.

Reluctantly she stepped outside and focused for a moment before vanishing between the veils. Beneath the Ascendancy's crumbling steeple, the wind howled and the snow flew. Inside, the two guards, now familiar with who she was and what she looked like, greeted her with nods. She wondered if they were the only two Uri Gallus left, and if they were, did they simply live in the lobby? Before she had a chance to turn back around and ask, the clomp of boots from farther down the dim hallway stole her attention.

A figure she'd only first seen the night before came around the corner. Jezreal. The way the soldier walked and put her hands on her hips gave her away in the darkness. "Follow," she commanded, and Angela did.

Around the corner, down the hall and past the old office of Kushiel Valadine, they came to the room once designated for storing the city's records and banned knowledge. The room had been rearranged since she'd last seen it. Red tapestries hung on previously bare spots of wall, and most of the furniture had been pushed around to make room. In fact, many of the bookshelves were missing entirely, but the lattices of spell-scrolls still rested in the places she remembered them being. All these changes were to make room for a large round table in the center with seven chairs surrounding it. It was littered with papers, books, even more scrolls, and pieces of scrap equipment like springs and the hollow shells of shifters. This room had become the Bui'dus' headquarters, so to speak.

Jezreal led Angela to a seat at the table next to the fireplace and pulled the chair out for her like she was the guest at a dreary dinner party. The flickering light revealed the woman's hard features better than the night before: an angled jaw betrayed her thinness, her nose was big for her head, her appearance was haggard and worn for her age, and a single scar ran down her cheek.

Angela sat as Jezreal found another place to sit. There were two other men in the room with them as well. A man, clean-shaven with a head of blond hair that stretched to his shoulders, reached over the table and shook her hand. In all these years of rough survival, he'd somehow managed to keep his teeth vibrantly white, his skin clean and glowing.

"Name's Gabe," he said in a velvet voice that made him seem far too young to even be here. He must have sensed the suspicion in her eyes. He said, "Yes, I am the youngest in the role." Gabe ran his fingers through his hair, leaned back in his seat. "And the most handsome."

Angela smirked. Jezreal laughed. The other Bui'du she had yet to meet scoffed from his kneeling position by the fireplace. He tore pages from a book and tossed them into the flames. His eyes were dark and cold, his skin a shade close to Sarosha's, and his frame thick. "You wish, Gabe," he said as he rose, "although I bet all those girls you've been with the last few years would agree with you. Oh, wait, there haven't been any." He flashed his teeth in a devilish grin, pulled the gray knitted cap farther down on his shaved head, and began to walk toward his own seat. Even the way he moved was stiff and rigid with tension.

"That's Samael," Jezreal said. "Sam for short. Or Sammy, if you like. He certainly does."

Samael groaned as he sat in his seat, waved Jezreal off with his hand, and ignored her. His voice was deep as he spoke. "If you hadn't already guessed, we're the Bui'dus. Or what's left."

Angela nodded. "Your squad functions independently of the usual chain of command. I remember."

He sat forward and weaved his fingers together, his shoulders like a fortress wall. "You were supposed to train us how to traverse the veils without shifters, but no one was expecting you to fall asleep like that. Or an ancient god to come out of the woodwork."

"It's a goddess," Angela corrected. "Ti'amat, that is. It's a she. I've seen her." That seemed to surprise the Bui'dus, who remained speechless. They must have never considered that a god could be female. Maybe there were gods out there that were entirely sexless entities. Angela was not sure but did not doubt the possibility.

"Sarosha said you were going to help us search for Ja'noel, right?" Samael asked.

Angela couldn't help but roll her eyes. Not at Samael, but at Sarosha. "I never said I would be able to or that I'd even try. If finding Ja'noel aligns with killing Ti'amat, so be it. But I'm not going out of my way to search for him when there's a goddess on the loose."

"Countless people have left Dingir," Samael said in a dark tone. "Even one of us. We already lost Rig. He left us because he had no hope that we'd get Dingir back to where it was before. We have to find Ja'noel. He's become a symbol for those of us that are left, and not just for us Bui'-dus. Without his leadership, I don't know how long the last of the Anunnaki can hold it together. We're *all* losing hope, especially that you're awake now. We know that a conflict is looming on the horizon."

Jezreal lifted a hand, stopping Samael from going on. "Hold up now. Sure, maybe her waking up is a sign that things are going to start to rumble, but it's the best thing that's happened to us in the last four years. If anything, people may just now begin to have hope."

Sam did not agree. He crossed his arms and asked, "Well, give me something palpable. A reason to believe. How are you going to kill this goddess?"

And that was the greatest question of them all. Just thinking about where to begin filled her gut with nervous bubbles. The way Samael's gaze never lifted made Angela feel uncomfortable, which was atypical for her. It made her feel as though she was not welcome at their table.

All Angela could do to break the tension was shrug. "The truth is, I don't have any idea how I'm going to do it. Ti'amat is going to rebuild her old world out of the ones we know, so she's definitely a threat. And until I can find a way to get an upper hand, we can only trust that she'll uphold her promise to leave us alone and not spy on what I'm doing. I've got a jumbled mess of memories that aren't my own. It will take time for me to sort through them, but I think the key to defeating her is somewhere in my head. Whatever shattered the Anchor Crystal before should be able to do it again."

Jezreal propped her head up with her arm. Her green eyes glimmered in the firelight as she asked, "What do you know from these memories?"

A sigh escaped Angela. "Not much. Dingir, Earth, and Kur are the worlds we know now. But the world before this, where the Nephilim came from, Vi'dinor, wasn't even the first. I've seen bits from so many different places it's hard to fathom, but I think all of existence has been re-formed and reorganized many times. Through trials and manipulation, Ti'amat is just a goddess who managed to play the game right. By devouring the souls of the others, she's held a position of power above all the other gods for a long time."

Samael asked, "How many gods were there?"

"Thousands, maybe? And many had unique abilities that Ti'amat's acquired by taking their souls. The things she *can* do outnumber what she can't, I think. She turned her own body into a massive crystal and anchored to it the souls she devoured. That's how she's survived through each world's destruction and the creation of the next one. Flesh and blood can't survive that."

The room was quiet for a moment, everyone searching

everyone else's expression for some sign of hope and waiting for someone to present an idea of what to do.

No one had anything to suggest until Jezreal finally spoke. "So we're up against a goddess that not only has the powers of a thousand or more other gods but is also literally the Anchor Crystal of Dalkhu myth."

Angela nodded, and Jezreal's expression went grim as she said, "That means she would have control over the weylines. Control over souls... Fuck. Just *fuck*. That explains what happened with Udug and Donny." She buried her face in her hands, distraught.

Angela placed a hand on her shoulder, drew her gaze back upward, and said, "Yeah, but she can only possess the souls she's come into contact with. I think we need to remember the most important piece of all of this: Ti'amat wants *revenge*. That means that I—or, more realistically, the person who had my soul before me—did something in my last life that destroyed her in Vi'dinor. All the tales about the Anchor Crystal shattering and creating these worlds, that wasn't intentional. I think Ti'amat was *defeated*. We just have to find out how and do it again. And I know someone who knows the—"

Samael chuckled from across the table and stood, his chair squeaking against the floor as he pushed it. The disturbance was so out of place that the room went quiet. "Clearly," he said, "the last time Ti'amat was killed, it wasn't permanent. Let's say you do manage to find the Anchor Crystal and shatter it. What will that do to these worlds? To all of us?"

Angela bit her lip and shrugged. "I don't know."

"And how would you even get close enough to her if she's connected to you? She touched you, right? Can she sense where you are? What you're doing?"

"I don't know that, either, but I do know someone else who was there when Vi'dinor was destroyed. I'm going to go have a talk with him."

REALITY RETURNED IN A CRUSHING BLAST. SHE STAGGERED but cleared the daze from her head quickly. It seemed she wasn't as recovered from her long stasis as she'd thought. An orange sun nearing twilight threatened to drop beneath the range to the west. The wind atop the mountains was wild but warm. Sweet-smelling cherry trees speckled the landscape below with spots of pink in the vast forests of green. Blue rivers snaked their way through bluffs and created cliffsides. Anyang rested somewhere down there, but her attention was drawn to the mouth of the cave before her.

A deep rumbling came from the darkness before the creature showed himself: clawed feet as large as her torso, a mix of purple hues gleaming from the scales on his pointed nose as he stepped into the sunlight, a forked tongue slipping between the hooked teeth of its maw and tasting the air. The Nephilim shook the ground beneath her with his weight, stopping close enough to loom over her. His breath smelled of rotten eggs.

"I'll hear the rest of that story, Gor," Angela said, unwavering as she looked into the beast's eyes.

He reared his long neck and huffed, amused. Gor's voice came deep and gravelly in her mind, rattling her. *The one that you cut short the last time we spoke?*

She rubbed her temples to ease the aches but knew she would get used to the Nephilim's speech again. "Yes, that one. Tell me how the Nephilim destroyed the Anchor

Crystal in Vi'dinor. Not only were you there when it happened, but you have always been a servant of Ti'amat, haven't you? You and Kuda are her pawns. Tools to manipulate me. That explains how a human had a soul."

The beast's laughter was deep and long, rumbling the air around him. *You figured it out, then. We are bound by shackles to an old goddess, I admit. We were instructed to aid you without giving away our purpose. You had to rise to the occasion yourself. Do you understand? Ti'amat wanted you to succeed against Maulkatu and the other Nephilim. A test, of sorts.*

Angela placed her hands on her hips and sighed. "I know I should have been more suspicious of your help. But here's the offer: you tell me how the story ends and I don't kill you."

Gor's lips twitched. Angela wasn't sure if that was a sign of anger, amusement, shock, or what emotion. His forked tongue licked the air once more, and he said, *You'll get no story from me today. She's changed her mind, given me restrictions. And you won't be killing me, either.*

A distant screech drew her eyes to the clouds overhead. From behind them, a winged figure came barreling down toward the mouth of the cave. At first, fright clutched her bones, and Angela grabbed the hilt of the sword over her shoulder, then came to realize it wasn't heading directly for her. The Nephilim's red scales glimmered, making it appear as a streaking comet before landing atop a boulder. It shifted its weight, claws grinding against the stone. Growled. Then glanced up at the councilman on his back.

Councilman Kanu, dressed in tattered black robes with a red cord, was smiling. Of course, his eyes were black, which meant he was only partially there at best—and more than likely entirely Ti'amat.

Angela clenched a fist and took a deep breath, demanding that her own nerves calm and her heart steel itself. "So how's this going to go?" she asked. "You pull your crystal shards through the veils and restore yourself. You regain control over the weylines, their souls, your energy. Then what?"

Ti'amat threw her legs over and slid down from the creature's back, then leapt off the boulder to land with bent knees.

"I still don't understand where I come into all of this," Angela admitted. "Why you're so bent against me. I'm not Antum or whoever had this soul before me. How am I, or anyone else you've killed, responsible for what happened in Vi'dinor?"

Ti'amat was still smiling. Her host's teeth had turned brown, and his black hair had grown long enough to reach his stomach, signs that she'd been in control of Kanu for some time and hadn't been taking care of his body. Angela remembered that Kanu had fled atop Lahmu the Red after the battle in Dingir. He likely became Ti'amat's pawn before he was able to return home to Kur, but there was also the chance that he enjoyed it, that he welcomed her presence and power in his soul and body.

In the councilman's voice, the goddess said, "You're not her, exactly. You're an echo. Half an echo, actually. When a person dies and their soul leaves their body, you know they return to the weylines, but what happens if that soul slips into another body? And another body after that?"

Angela couldn't answer that. The goddess walked like the man she inhabited, displayed the strong, proud gait of a councilman in every way, and placed a hand on Gor's leg. She tapped his purple scales with her fingers as though she was waiting for an answer, then resumed. "Every time a soul leaves a person, it takes a handful of that person's memories along with it, clinging to the most important things. Souls carry nature, attitudes, and moods that affect the next person they are born into. While they don't define who a person is or the choices they will make, they can have a resounding influence on a person's nature because of the echoes that still live on deep inside the soul."

Something clicked in Angela's mind. "So I'm half an echo because Antum existed before the Anchor Crystal broke? Her soul was split apart, just like the world, and I only have a portion of it."

A wide smile stretched across the goddess's face. "Very good, Angela. I wasn't the only one that turned my body into crystal. Vi'dinor's destruction was my final act of revenge, I admit. I expelled every ounce of my being into shattering all things around me—including the remaining gods' crystals. The ones who I'd thought were not poised against me. Antum was one that I had considered a friend, yet in the end, she betrayed me—the Anunnaki part of you betrayed me. If you find the remnant shells of the other half of you, you'll awaken that part of you, and maybe Antum's echoes will have what you're searching for." Ti'amat smiled devilishly like there was something more to it. Something she would gain from it.

Angela's brow furrowed. What would it be like to awaken an echo of someone who had her soul before her? How would restoring a goddess's soul affect her? She wasn't sure how to even picture an echo. Frustrated, she asked, "How could I even find a half of me I've never felt before? I couldn't scry that soul."

"You're right again." Ti'amat held out a dirty hand, palm up. "You'll have to search for it. But in order to find it, you'll need a gift." Her black eyes glanced down to her open hand, then back to Angela as though she wanted her to take it, wanted to show her something like she had before.

A nervous buzz developed in her belly, but what would the goddess do that she couldn't have done to her already? Angela stepped forward cautiously and took the goddess's hand.

The whole world fell out from under her. Her knees buckled and crashed into the dirt, but she barely felt it as the sensation of touch melted away. The smells of the earth and the Nephilims' breath disappeared. Birds and wind grew quiet as a whole new sense developed. The more she grew aware of the surrounding veils and this world, the more she forgot the boundaries of her own body. The veil was a spherical net cast around her. She could always push on it, slip outside it, and travel around it, but now, somehow, she could feel the nets of other worlds beyond her own.

There were Kur and Dingir; she recognized those because she'd been there countless times before. Their positions in the veil were relative to Earth, and their tunes were distinct. But now, there was an expanse beyond what she'd known before. She could reach far off into existence and feel the veil of a different world, foreign and alien. Beyond it, there was another. The further she stretched, the more she found. On and on. Existence was simply world upon world, stacked on top of one another, and there were more out there than she could hope to count.

The sharp sting of a slap drew her back into her head. Ti'amat-possessed Kanu was standing over her, impatient. For a moment, Angela was unsure how much time had passed. She felt dizzy, rolled onto her back, and played with a rock in her hand, feeling the sensation of its sharp edges as everything came back to her.

Ti'amat said, "The gift I've given you is an awareness of the boundaries of worlds. As you no doubt can feel, there's more than just Dingir and Kur out there. Whole civilizations you've never met. Fragmentary passages and dimensions barely inhabitable yet home to creatures dark and lurking. But somewhere out in the shattered remains of Vi'dinor's corpse, you'll find the crystalline remains of Antum, where the other half of you sleeps. Go forth and repair your soul. The answer you seek is buried in the deepest parts of it. Repair her and let her out, Angela. Let me see Antum once more."

CHAPTER FOUR

A ngela sat at the round table, tapping her fingers impatiently as the others gathered. Jezreal, with her copper hair tied into a ponytail and sleep still in her eyes, sat opposite her. Young Gabe and cautious Samael sat at Jezreal's sides without a word as well. On long strides, Sarosha was next to walk through the record room's doorway, holding her head up higher than she did the last time Angela had seen her. It seemed that their previous conversation and Angela's reluctance to prioritize her lost partner had put her in a mood. Finally, Donny was the last to answer her summons. He sat to Angela's right, leaving only one chair open.

The fireplace crackled, its light casting shadows across their faces as everyone tried to discern one another's expressions in the darkness. It was Angela who took a deep breath and broke the silence. "Thanks for coming and listening to me. I'll get right into it. I know what I have to do to defeat Ti'amat, or at the very least, I have a path to follow now."

The faces around her were a mixture of confusion and

outright disbelief. Even saying the words aloud didn't help Angela herself believe them any better, but as far as she was aware, it was true: Ti'amat could be killed again, only this time she hoped it could be more permanent.

"In the many worlds before this one, gods survived destruction by turning themselves into crystal. They understood that certain crystalline structures could house their souls longer than their flesh could. But this last time, Vi'dinor's expansion into smaller pieces was different than all the others. As a final act of revenge against the gods who wronged her, Ti'amat shattered everything: the whole dimension and the other gods' crystals." Angela softened her voice as she said, "Some of those souls slipped from their moorings and drifted to the weylines, and it turns out that I have half of one of those gods inside me. Her name was Antum."

Samael's white teeth flashed as he bellowed, "You can't be serious." The way he looked at her, like she was joking, upset her.

"I wouldn't lie about this, Sam. I can't explain everything I've seen in dreams and memories to you, but I'd ask that you believe me. This is why Ti'amat has such a great interest in me. Ask Sarosha or Donny if I have the capacity to fabricate something like this."

Samael glanced at Angela's oldest friends, who shook their heads, but that only seemed to strengthen Sam's suspicions that it was an ill-timed joke. He crossed his arms and asked, "I'm not the only one here who's hesitant to believe this nonsense, am I? Jezreal? Gabe? What do you think?"

The blonde Bui'du shrugged, seeming uncertain what to say but not dismissive of the possibility that Angela was telling the truth. Jezreal put on a steel expression, refusing to let anyone get the slightest hint that she was feeling anything about the matter.

Sam did not seem to like their lack of input. He frowned like a child, began to fuss up a storm of mumbling.

Before he got too deep into his rant, Angela cut him off and changed the topic. "Now that I think about it, why wasn't a single one of the Bui'dus seen when the Nephilim attacked Dingir? I can't say I recall any of you helping in the battle, but this squad was certainly formed before I even returned."

Samael crossed his arms, his eyes unblinking. As his lip curled and he opened his mouth to speak, Jezreal lifted her hand to cut him off. He needed a muzzle, it seemed. "We were afraid," she said. "A few of us I won't name wondered if it would be better if we stayed back and launched a surprise attack, but the rest of us knew we were just being cowards. But what could we have even done? Even now, after all these years, we're little better than Etlus. Sure, we can steel our minds and resist the mental grasps of one another, but we know we're nothing compared to you or a Dalkhu or a Nephilim. It would have been suicide."

Angela crossed her arms, reading Jezreal's expressions as she spoke. She had heart, that was for sure. But heart had never been enough for her, so why would it excuse the Bui'dus? "Suicide or not, it was your duty to defend this city. You took the same vows I did. Did you not mean them when you swore your life? So far, that was Dingir's most dire hour, and you failed to defend it. I think all the soldiers who died that day were more devoted to this city than you are, and you were hand-picked by Ja'noel. Despicable. What a disgrace."

Sarosha seemed to wince at the mention of her partner's

name. She looked away, into the firelight, while the Bui'dus trembled with mixed emotions. Gabe let his head slump in dejection, feeling sorry for himself and full of regret. Sam was seething, his clenched fists on the table in front of him.

Jezreal's lips were trembling in so much fury a tear streaked down her cheek. Angela could see through her. She was ashamed, stumbling with words in hopes of defending herself and the honor of her squad. "I-I think you're missing something here, Angela. For us, this city hasn't decayed and crumbled into this sorry state in the blink of an eye like you've experienced it. We've been sitting through all of this, with no hope and guilt on our consciousnesses, waiting for something to change for *four years*. One of us may have abandoned our post, and we may not have been as strong as we should have been when the Nephilim came, but we are still here now when so few others are. You have no right to question our devotion to this city when we have watched it fall apart as you just slept through the decay."

Angela was a little surprised. In a good way. Michael had once told her that a good way to gauge someone's character was to pick on them. Maybe even embarrass them. How they handled the criticism was a good indication of their resolve, and Angela was impressed. Jezreal would make a fine leader someday, Angela mused, and she would need that strength moving forward. "I won't anymore," she promised.

Jezreal relaxed, leaned back in her chair with a deep breath, but Samael didn't seem any more pleased than he was before. Sarosha kept her thoughts to herself, nibbling on her fingernails.

"Like I was saying," Angela began, "all of us only

really have half a soul. The story we know is that the world broke apart and the weylines separated souls like magnetic fields. The Dalkhu and the Anunnaki are the two distinctly different pieces of these old gods' souls, plain and simple. If I can find my other piece, there's a chance I'll be able to remember more from the last world, discover where the Anchor Crystal is, and learn how to defeat Ti'amat. There's also a good chance that Ja'noel will be wherever her heart is, too."

The room grew still and quiet as Sarosha's eyes sparkled. Even Samael relaxed and pondered the possibility.

"It makes sense," Jezreal announced.

Donny reached out to take Angela's hand, but he stopped himself. "We… We're here to help." The eagerness in his eyes was palpable, but all it did was twist Angela's guts into a knot. He would not be coming with, no matter what, but she felt the need to be careful with how she let him down. Her old friend was too inexperienced and too dear to her to risk.

He leaned in closer and asked, "So what's the plan? Where are we looking?"

Angela took a deep breath and stood. "I don't know, exactly. Ti'amat has given me an awareness of sorts. There are other dimensions out there never seen by Dalkhu or Anunnaki. I'm just going to head where my soul tells me to go. It could be a waste of time, but if Ti'amat wants to bring me up to her level and fight it out, I say all right. Bring it."

"Unknown dimensions, huh?" Samael clacked his tongue, stared at the ceiling as he thought. "I guess we'll see what you're made of, *Antum*."

Angela rolled her eyes. Nothing but proof would seem

to convince him she was not lying, but even Angela doubted it was true. It seemed too unreal to believe. She shrugged. "You're not the only one suspicious of all this. Even I don't know if I really am Antum, but it doesn't matter if I am or not. I'm done grieving over what Ti'amat has taken from me. I think of Neti, Ja'noel, Kushiel, and all the damage she's done to this city. I'm out for revenge now. And I could use some help. Will you come?"

It was quiet for a moment as the others considered it. Angela could give them no certainties or promises of success, but Jezreal was the first to rise. She threw her arm across her chest in a stiff salute. "I will go with you."

Gabe followed suit, mirroring her. "I will come with, too. Ja'noel formed the Bui'dus to fight for Dingir in the best way we see possible, and I think your success is imperative for the city's survival. I will not sit by and let you go this alone."

Angela almost blushed. The zeal in his voice was moving, and for being such a new soldier, he certainly took his oath seriously. *Youthful passion, perhaps.*

Samael was less eager; he grumbled quietly as he rose to his feet and placed a closed fist on his chest, albeit less enthusiastically, of course. "I follow, too," he said.

As Donny began to move in his seat, Angela was quick to speak and cut him off before he had a chance to rise and say his piece. "Pack up your things," she said. "We leave in an hour."

In a passing glance, she saw the confusion in Donny's expression but could not bring herself to explain. She turned to leave, still unsure how she would tell him he wasn't coming.

THE BITTER WIND WHIPPED ANGELA'S HAIR INTO HER FACE, distracting her. She scooped it up, tied it into a ponytail, pulled a knitted cap from her jacket's inner pocket, and put it on. Breathing slowly with her eyes closed, she stretched her mind out into the vast expanse of worlds around them. She could lightly trace the veil of world after world, feel their borders and estimate their size, but she couldn't see into them. There was no telling what was inside each bubble and where she was about to lead the Bui'dus.

A hand touched her. She jumped.

"Sorry," Sarosha said from behind a whirlwind of black hair. It was just the Grand out in the cold with her; the others hadn't come yet. "I... I wanted to thank you before you left. I know I haven't been fair to you. Been expecting too much. I just—"

"Don't worry about it. I know it's not personal. Turns out there's a lot of stress on everyone when we're looking at the end of everything we know."

Sarosha swallowed. "Is that what you think will happen if you lose?"

A deep breath, and she let it out slowly as she thought. "Ti'amat might do anything, but I can't imagine she would want to keep things the way they are or do nothing at all considering she did say she wanted to rebuild Vi'dinor. And that probably means these worlds would be swallowed to create it."

A gust took the Ascendancy's door, slamming it against the brick wall behind it and cutting the conversation short. Donny cussed as he heaved against it until it closed. A satchel hung at his waist, and he wore a large pack on his back. By the way he carried them, they were stuffed and heavy, making him struggle through the snow.

He huffed and puffed, sucked air. The skin on his

cheeks was thin and sunken, and his cheekbones were prevalent. With the lack of food in Dingir and his own lack of exercise, Donny was thin, weak, and frail. He would not be an asset on their journey, but a burden. Guilt bit into Angela's heart, and there was no more hiding from it. The sooner she said it, the better. "I can't let you come with us, Donny," she blurted.

He stilled, looking at her incredulously with his icy blue eyes that seemed to ask why.

Angela showed her palms. "What did you think I was going to say? We're going off into worlds that none of us have ever been in, and you have no combat experience beyond manning a turret. You're thin. Out of shape. And I can't risk you like this."

His brow furrowed as his eyes reflected an angry fire she'd never seen in them before. "You think that I'm going to let you keep me here? That I can't make the same sacrifices as you? Let me remind you who broke you out of the Ascendancy's cells, who waited fifteen years to be free again, and who watched over you for four more while you slept. Praying and praying and hoping and dreaming that someday you would wake up and we'd set things right. Together. Like how things should have been from the beginning, Angela. *You* and *me*. I—" He turned around, hands trembling in rage. Screamed into the freezing air, his curses turning into fog.

Sarosha stepped back, unsure and awkward. Angela felt it, too, but stronger yet, the guilt in her chest had ripped open like a wound. For a minute or more, he looked away, and neither spoke. How was she supposed to react to that? The way he had implied that he and she were supposed to be together... It never happened, but it was true. She'd smothered that feeling for so long she had no choice but to continue to suffocating it. Out of regret. Shame, even. If she didn't, it would almost be like giving up on Michael, who had stolen everything about her from Donny so long ago: her attention, her time, and finally her heart.

But Angela swallowed. There was no middle ground in this. Still, she struggled with Neti's death. If Donny came with her and something happened to him, too, she would never forgive herself. Yet if she left Donny behind, if she controlled him like she had Neti and then lost him anyway, she wouldn't forgive herself for that, either. She sighed. *To love is to let free.* And she did love him. Not the same as she had Michael, but there was something there. Why was it that, so close to the end, she had to feel this way so strongly?

"I'm sorry," Angela said, and the dark oak door to the lobby swung open again.

Out came Gabe, Jezreal, and Samael, bracing themselves against the wind and shielding their eyes from the flying snow.

Donny cleared his throat and wiped at his face. "About time. We were about to leave you," he jested, and the Bui'dus smirked.

What a stubborn fool, Angela thought. *He will not give up willingly...*

"Go right on ahead," Gabe said from the back. "We'll catch up."

Angela couldn't help but smile as they waded down the narrow path of shallow snow. She looked over all of their gear. For cold weather, they brought extra furs and pelts, a bundle of firewood, and the flint and steel to start it. They carried clothes and hats for warmer, sunnier places, goggles for windy places, and fifty feet of rope and a folding telescope for seeing things far away. There were knives and hand tools, of course. With all the mystery of traveling to new dimensions, there was really no knowing what they would need in a pinch.

When everything was settled and Angela was as ready as she was going to be, they formed a line, taking hands. Donny stood on her left, his eyes seeming both sensitive and emotional as well as firm and asserting. He still believed he was coming, thinking he could force his way into this, but Angela could not allow it.

The Bui'dus locked arms to her right. It would be a lot of weight for Angela to carry between the worlds, but an inner voice told her there was nothing she couldn't handle.

"Not sure how long this is going to take," she admitted.

The others nodded. Angela took a deep breath to think and reaffirm that this was what she wanted to do, then smacked Donny's hand away and planted her boot on his stomach. With a kick, he fell out into the snowbank several feet away. Confusion and anger rippled across his face before she closed her eyes. A quick slice of the veils and a push with her souls was all it took to leave him behind. She and the Bui'dus disappeared, the snow puffing into the air at the blast of their disappearance.

The veils froze her to the bone, but not as much as Donny's expression had frozen her heart. She felt terrible, wading between Earth and Dingir for what felt like a hundred years before finally righting herself and expanding her awareness outward. Beyond the three worlds they knew were many more. Which was the right one? She had no idea, and no inclination or guidance from inside her soul made itself known. She wondered what it was like for the Dalkhu to find Earth in those ancient times.

The Bui'dus never reached out to aid her. They tagged along, completely at her will as she pulled them forward, and as time passed between the veils, it grew more and more unlikely that the goddess had given her more than just the awareness of other dimensions; the black hook in her soul seemed to bolster her reserves of energy.

Before her mind wandered for another hundred years, she decided on a relatively close world. While most felt spherical in shape and massive in size, this one was more cylindrical and smaller. Not only did that pique her curiosity, but it would also be a faster search. When she put her mind to it, they passed through its barriers quickly.

A gust of air slammed against them. Angela breathed once. Then a second time. That was good. Nothing was toxic, but everything was pitch black. Stepping forward with a hand outstretched, she felt nothing but heard the clomp of her boots on solid ground. The sound carried off into the distance, and its echo returned somehow amplified and louder than the source.

The Bui'dus shuffled behind her, grabbing and trying to find themselves. A flash of light brought Angela to squint and look away for a moment. When the match steadied and lit a gas lantern, she could make out Jezreal's face in the yellow glow. Her nostrils flared, her lips thin. "What the hell was that?" she asked. Her voice boomed, each echo getting louder. "Kicking Donny to the side like that was uncalled for."

Angela swallowed. "I... I know. I just couldn't... couldn't form the right words to convince him he couldn't come. He has to be free of all this, whether or not he understands. I won't risk his life again. He doesn't have the experience that you all—"

"Experience doesn't matter anymore," Jezreal said. She pointed at the ground, shaking mad. "There are so few of us left that we need everyone we have. He wants to fight this fight, make whatever sacrifice is necessary to get this done like the rest of us, and he has every right to. We're going to go back and get him."

Angela stiffened. Crossed her arms. Who was this girl to order her around? "Donny has no place on the literal frontier of dimensions unknown, in a fight against an ancient goddess. We are going to have to agree to disagree on this, because while you have crystals to get back to Dingir, you don't have a crystal to get you back here, and I'm not going back to carry you." She held out an open hand. "Give me the lantern and follow or go home."

Jezreal's eyes narrowed, the look of disgust washing over her as she handed the lantern over with a shove. She was a proud fighter, too, and Angela wondered if this was a sign of more arguments to come.

She'll just have to learn. This is my fight more than theirs.

Raising the lantern, Angela stepped into the darkness. The flickering yellow light was bright, yet it couldn't seem to reach farther than twenty yards. The ground was smooth, sheen black, and dully reflected the lantern's glow. Looking down, she saw a version of herself upside down in the reflection. It made her gut feel like she was falling until she looked away again.

For a while, the sounds of their footsteps coming back toward them was all that they encountered. The clanking of their gear and the clomps of their boots grew louder and louder until they were forced to pause so the sounds would die out. It slowed them down, but if they walked for longer than ten minutes, the reverberations grew uncomfortably loud.

"I'm worried about being detected," Angela explained.

"What could possibly live in this?" Samael asked. "It's

just darkness. No plant life or food or anything. Are we in a basement or a dungeon somewhere?"

She shook her head. "Not sure. All I know is that this world is shaped more like a tunnel than a sphere. I can feel the borders, not what's inside, but I think we're getting close to the edge. Just a little farther."

When the sound was no louder than a whisper, they resumed their search again. Angela was almost certain there would be no crystal shard of her soul's former owner here, but she led them on nonetheless with nothing more than curiosity to guide her.

What does the edge of a world look like?

The answer surprised her. Lantern light reflected off what seemed like a wall of shifting glass panels that shimmered as they approached. Jagged pieces broke off the floor and floated into the air, rotating to create a kaleidoscope-like effect, but each panel was more than just a reflection of the black that surrounded them; they were windows.

As they neared the edge, the pieces lit up like their footsteps had awoken them. Each tumbling and twirling panel was different. A valley of reddish rock and broken crust. A lush forest with bright colors. A sea as far as the eye could see. There were so many images moving about that they were hard to keep track of, but Angela focused on one and reached out into the expanse between worlds.

A minute passed before Gabe broke her dumbstruck silence. "This is incredible," he said, stepping to Angela's side. He reached out a gloved hand, poked one of the panels, and watched it jitter. "I've never seen... never imagined something like this. These are...?"

"Other worlds," Angela said. "But I can't seem to

connect these images to their veils. They're just peepholes, not doorways."

She watched a city unlike any she'd seen roll by. Tall, windowed structures with sharp angles. They stretched out into the distance, with glowing lights of so many colors and—

The image disappeared.

"Do you think every world has a physical border like this?"

Angela shook her head. "I don't think so. Something tells me this tunnel of dancing glass is special."

"What if," Jezreal began as she lifted a hand to her lips, "this isn't a random dimension created by the expansion—or destruction—of Vi'dinor? What if someone, or something, created these windows to watch other worlds? Do you think it would be possible with some advanced kind of technology, or is this something more of a god-level creation?"

Angela shrugged. "Either way, it was done with methods I don't think we could even begin to comprehend. There are so many different worlds on so many different timelines, each one starting off differently. It's hard to guess with the bits and pieces of information rattling around in my head."

Samael crossed his arms, glanced over the wall of images in front of them without a word. He'd been quieter than normal, and Angela wasn't sure how to take that.

"What's on your mind?" she asked. "You're input could be valuable."

Sam sighed, ran his palm over his face. "So we have all these worlds and no hint of where to look. If we can't connect these images with their worlds out there, how are we going to find this crystal shell of Antum you need? We can't possibly search all of them."

"I was thinking the exact same thing." Angela walked away from the wall a dozen steps, then sat cross-legged on the ground with the lantern in front of her, the light warming her cheeks as she took a deep breath and closed her eyes. "Watch over me for a bit. I'm going to reach out to her."

"To who?" Gabe asked.

"Ti'amat."

TWELVE CRYSTAL GODS HOVERED BETWEEN THE SCATTERED worlds, in a place that did not exist on its own volition. Held together by her energies and strong hand, this was where she gave shelter to gods she found still palatable and mostly controllable.

No matter how much time passed, Ti'amat still had a need for attention and entertainment. An eternity with no one but herself was uneventful. Boring. So over the eons, she'd picked favorites, extended offers of partnerships, and eaten enemies. Other minor gods existed out in fringe dimensions, fleeing at the first sign of her pursuit or finding ways to hide from her entirely, but she did not mind those elusive ones as much as those floating before her. These ones were with her to be watched and played with. All gods of any importance were here with her.

Half were considered her brothers and sisters, having come to be at about the same time as her, and four were their offspring. Most of their abilities varied but none compared to the vast array at Ti'amat's disposal. She reveled in the knowledge that she'd even acquired some of theirs, as occasionally there were twins and generational abilities that Ti'amat had gained through the consumption of one of the twins or their children.

Lahamu and Marduk were her and Abzu's own offspring. Marduk, the rebel, she kept quiet and imprisoned inside his crystal with no way to reach out. Motherly love was the only thing that kept him alive. Even though he had destroyed the first world and ran off to create his own dimension for a time, Ti'amat could not bring herself to crush him. A part of her respected his tenacity, so she held him close, pending her decision on what to do with him.

Surely, most of these gods and goddesses hated her, or at the least disliked her, she knew, but she'd offered to turn them into crystal so they could survive and she could keep things interesting. None but Marduk were direct threats; the rest were just sneaks.

How long have we been here? Ti'amat asked the others. *I grow bored in this timelessness.*

A long time, one of the others answered. *Perhaps you could let us free and we can go our separate ways.*

With all the strength I have taken, I still desire something... something that you others will never give me. True companionship. Servitude.

Perhaps worship is what you seek, another crystal said.

Ti'amat laughed but was not above admitting, *Perhaps.*

Another said, *I assure you that all of us are indebted to you, one way or another. We favor you. Even in our private conversations, we speak of how we might create with you again someday.*

Oh, please, Ti'amat began. *Don't even try to convince me that the eleven of you love me. You do not care for me any more than I do you. I know. That's how it's been for a long time. But please, continue, if you would, your tale of creation and partnership. What would we do?*

The others mumbled to one another for a time. Some conversations were discrete and quiet among the crystal gods. It had been a long time since they had discussed doing anything at all, so before long, rumors and plans began to form. Ti'amat allowed them to continue to think she could not sense their secret messages but guessed they knew she was listening. While none of them said it directly, there was the underlying desire for freedom. She could not hold that against them, she supposed. If anything, at least she would not be bored anymore.

After some time, she made up her mind. The others would squabble for eons if she let them, so she began to pull worlds together. As she worked, one of the twelve spoke: *Matter shifts, Ti'amat. I assume it is your doing?*

It is, she said.

The thinnest veils were the first to dissolve as she combined small, desolate dimensions around them. When she had gathered enough, the primordial chaos she ruled spawned the stars, and earthly bodies were formed. Most she allowed to remain how they were born, except for one she chose at random.

Dirt was carved from the surface to form canyons, rock crushed together into mountains. Water pooled, filling basins across the globe. Fire rumbled from the belly of the planet as she shaped this particular one to her liking. For a time, chaos reigned on the surface of that world.

The veil around them began to solidify and form. She had drawn upon her memories of Mulki as inspiration. This one was similar, but its own. At her command, the crystals fell, cutting through the atmosphere in streaks of heated air until they reached the barren surface of rock and dirt not yet completely cultivated. It was an empty canvas, and she said, *Let us separate to opposite ends of this world. We will form our sections as we wish, aid or hinder one another, and create new life for us to dabble with.*

As you wish, the others said. They tried to hide it, but Ti'amat knew they were filled with glee. They scattered like birds taking flight, their colors shimmering in the sunlight as they went off to find their own slice of her new world. Within hours, the surface began its transformation. She could feel things shifting in the distance. Hungry trees and plants dug their roots into the soil. In a fortnight, the first living creatures burrowed in caverns and walked on land.

But I will have the seas, Ti'amat decreed. *The seas of water and of air.*

She made her creations with serpentine bodies of all sizes. Some with claws and fangs, some with just one or the other, but most were just like her old flesh. What goddess wouldn't create after her own image? She worked alone for a time until a presence touched her.

I've thought of what you said, a soft voice said. *You think that no one could love you, but I think you are wrong. Your wrath is wicked and your judgment harsh, but your grace and wisdom withstand the tests of time. I know your anger is sparked by all the good you see lacking. You mean the best by establishing order. I might not love, but I do serve, and none know what the future holds.*

Ti'amat was amused. The voice came from the crystal goddess closest to her, the one that did not go far: Antum. These were not the sweetest words she'd ever heard, but they were the best in a very long time. This goddess hadn't said anything to the others in secret. Either she was sincere or very smart. She had always been quiet, and there was a wisdom in that, but could Ti'amat trust her?

They are beautiful creatures you've made, Antum said. *What do you call them?*

What does that matter to you? Is it all a game to get close to me? To crawl into the light of my favor? Tell it true, I warn you.

Antum paused. *No, I swear. I mean nothing ill or self-serving. A genuine curiosity drives me nearer.*

Ti'amat gauged her soul but found nothing off. If Ti'amat had lungs, she would have sighed. *A game of wits is about to begin, Antum. A war fought with pawns where we do not get directly involved. These creatures we create will be our tools. Our toys. We'll teach them faith and devotion, wrath and war, order and peace. They will strive, as we have, to create and commune, but like us, they will not succeed. Fate would see they follow in our footsteps. All offspring of fallen gods will be known as Nephilim.*

PHYSICAL SENSATION RUSHED BACK: THE COLD BLACKNESS around her and the dingy glass-like floor under her hands. The stale air filled her nostrils and all seemed as it had been when she had begun her meditations, but when Angela saw the Bui'dus frozen in stasis in front of her, she was certain that she had brought someone else back with her. Rising to her feet, she checked Jezreal's, Gabe's, and Samael's eyes for signs of the goddess's presence, but there was still color to them.

Maybe she's playing a game with me.

No, she was just a bit delayed. As Angela spun to search the darkness, Ti'amat came walking closer with wisps of smoke trailing behind her. The goddess threw her hair behind her shoulders and stopped. This time, she wore a dark blue dress, a copper-chained talisman embedded with lapis lazuli stones, and earrings of silver. In the dark, she seemed to glow.

"You reached out for me?" Ti'amat asked. She seemed confused as she put a hand on her hip.

"I need you more than I'd like to admit."

Ti'amat smiled, taking pleasure in that. "This is an interesting world, isn't it? I take it this is your first step into unfamiliar territory?"

Angela nodded.

"I figured, and I see you've brought company along with you. The Bui'dus. Ja'noel's final effort to stabilize Dingir. A lofty and improbable goal, but honorable. That city is on its final throes of death. It's just too sad the city he's devoted his life to won't recover to its former glory. But many of us live for a purpose or a dream only to have it squashed right in front of us. That kind of horror is heart-wrenching. I felt it myself when all the work I put into developing Mulki was ripped apart before my eyes." Ti'amat paused, then shrugged. "But all things begin and end in the cycle of chaos. Even I cannot deny its power over all." The goddess's gaze drifted into the distance as she pondered something.

A thought came to Angela's mind. She wondered if she could use a different approach to try tricking the goddess into telling her where she was. Angela asked, "Where is Ja'noel?"

A grin. The goddess knew better than to give him up. "He's with me. Resting in body and soul until I have further use for him. But we digress, unless that is what you reached out to ask me."

"Not exactly, but we'll get to that. How long do you expect this journey to take me? If I'm to find Antum's remnants across the dimensions in any timely manner, I'll need more guidance than you just setting me free to roam. We both know where this conflict is headed. Why not just get us to the end? Where is Antum's crystal?"

Ti'amat placed an arm across her stomach and lifted a finger to her lips. "Even if I knew, I wouldn't say. To find the rest of you is to complete yourself, and it benefits you just as much as I want to see it happen, but it is imperative that you earn this by your own means. So what else might I do? Reach out and bring fragmented worlds together to hasten your search? No... That would make the worlds larger and lengthen the search. How might we cut the fat? Remove the unnecessary dimensions?"

She paced for a moment, her long black hair bobbing at the middle of her back. Suddenly, she stopped, turned to face Angela with a vibrant smile full of beauty and mischievousness. "Instead, perhaps you should draw upon me. For this, I'll allow it. A portion of my energy will be at your disposal and heighten your awareness of the other worlds. Beyond your current ability to detect the many veiled pockets, you may be able to sense the energy inside them. You will root out most of these dead worlds."

Ti'amat motioned to the space around them. "Yes... That will save us some time. In fact, maybe as we go along and I collect more of my crystal shards and souls, I'll grant you more and more of my power. Yes... I think I'll do that. Draw upon me in your times of need, and I will see if the situation justifies my divine intervention." Ti'amat twirled her finger in her hair, smiling devilishly as she said, "But of course, don't think it will come without a cost."

Angela was afraid of that. She had expected the

goddess would not play nice when given the chance. She sighed. "What cost?"

"I'll have to think about it," Ti'amat said. "But when you need a boon, I'll be there. Until next time, Antum." The goddess winked, and the black hook inside Angela's soul swelled.

She clutched her chest as a rush of foreign strength flooded into her. It burned yet invigorated her. Got her heart racing. She closed her eyes, hard. Fought to keep her breath as the connecting bridge between her soul and Ti'amat's immense being widened like opening floodgates. Ti'amat's presence in her soul was like the root of a tree burrowing itself deeper into her, but only now could she faintly sense the size of the tree looming over her, massive and over-shadowing. The black stain in her soul had grown to nearly double in size, and this gift of energy was nothing compared to all that Ti'amat had at her disposal.

The flow slowed, and so did Angela's breathing. When she opened her eyes, she was on her ass but couldn't remember sitting or falling down. Jezreal was looking down at her, blinking. The woman reached down and slapped Angela across the cheek. It stung. Time had resumed.

"What was that for?" Angela lurched to her feet, perhaps too quickly.

Samael shoved his partner out of the way, rushing to get into what he must have perceived as a fight in the making. There was a knife in his hand. He stood defensively at the ready, the blade pointed at Angela's chest. "Your eyes were black," he said. "You would not respond, no matter what we tried. We could not reach you. Ti'amat had you so hard I was afraid you were hers. Give me one reason why I shouldn't slit your throat."

Angela stiffened, angry and completely blown away. Gabe and Jezreal appeared just as shocked. They rushed forward to take the knife away. He evaded them and stumbled back. "You saw it, too," he said, pointing the blade at both of them. "Those were the goddess's eyes, and that means that Ti'amat is with her. We cannot trust her." His knuckles turned white as his grip on the dagger tightened.

"I reached out to her, had a vision, and she came to me," Angela said. "Is that so surprising? As much as we are against her, we need her, too. She has all the cards, and we're fighting to level the playing field. Put the knife away. Have you ever threatened Donny's life for the time he was taken over? No? I thought not. This is the game we play, Sam. So calm down."

His brow furrowed. He let the knife fall to the side of his leg but did not put it away. No one liked the situation, but drawing a knife was stupid and unacceptable. He asked, "How... How do we know she's not watching through you now?"

Angela shrugged. "How do we know she's not watching through *any* of us? All we can do is hope she'll keep her word and keep pushing forward. Until we find how the Nephilim defeated her, we have no option but to trust her and each other. Now put that knife away. I'm serious. We're moving out."

CHAPTER FIVE

The journey between worlds was longer than Angela had anticipated. Conservatively, it seemed as though months had passed in those icy halls of the void. The others she was dragging along with her were probably upset with her and impatient, but how was she to choose a destination among a seemingly infinite number of worlds with at least some spark of energy inside them?

The strength that Ti'amat had lent her was no joke, and the new vibrations she could sense on the surfaces of those worlds' veils were signs of life just on the other side of them, she knew. Some quivered like a leaf in the breeze, while others seemed to shake and tremble like a quake. But then she had to take the world's size into consideration. If it was small and the veils seemed to thrash, it was densely populated. Large ones seemed to only shiver, if move at all.

The debate raged on inside her, and when she finally decided and pulled them through, she was greeted by a hot blast of sand on the wind. It whipped at her eyes, stung her skin, and almost pushed her to the ground. When she covered her mouth with her cotton undershirt to filter out the dirt, the air was breathable enough. The Bui'dus had a harder time than her; moments in and they were already on the ground, shielding their eyes and fighting to regain their feet.

Just barely audible over the howl of the storm, Jezreal shouted, "Why here? We can't—" She tripped. Ate a mouthful of sand, spat, and swung a fist at the ground in anger.

Angela pulled the goggles from her bag and did her best to bring the soldiers together and get them their gear from their bags. When they were seated with their backs against the wind and huddled side by side, she said, "About three miles away from here is a big well of energy. I want to see it from a distance before we get close."

Jezreal scowled.

"That means we wait out the storm," Angela said.

"I know." She sounded defeated already but kept her opinions to herself.

So they sat at the bottom of a dune and withstood the blowing red sands for hours until the air began to slow and they could finally make out the giant orange sun in the sky. Holding up her fist between her and the horizon, the sun was still larger. It had been warm before, but now it was *hot* as they shambled to their feet and stretched their limbs.

They were standing in the valley of two dunes speckled with craggy rock showing through the sand. Before the others asked which way, Angela closed her eyes and focused for a moment. Blooming outward with her mind, she stretched out over the land until the electric tingle of energy brushed against her. It was like reaching out over a field of wheat and touching every kernel, an imprecise sense that allowed her to know that there were many small sources, but she was unable to make distinctions between them or identify them.

She pulled herself back together, having felt enough to know which way to go and knowing she didn't need to cover it all. Perhaps getting closer would help her differentiate the sources.

The others followed her up the dune without a word. Even at the top, sand stretched in every direction but one. In the distance, jutting red sandstone towers stood above the dunes like fingers. That was where they were headed. Up and down the shifting hills, they pushed on, through the heat and into the fields of stone.

Gabe dropped his pack and rubbed his back against a rock, scratching himself where he couldn't reach. "I've got sand in my crack, I think," he complained.

Jez laughed and beamed. "You're such a child."

He shrugged and did not deny it as he threw his bag onto his back again.

All around them, the red towers loomed, holding back the wind and the sand but radiating the sun's heat back at them. The Bui'dus trailing behind Angela were breathing heavily, leaning against the rocks whenever they could to conserve every bit of energy. Before long, Jezreal's hair was soaked in sweat. Gabe's legs shook and wavered, and Samael was too tired to find something to argue about. That was nice. The stones were a labyrinth and an oven, but they were close now. Angela could feel it.

They walked under red arches and squeezed into a crack in a wall of stone. For thirty yards, they walked sideways, shifting, bending, crawling, and sucking in their stomachs to fit through. Even Angela began to have doubts they would make it through the narrow passage.

When the stone finally opened up to them, the party

took a moment of reprieve. They were standing in a hollow cavity the shape of an open bowl. The walls were smooth, and other cracks and tunnels led off in different directions. The dimming sky hovered above them: a view to dusk and a sky filling with more stars by the minute.

"Here," Samael said, kneeling near the side of the bowl. Over his shoulder, Angela could see bits of scrap on the ground and the black charcoal remains of a fire. He pulled blankets and clothes from crevasses in the rock. Tiny bronze disks shimmered in his hands. "I'll take that as a sign of life," he said, amused. "And not just animal life, either. This is coin. There are intelligent people in this world."

She nodded. It made sense. The vibrant specks of energy she had felt out in the desert were the sparks of souls, and that meant they were not the only people here. "Take whatever clothes you can find. There's a lot of life up ahead and I don't know how they will take—"

Her breath escaped her. A star that had twinkled blue and white in the dusk sky grew and wavered like the flame of a candle before stretching downward into a pillar of light. Far away, it reached the bottom edge of their view, disappeared behind the rock, and presumably crashed into the earth when the ground began to shake and the loose stones around them rumbled. Dust filled the atmosphere, but the light did not fade.

"What in the old tongue is *that*?" Jezreal asked. Her hands were trembling at her waist.

"Energy," Angela said, voice shaking. "So much of it."

Gabe stepped forward. The bluish glow lit his boyish face, revealed the sand and dirt clinging to every fold of his clothes. He turned to Angela, concern on his face. "Is it a god?"

It felt like a rock had hit Angela in the gut as she considered it. Even from their distance, perhaps several miles away, the subtle heat warmed her face. In moments, a breeze carried a cloud of dust over the alcove, filling the air with the smell of pine and earth. The skyward obelisk *was* pure energy, Angela was sure of that, but all she could do was stare at its brilliance in stupor.

If not an old god, who or what could conjure this? Angela wondered. But as quickly as the pillar of light arrived, it disappeared, fading until it became transparent, and its mystical blue light vanished into dark night again. It took a moment for their eyes to readjust to their reddish surroundings, and they stood staring at one another in silence for a moment, soaking in what they could not understand.

"We should leave," Samael said. "We don't need trouble with another god."

Angela bit her lip. "I agree with you, but we don't know if it really is a god."

"Maybe this other god has a beef with Ti'amat," Gabe suggested.

Angela pointed at him, smiled. "I like where your head's at, Gabe. Maybe you're more than just the most handsome."

He wore a vibrant smile. "The smartest, too? Oh, Angela, you really should watch how much you notice my usefulness to the party and compliment me for it. I might just fall in love with you."

Jezreal laughed as she shook her head. "Don't encourage his behavior. Are we moving on or what?"

"Yeah, we move on," Angela said. "Toward the area where the light touched the surface. I think we'll find something there."

Samael stepped forward again. He was shaking in either rage or fear; Angela couldn't tell which. "No, we should leave. Unlike the last world, where black halls of mirror-like images were cunning and full of shrouded mystery, this place is unafraid to show its power and terror in sandstorms and brilliant beams of light. Mark my words, if we press on and something happens, I will remind you all that I was the voice of reason you chose to ignore."

Angela sighed. She could not get Sam on board with anything, it seemed, but he did not say he would stay behind. She said, "Even though we are all afraid, we have to carry on until we know for certain that this place has no remnant of Antum's soul."

Samael furrowed his brow. "If there are other people here, what is the chance that the other part of Antum's soul is inside one of them? How are you going to know where it is, and do you have it in you to take it from them?"

Angela hadn't thought of that. Taking a soul from someone was the last thing she wanted to do. The thought opened old wounds. She remembered what it was like when Udug had taken her soul, as well as the feeling of taking it back and watching his lifeless body fall into the blue expanse beneath Dingir.

But lifeless he was not, she thought as she remembered his return.

"I haven't felt prepared for anything in a long time, so it doesn't matter how I feel about it." Angela walked through the Bui'dus and to the stone wall around them. Standing sideways to fit between a crack, she looked back and said, "All I know is that there's a goddess who will destroy everything if we don't do what she says. I'll do whatever I can to avoid taking anyone's soul, but if we are going to find our own way out of this, we're going to have to make it seem like we're moving toward what she wants until we figure something out."

The soldiers wavered, eyes dropping to the ground as they thought about it, but Angela didn't stick around to see their final conclusion. The enclosing red stones were beginning to cool, and the lack of sunlight grew more and more apparent as she continued on. There must've been ten yards between them before Angela heard the first sounds of the soldiers following after her. For a moment, she had feared that they would not.

Slowly, the crack they traversed expanded into a fissure twenty feet wide and growing. Red sand spilled down from the cliff above them in steady streams that reminded her of hourglasses. Other tunnels began to appear, jutting off in other directions. The farther they went, the passageways appeared more and more frequent until there was more air than stone, it seemed. The path was leading them downward, beneath the surface and into a cavern riddled with pillars and strange rock formations, a maze of tunnels and passageways that went off at strange angles.

"Feels like we're walking through a giant piece of cheese," Gabe muttered.

Everyone was amused at that, and Angela took it as a good sign. Joking around would keep their spirits up, keep them connected with one another even when they had their disagreements. Morale was always a tricky thing to improve for any enlisted person, but the effects of its lacking were always apparent and dangerous. With things as desperate as they had ever been for the Anunnaki, the last thing Angela needed was for the party to rip itself apart. That, and the mass grave that lay before them.

Between cragged columns of red stone and beneath the circular skylights above, piles of dead bodies were rotting.

Dirty ribcages in torn, bloodied rags. Dismembered hands and limbs. Most of the flesh was already gone, other than the occasional bits of hair and meat that still clung on, but the stench remained strong. There were gnaw marks on some of the bones. Some skulls were big, and others were smaller, suggesting that the age of these victims was not important to their killers.

As they stumbled up to them, the soldiers gagged. Samael tried to speak, tried to convince Angela it was finally time to turn around, but she shushed him. They needed to be quiet now, but Gabe choked and retched. When he regained control of his guts, looking sorry, Angela could only shrug. She was having a hard time keeping in her own acid. Covering her nose with her shirt only helped a little.

She didn't dare walk through the remains and instead led them to the side and around the mound to avoid disturbing it. After they reached the other side of it and were out of range of the stench, they took a break on a cluster of boulders.

"I don't like this," Gabe said. His breath reeked of vomit.

Samael sat and ran his fingers over his sweat-coated scalp, sighing slowly. Angela could barely make out his face in the darkness. The last of the dusk light was gone now. Down at the bottom of the cave, there were only the faint rays of what must have been moonlight peering through the holes above. The light was dying in the catacombs, and as the soldiers stilled, a quiet noise became apparent: a scuttling, scratching sound from beyond the pile of bones behind them.

"Did you hear that?" Angela asked. The others looked at one another, then the cavern around them, wary.

"Is someone following us?" Jezreal asked.

It was quiet but for the thrumming of her heart and their heavy, nervous breathing. Assuming it was nothing, a trick their own minds had played on them, the Bui'dus allowed a few sighs of relief to escape them. Then came hunchbacked figures descending from the cavern roof by scuttling down the red stone columns. Humanoid in some regard, the monsters clambered with thick bipedal legs but had more tiny arm-like appendages than Angela could count. On the ground, they stood upright, stepped onto the bone pile without heed for the dead, and came into the rays of moonlight.

Their insectoid form became clear: a conjoining of man and cricket or roach. As they crept closer, the exoskeleton on their limbs rubbed, creating the scratching sounds that haunted them. Mandibles chattered back and forth like they were communicating to one another as at least fifteen of the creatures began to surround them.

Gabe and Angela were just too stunned to react. Samael was trembling as he fumbled with the knife at his belt while Jezreal was steadier and drew her tether gun. "Group up," she commanded. That helped snap the others out of their daze. Angela drew the sword from its over-the-shoulder scabbard and placed her back to her comrades as they formed a rough defensive circle against the encroaching creatures.

"Wh-What do we do?" Gabe asked as he fumbled with his own gun. "Shoot and make a run for it?"

The creatures continued stalking closer, their bug eyes shimmering wet in the moonlight.

Twenty yards, Angela noted.

"They clearly aren't friends," Samael answered.

"Well, no shit," Jezreal added. There were too many

targets for her barrel to jump between. Standing upright, the tallest were just over seven feet and bulky, and they did not seem to take the threat of her gun seriously.

Fifteen yards.

"Stay back," Angela commanded. She shook her blade, swiped at the air, and the creatures took another step. They seemed intelligent enough to communicate with one another but either did not comprehend their language or did not care.

Ten yards.

They were too bestial. That much was clear. Strings of saliva dripped from their mandibles. This close, they were more like insects than men. Before this, Angela thought that brandishing a sword was a universal language, but apparently that was not understood here.

One screeched and leapt for Jezreal. In a single bound, it covered the distance. She sidestepped and fired, missed, steel dart tinkering off the rock. The creature landed in the middle of them with a thud. The Bui'dus stepped away, spreading out. Standing upright again, the creature hissed. Its gaze bounced between them all, the creature uncertain who to go for next. Angela took advantage of its indecision, rushed forward, brought the blade up. She pierced its exoskeleton and made a long cut up its abdomen. The beast's spindly arms writhed against its chest as green innards spilled out. As it toppled to the ground, the others screeched for their fallen brood-brother.

And they came rushing like a tidal wave, slamming into Jezreal and Gabe and tackling them to the ground. They rolled, screaming and kicking as mandibles snapped and legs scuttled over them. The pop and sizzle of a tether gun filled the air, and the one atop Jezreal seized and shook. Samael pushed it off her with a kick and helped her to her feet while Angela pushed into the veil. These things were fast. Appearing again in a blast of air, Angela saw the creatures pause. They didn't know what to think of her teleportation. She thrust down at the creature on top of Gabe and severed its head with a flick of her wrist before they continued their assault.

"We're not going to win this," Angela said as she pulled him up. "Retreat." She ran.

Gabe and Samael were quick to follow. Jezreal stayed in the back of the group, firing her tether gun hopelessly behind them as they ran.

"Teleport us out of here!" Samael demanded.

Angela thought about it but decided against it. With the heightened awareness that Ti'amat had given her, she reached out as she ran. Not a quarter-mile ahead, she felt the thousands of pinpricks of energy just barely above their heads. The insectoid creatures were dull and lifeless compared to what lay ahead of them. They had not seen what they walked through sandstorms and intense heat to find.

"Not yet," she said. "Follow me. Keep running."

The cacophony of scuttling feet behind them was terrifying, and the clunking of their boots could not go fast enough. They raced through the cavernous catacombs. Even Jezreal gave up trying to fire behind her when she could not hold her gun steady and land a good hit while sprinting. The monsters began to fall behind as they ran bipedally, so they shifted their weight onto arms and legs like apes in order to keep up.

At least they are slow and can't fly, she thought.

They took a tunnel that led up toward the surface. The star-filled night sky and the pale glow of the moon ahead urged Angela forward. A small part of her hoped that the creatures wouldn't follow them on the surface, but she knew that was a foolish dream.

A scream erupted right behind her. She turned. Jezreal was on the ground. Too frenzied and too afraid to move, Gabe and Samael looked to Angela, who said, "You two need to toughen up," as she ran past them. The roach-men made their way up the tunnel toward them, clinging to the tunnel walls as they snapped their mandibles and screeched. One she did not see dropped from the ceiling, its weight crashing down on her as something sharp cut into her shoulder. With a groan, she heaved the creature off, throwing it against the wall. Fury took hold of her. She pulled on the energy inside her, formed a rippling purple light around her left hand, and swung. Her fist broke through the exoskeleton as easily as her sword did earlier, its innards smoking and filling the air with a terrible stench. The creature hissed and shuddered to its knees as its spider-like appendages raked against her in retaliation. For a moment, she was glad that she did not bring Donny along to face these things.

Angela cut off her light and withdrew her fist, grabbed Jezreal by the arm, and left the creature to clutch at the crater in its abdomen before the others caught up. Jezreal kept pace. That was good. Her ankle hadn't twisted and nothing was broken. The creatures paused long enough at their dying brother that Angela and her team were able to break through to the surface and onto flat land. She wondered if they would eat the ones they had wounded rather than continue to chase them, but in moments, the answer was clear. They came swarming onto the surface, more of them than she had thought there were to begin with. It seemed they did not enjoy an easy meal.

Ahead was something none of them expected to see.

Vibrant lights traced the outer edges of blocky gray buildings set into red cliffs, some blue, red, green, and even
white. This place was so bright that the stars were drowned
out. As the sounds of the creatures behind them continued,
Angela urged everyone to pick up the pace and rush toward
whatever safety this strange village could offer.

She led them into the open canyon with a bad feeling in
her gut. Silver doors with no handles and black glass
windows lined the main thoroughfare. Strange symbols
hung over doorways in colored light-tubes. The insectoid
creatures chasing them had newfound strength, kicking up
sand and dust as they rushed closer. For some reason, the
roach-men were growing desperate, and Angela realized
that they knew they were running out of time to catch them.
Red lights were flashing atop the buildings. A siren began
to wail. Before Angela could determine if that was a good
or bad thing, movement ahead caught her gaze.

Three people in heavy, colored cloaks that dragged on
the ground rushed out onto the main road. Their heads were
shrouded in a cloth that matched the red sands, but the
gloves they wore were blue. Each of them carried a thick
silver staff, the end in a flanged mace. Gabe and Samael
were waving their arms, shouting for the guards' attention,
begging for help as they ran toward them. Unlike the beasts
behind them, they appeared to be civilized people.

Before Angela and the Bui'dus reached them, the
strangers stopped, pulled up the colored sleeves on their left
arms to reveal a single golden bar that ran along their forearms. It was not their gloves that were blue; it was their
skin, and their hands seemed slightly off in shape and size.
The golden bars swung vertically with a whirring sound,
then clacked as they locked into place. Blue light formed a

disk like a shield in front of them. They readied their staves like they were going to strike.

"Stop," Angela said, not fifteen yards from the strangers. She wished she could see their eyes and faces behind their wrappings and discern just how human they were.

Bolts of bluish light raced from the ends of their staves, flying fast between her and the Bui'dus. Samael cursed and dropped to the ground. Angela spun around to see the impacts. If they wanted to kill her, they would have. The bolts slammed into the sand, kicking up the earth in blasts around the incoming creatures. One bolt hit a creature squarely in the chest, liquefying its abdomen. It flailed before falling face-first into the dirt.

That seemed to be all it took to turn the tide. The rest of the creatures hissed and turned on their heels, speeding back toward the system of caverns they had emerged from as more blue balls of light followed them all the way there. When the dust cleared, Angela saw the bolts had hit the sand had turned it into glass mid-explosion. They were frozen in time, like little glass trees that peppered the ground.

"Gods…" Jezreal muttered, out of breath. "What kind of world have we stumbled upon?"

"I have no idea," Angela said as she watched the last of the cockroaches slip into the tunnel. "But I'm glad we stopped here. I never would have guessed that—"

A sharp pain washed over Angela's head, and everything went black.

CHAPTER SIX

A ngela awoke with bright blue light cast across her vision. From the rigid bed, she could look across the small room and see that the light was less a means of illumination and more of a barrier. It was the same kind of light as the shields of those strangers who had assuredly knocked her out. While they had saved her from those insectoid creatures in the caverns, those guards were now her wardens. Clearly, they had thrown her in a cell, and she would have to decide if their help outweighed their impedance.

Putting her feet to the ground and sitting up, she groaned and rubbed her temples. Shifting her weight seemed to hurt her brain. A stride across the room and she put a theory to the test by poking the field of blue light with the tip of her pointer. She jerked back, put her finger in her mouth. It burned badly. Without touching it again, she moved to the left and the right, trying to get the best angle for looking down the grayish halls, but to no avail.

Turning her attention back to the walls that imprisoned her, she noticed that there was nothing too fancy beyond the blue light. The place was made out of the same hard-as-rock grayish material as the homes out in the canyon. There were no blocks or bricks in the floors or wall, and it appeared that all of it was made from the same stone, but not in the grandeur style of the Kissum. Nor did it seem that this place was carved by hand. The room was too perfect, sharp, and square. How it was made with such precision, Angela couldn't guess, but she now understood that she was standing in a world where technology reigned supreme. It made the Ascendancy's shifters, lights, boilers, and steam-powered utilities look rudimentary. And perhaps they were.

She made her way back to the bed, realizing that it was actually a twin bunk. White sheets, light blue blanket, a single pillow. The simple nightstand didn't have anything in it or on top. There were no windows, but at least the toilet in the far corner had a privacy drape. It was particularly comfortable as far as cells went, but Angela had no intention of prolonging her stay.

Sitting lotus on the bed, she closed her eyes and reached outward. Instantly, she felt the buzz of quiet energy all around her. The auras of the Bui'dus stood out above all the other noise in the area. She thought about the natives of this world. The insectoid people were purely animal and had no souls attached to them, but she was not sure if the armed villagers with blue skin did or not.

There would have to be guards wandering the halls. If she was going to free her partners, she would have to move quickly. But just before she pulled herself back into her body, the forefront of her mind brushed against something she had not expected to find. Not a half a mile away was something profoundly *loud*: the aura of what had to be a spirit, deeper and stronger than even the Nephilim, humming like an engine. She guessed that she, with the goddess's gifts, was the closest comparison to an aura of similar magnitude.

What is that? she wondered. Her curiosity of this strange place and the wonders within gripped her strongly. *Only one way to find out.*

Angela rose from the bed and faced the glowing blue barrier in front of her. A quick jaunt through the veil and she was on the other side, standing in a long hallway that spread out a hundred yards in both directions. The boom of her teleportation reverberated painfully in the confined space. Certainly, that would draw someone's attention.

A few silver doors without handles lined one side of the hall, similar to the ones she'd seen when they entered the canyon. The other wall was partitioned by the glowing blue of more cells. She rushed to the closest one and found it empty and identical to her own. In the second cell, two concerned faces looked out from their vertically stacked beds.

"Angela!" the woman whispered. She threw blankets to the floor and raced to her feet. Angela had never seen Jezreal's hair out of its ponytail; she hadn't recognized her at first. The Bui'du slunk to the blue barrier with gentle steps like she was trying to be quiet, and stealth most certainly did not matter now. Jezreal's armor and pack had been removed and she'd been stripped down to her under-armor lining. To Angela's surprise, there were no visible bruises on her skin. In fact, Angela couldn't spot a speck of sand on her, and it even looked like she had bathed at some point.

"How did you get the royal treatment when I got clubbed in the back of the head?" Angela asked.

Jezreal strained, seeming surprised that Angela was

complaining. She shook her head, ignored the comment, and asked, "What the hell are you doing?"

Angela shrugged. "Getting us out of here. What else?" She sliced her way through the veils and teleported into the cell without warning. A man on the upper bunk jolted upright in a frenzy of matted beard and curses when she appeared. He tried to use his blankets as a barrier.

"You bitch," he said, peering from the security of his fortress. "The fuck was that?"

Angela's jaw went slack. Not only did the man look mostly human, but he spoke a language close enough to her own dialect that she could understand him. "How... How is it possible you and I can speak the same language? As far as I know, our worlds never came in contact before. But..." She bit her lip, thinking for a moment until the answer clicked in her mind. "A god that must have escaped the destruction of Mulki must have made all this..."

A blaring sound flooded the room, grew high-pitched and oscillating, then repeated itself. *Shit*, Angela thought. *An alarm.*

The man's brow tightened. He gestured and shouted, "Fuck off with your gods and fuck off with you." He threw the blanket over his head and began to burrow into it as though it would protect him.

Jezreel wobbled on her legs, nervous. "About getting out of here..."

Angela nodded. "Right." She grabbed her elbow and pushed them into the void, then into the hall just outside the cell. They ran, their boots heavy and loud until they reached the next cell. A blue-skinned person was standing just on the other side of the barrier. Dressed in simpler clothes, its skin was mostly bare and the sex undiscernible. Dark marks almost as black as pitch were sprinkled about like freckles. Its frame was thin but muscular, and its limbs were disproportionately long compared to its torso. And then fear squeezed the life out of Angela, freezing her in place. Beyond the wall of light, the prisoner's eyes shimmered like pools of black water.

Are they naturally like that? Or is that Ti'amat watching us?

Jezreal pushed against her, urging her forward. "It doesn't matter if she's there or not," she said, reading Angela's mind. "What matters is that we find the others and get the hell out of here. Fast."

Angela let out her breath slowly, calmed herself. Jezreal was right; they had to move. "Split up. You search for Gabe and Samael. I'll look for our gear in one of these other rooms. If you run into trouble, just yell, I guess."

Jezreal laughed weakly. It was hardly a good plan, but it was the only plan they had. She turned and took off down the hall, so Angela went the other way.

The next silver door she came to had a little black square to the side. In fact, every door, including the glowing blue prison cell fields, had one of these black squares next to them. She hadn't considered them before, didn't think they were anything special. When she touched it, its surface was smooth like glass, and the black square chirped and flashed red suddenly. Angela pulled her hand back. It was a locking mechanism of some kind, but she could only guess what opened it since there was no keyhole.

A calm male voice spoke from behind her. "What's a little bird like you doing outside your cell?"

Angela's breath caught in suspense at first, then confusion. She turned and beheld a man behind the closest blue field. He was dressed in a long leather coat that reached his knees and black boot-cut pants. Double silver earrings looped around his earlobes. Picking at his teeth with a toothpick, he sauntered up to the blue field between them and rested a shoulder against the wall. Over the buzz of the field, he said, "I can help you get out of here if you get *me* out of *here*." He pointed to his feet, and in the brief seconds she had, she made a decision.

"Sorry. Don't know you." She turned back to the silver door and pressed her hand on it once more. Again, it made a noise and flashed at her. The door did not open.

The stranger scoffed behind her. "You won't get in that way, little bird."

Angela curled her fingers into a fist but ignored him otherwise—until his comments began to pick at her looks and explain how the color of her hair hinted at the size of her brain and her inability to open the damn door. She faced him, irate. "You're hurting your own chances, you know."

He lifted the edge of his thin lips in a smirk. "If I can't come out there, why don't you come in here? There's a bed." He motioned to it.

Angela's jaw might have hit the floor. She wasn't sure; she was too busy teleporting into the cell and slapping him across the cheek. The man came back up, holding his cheek, which had turned red from the blow. His uncertainty of what just happened only lasted a moment. He groaned, "What a sweet gesture from such a little bird."

Angela gave him a boot to his chest for that. He dropped onto the bed and stayed there, huffing and fighting to catch his breath. She said, "Your attempts to be suave are more irritating than anything." Hoping he'd received the message that time, she turned her gaze back to the door across the hall, and he proved her wrong.

"I knew I could get you in here," he said, patting the

bed, that smug smile returning. A single silver tooth glimmered in his mouth. "Name's Ibarra, partner. I knew a pretty lady like you once before. Tough as nails and an appetite for crushing nuts, if you know what I mean."

Angela shook her head and turned away, trying to hide her smile. *This guy is ridiculous!* she mused. "No, I don't know what you mean. I think you must have been looking in a mirror when you made that comment about intelligence, but you're persistent and confident, I'll give you that," she said.

He shrugged overenthusiastically. "Well, I am a captain. What do you say? How about the two of us get out of here? You got a knack for being somewhere one second, then being somewhere else the next, and I know this place like the back of my hand. The places we need to go. We could work together. Get out of here and off this rock. Go wherever you like."

A sigh escaped her as the ringing of the alarm reminded her of the severity of the situation. "Sorry, got to keep moving." Besides, she didn't know what Ibarra was in a cell for. And even if a small part of her secretly did feel vexed enough to help him, what would she do with him? She couldn't take him with her to other worlds.

An idea came to her. A bad, reckless idea. Angela guessed the silver door was a foot thick, tops, so she closed her eyes and pushed between worlds. With nothing more than the perception of where she came from, she traversed the veils to the place she thought would be on the other side of the door and went through again. The air slapped against her, hot and humid like a rainforest, but there were no trees there. Corrugated steel greeted her. Railings and pipes surrounded a dozen giant metal tanks. The symbols on the gauges and valves were foreign, but the heat and gurgling sounds told Angela that this was a boiler room.

She looked around her feet and swallowed nervously.

Not a foot away was a bucket filled with stinking rags. That was the risk with teleporting into places she'd never been before. Even with Ti'amat's gift, she could only gauge approximates, only faintly feel the physical makeup and size of a room or world and the amount of energy in it, but she could not detect specifics or small things. If she would have come into that room just a little to the left, or if the person who had last used that bucket had innocently left it just a bit closer to her, she would have had a very painful arrival. Meshing leg and bucket was not something she wanted to experience.

Taking a deep breath and holding it, she cut into the veil again and disappeared. Upon arrival, she shivered. The icy sensation was a feeling she just couldn't get used to. Behind the blue energy field in front of her, Ibarra was still leaning against the wall and picking at his teeth. He waved to her with a smile but did not say a word.

Faintly, underneath the trilling sound of the alarm, Jezreal was screaming, grunting, and groaning from some-where down the hall. Angela cussed, gauged the direction, and teleported. Around the corner, six blue men with staves in hand surrounded Jezreal. A quick blow across her cheek and blood sprayed from her mouth, staining the gray walls and floor.

Not a second passed and Angela was on top of them, clubbing a fist into the back of the closest one's head. He toppled face-first onto the floor. She scooped up the staff and twirled around, whacking the side of a second one who was too slow to react. Jezreal recovered, roaring as she swung. That one fell, too. The guards drew back, formed a line, and activated their glowing blue shields. Their language was guttural and strange, but Angela could tell they were pissed by the way they shook their weapons.

"How are we going to get out of this?" Jezreal asked. She wiped at the blood on her cheek and lips.

Angela had no idea. She asked, "Did you find the others?"

Jezreal shook her head. "This place is a maze."

More clomping footsteps and grunts were coming up from behind them.

Gods be damned. As much as I hate to admit it... She took Jezreal by the arm and made them disappear. In the icy void, she took her time to make sure the plan she was forming in her mind was truly the best way forward. When no other alternative came to her, they broke through again inside the cell of one particularly surprised man.

"You're back, little bird." Ibarra beamed, pausing to see if she would hit him again. If necessary, to shut him up, she would. But now she needed him, and the threat of physical violence did not damper his demeanor anyway. Suave like before, he leaned against the bunk and picked at his teeth as he scanned Jezreal up and down with hungry eyes. "Making a nest in my cell, little bird?" he asked. "Or maybe you just missed me."

Angela groaned. For him to ogle every woman he came across, he must have been jailed for quite some time. "Hardly either," she said. "I just need a hand finding my friends. You said you were familiar with this place, so I've come to barter."

"Barter? What is there to barter? Get me out of this cell and I'll do my best to get us off this planet."

Angela furrowed her brow but persisted. "Before we go anywhere, I need your word that you'll help us find our friends. Two of them. One's a sour man, thickly built and with deep brown skin. The other is taller, thin-framed, and has straight blond hair to his shoulders. After we get them, we'll need our equipment and bags. *Then* we'll see about getting you to your ship."

Ibarra tapped his lips, thinking for a moment until he couldn't contain his thoughts any longer. "Sure. I think I might know a way to help you and your friends. But first, two things. What might your name be, little bird?"

"Angela," she said, rolling her eyes.

He smiled. "Your accent is so strange, Angela. Might I ask where you're from?"

Angela shrugged. "My home."

He smirked. The look in his eyes told her he liked difficult women. They were a challenge to him, and he loved a challenge. "Very well, let's be on our way, yeah?"

What am I getting us into?

Taking Jezreal with one hand and locking arms with Ibarra, Angela closed her eyes and reached out with her mind. She was about to carve them a path into the veil when she realized that he was trembling. He was nervous, anxious, and it hit her: Ibarra had never teleported before. And if he had never teleported before... She reached out, brushed her mind against him, and felt... nothing. Ibarra had no soul.

A curse slipped from Angela's lips. She released them and began to pace the room. "I can't take you like that. Your body can't take it. You'll die."

Jezreal nodded like she understood, but Ibarra narrowed his eyes in confusion.

She couldn't tell him he didn't have a soul. If he believed he did, the news would shatter him, and if he did not believe they existed, it would only send them spiraling into a debate. She said, "I don't have time to explain. You just don't have the energy to withstand the void, let alone the reentry. It's like taking a hundred punches at once."

He sat on the bed, defeat and disappointment spreading across his expression.

"We're not giving up yet," Angela said. She still needed his help and swore she would see him out of this cell. Staff in hand, she jaunted through the veils and appeared outside the glowing blue cell wall. Down the halls, there was nothing but the ringing of the alarm. No footfalls of angry blue guards. That was good.

Before now, she hadn't had a chance to thoroughly examine the weapon in her hands. It was completely silver and featureless other than the mace-like head on the one end. She shook it, tried pulling it apart, but nothing happened. Searching its surface, she found a small circle in the otherwise smooth surface and pushed on it. The button fell in, and the flanges at the back of the staff clicked and folded outward on hidden hinges. Flipping the thing around and pointing the end of the staff at the black panel outside the cell's field, Angela couldn't help but be proud of herself for figuring it out. She pushed the button again, expecting the thing to launch a ball of light like she'd seen before, only for the mace-like head to close up again. Her glee vanished in a frown.

"Twist your back hand," Ibarra shouted over the hum and blaring sirens.

Angela tried again, and it worked. The staff hummed in a rising tone, then fired a screeching bolt of energy. It crashed into the black panel, melting it into a mess of oozing glass and metal. Most importantly, the blue glow of the cell wall faded. Jezreal and Ibarra came out with smiles on their faces.

Clapping her on the back, Ibarra said, "Very good, but we've got to go. There's bound to be someone watching." He pointed up to a small black dome in the corner of the ceiling, then took off down the hall, his long coat billowing behind him. Jezreal shrugged. They followed. Two corridors down and they turned to the left, only to be greeted by two guards bearing down on them. They chattered, must have known they were coming this way. Ibarra squealed and spun on his heels to head back toward Angela and Jezreal.

Taking Jezreal by the arm and preparing to teleport them, Angela paused when a screeching bolt of energy crashed next to her and melted the floor. The smell was terrible.

Ibarra called out from the corner he hid behind, saying, "What did you think was going to happen? They know you know how to shoot that thing now." He ducked behind the corner again.

Angela groaned and pushed them forward. Appearing behind the guards, she surprised them enough to take out both before they knew what was happening. They were good fighters with their staves but slow to react and unable to predict her movements.

Jezreal picked up a staff when the group was dispatched, and Ibarra came out of his hiding place with a smile. He sauntered closer, his hands on his hips. "Little bird is nasty when she needs to be."

"Little bird's going to pick you up and drop you off the nearest cliff if you keep calling her little bird."

He showed his palms. "Now, now. We're almost to your friends." He moved past them and toward a set of silver doors behind her. These double doors were not like the others. They seemed thicker, and two black panels rested on both sides of the doorway. It was definitely more secure.

"You can't go blasting through these," Ibarra said as he dropped to a knee. "I've got to fake it out. Here, let me borrow that for a moment."

Jezreal handed him her staff, and he used the flanges at one end to pry the black panels on both sides free from the wall. Behind them were green panels and a confusing array of colored wires. He handed the staff back and said, "Cover me."

Seconds piled up, but they never reached a full minute of peace and quiet. Five more blue men rounded the corner, planted their knees on the ground, and readied their staves. Before their bolts came flying, Angela and Jezreal loosed theirs. The blasts smashed into the ground and the walls and zipped over their heads, but none of them came close to hitting the guards. They chattered and returned fire. Light and melted bits of metal began splattering all around them as they tried to avoid the balls of energy.

"I know imperial soldiers who shoot better than you," Ibarra screamed as he shrunk and covered his head.

Angela raised an eyebrow. "Is that supposed to be an insult?"

"Yes! They're *terrible* shots."

She groaned. It was her first time at such distance, let alone using these weapons. What did he expect? But the scuffle needed to end before someone got hit, she admitted. A quick teleport behind them worked again; they were caught so off guard that Angela was able to knock them unconscious with quick strikes to their heads. Looking down the corridors, she saw no more coming, but when she turned back to Ibarra and Jezreal and noticed the silver double doors sliding open behind them, she fired.

The bolt flew through the air, zipped over Ibarra's shoulder, and slammed into the chest of a guard just beyond the opening door. His staff had been raised as the sliding doors revealed him; he was so close to bringing the weapon down on Ibarra's head. The guard toppled over, clutching his chest and gargling fluids. A wave of satisfaction washed over her.

"With your track record, don't you ever fire over my head again," Ibarra said. He was pissed, and probably rightly so.

Angela shrugged as she passed him. "I saved you, though," she said as she stepped over the body and into the room. She had not realized that their blood was a strange purplish color.

This room reminded her of the last world they had explored, where panels of light revealed pictures of other places. One of them flashed with a red border, catching her eye. She could make out the melted remains of the black panel outside Ibarra's old cell. On another window were the first guards they downed, and even more showed places they had not yet seen inside the prison.

Ibarra took a seat and rolled up to one of them, where he pushed buttons on an incomprehensible panel with practiced speed. The screen in front of them changed, displayed different symbols at a dizzying speed. She couldn't help with whatever Ibarra was doing, she knew, so she turned her attention back to watching the other windows.

Occasionally, she would point out guards running through the halls. Ibarra was able to somehow identify and triangulate doors through the windows and close them. That pissed the blue men off even more, forced them to reroute down different halls. A few had even taken to shooting the windows and destroying them from their side. How many of these things actually worked, Angela had no idea, but she was glad that she was able to help a small bit.

"Is that one of 'em?" Ibarra asked. The wall of symbols in front of him had changed to another window, this one peering down into a cell. Through the glowing blue field, Angela could see the familiar blond hair atop the prisoner's head.

"That's one. That's Gabe," Angela exclaimed.

Ibarra leaned back in his seat, motioned to the screen, and said, "Well, go on. Go get him."

Angela wrinkled her nose. "It doesn't work like that. It can be dangerous if I try to go somewhere I've never been before. I can't just look at this and know where I need to reappear, especially when it's such a small, confined space."

Ibarra sucked on his cheek for a moment, thinking. "All right," he said. He rolled back up to the buttons and began clacking away. "By getting that cell number, 3316, and coordinating our position on a map... There." He pushed himself away from the window. "Does that help?" The map on the screen was harrowingly complex. Doors and extra rooms. All the countless cells.

The sight of it reminded her of a toy Neti once had. The first time she had met him, he was lying on the bed, playing with a stone bowl. A small marble rolled through a maze inside it. Just the thought of Neti filled her with grief, but she forced herself to ignore it, knowing that contemplation was better saved for another day.

There were two blinking dots in the maze, and Ibarra told her which was them and which was Gabe.

Angela groaned. "I mean, yeah, it helps, but not very much. If I'm going to have to go find him, you may as well find Samael while you're at it so I can get them both at once."

Not another minute passed before Ibarra was able to locate Samael as well. He said that since he'd found Gabe, he was able to cross-reference prison reports, and finding Samael was simple. Angela just took his word for it. Studying the map for another minute, she felt confident she would be able to find her way to them. Hopefully.

She stepped out into the hallway and turned back to face her new companion and Jezreal. "Can you close this door behind me? Lock yourselves in?"

Ibarra nodded, rolled his way up to a panel of buttons.

"Stay to the sides of the room," Angela warned, and she turned away from the door. She waited until she heard it whir closed behind her, then teleported to the four-way corridor in front of her. First it was left for two, then right for one, if she remembered correctly. Normally, she thought she had a pretty decent memory, but now it was being put to the test. This prison was massive, but she followed the pattern she was supposed to as best as she could, preferring to jump in and out of the veils to speed up her progress. Eventually, though, she got lost and had to return to the window room.

Ibarra jumped out of his seat at her concussive arrival. He fumed. "Next time, wave to the cameras or something." Angela raised a brow. He had to explain what a camera was, and the great big mystery of the place died a little. Reality was often somewhat disappointing.

After referring to the map again, Angela was back out in the halls, navigating the maze as quickly as she could. She started to learn the pattern and the numbering system for the cellblocks. Never again did she run into more blue-skinned guards, but she did occasionally peek into cells and behold some of the strangest creatures she'd ever seen. She never stared long; the lack of armed company would not last forever. She could move faster than them and there might not have been a lot of them to cover such a massive prison, but eventually, she would run into them again.

What felt like ages of searching had, in truth, only been minutes. Jumping through the veils so frequently just made it feel so much longer. But with patience and a scream of glee on the edge of her lips, she came to a cell numbered 3316. Inside, Gabe rushed to the blue field with the biggest grin she'd ever seen the young soldier wear.

"It's about time," he exclaimed.

Angela sighed. "You've got no idea what it's taken to get this far."

He pumped his fists, eager to go, and accidentally brushed his knuckles against the blue between them. He cursed and drew back as Angela laughed. She had to calm herself before warping into the cell and taking him back to the window room. Gabe introduced himself to Ibarra, but Angela did not stay afterward; she would leave Jezreal to explain what had happened thus far. In moments, she was back out searching the maze, this time for Samael.

As time went on, Angela found herself moving slower and slower. She was growing tired. The gray halls were beginning to blur together. If it weren't for cell numbers, she wasn't sure she'd be able to recall which points she was supposed to turn at. As fearful as she grew, the blue cell she was looking for was just after her last point of arrival.

Angela jogged up to the barrier. Samael lurched to his feet from the bed. He wiped the glistening sweat from his brow and rushed up to her. Over the hum, he spoke exasperatedly. "Thank goodness. I was worried we were dead." He seemed a bit more nervous than usual, but Angela didn't question him. She entered the cell, took him by the hand, and pulled him through the veils.

Back in the room with the others, he gasped for air. Panting for no reason, it seemed.

"What's got you in such a tizzy?" Angela asked.

There was fear in Samael's eyes, plain as day. "I-I watched them beat a man who tried to escape right in front of my cell. He was screaming, 'Please, no. Don't feed me to that thing.' The man kept going on and on. Gave me a really bad feeling about this place."

A knot formed in Angela's belly. Being fed to something was terribly cruel. To think that the blue people would do such a thing... It certainly wiped away the pangs of guilt she'd felt about clubbing and blasting the living heck out of them.

Angela placed a hand on Samael's shoulder. "We're all getting out of here. Isn't that right, Ibarra?" She turned to him. Completely relaxed, he was still seated in his chair like it was a recliner in his own living room.

"Of course," he said. He spun back to the buttons and began pushing on them. "We just need to find your gear, yeah? Then get to my ship, and we'll be right as rain. This is just about the easiest prison break I've ever been in."

"And how many have you played a part in?" Jezreal asked, crossing her arms.

"Just this one. The rest were accidents with happy endings."

Jezreal laughed, incredulous.

"Don't be getting too chipper," he said. "We aren't out of this yet, and your friend's not kidding about getting fed." Ibarra spun around, looked over everyone's faces. The room was quiet for a moment. He raised a brow. "You knew about that, right? Feeding the convicts is kinda their thing. Well, not really feeding them. Well, they do feed the convicts obviously, but—"

"We get it," Angela blurted. "They feed the convicts to something else. What is it?"

His eyes narrowed. "Do you even know what planet you're on? This is Exaltia, home of the Grude? Either of those ring a bell?"

They all shook their heads slowly, and Ibarra's eyes grew wide. He threw his hands in the air. "Well, if this isn't the saddest group of criminal scum I've ever seen. What even got you put in here?"

That would be a hard one to answer. Angela wondered if she should lie about it. As far as she was aware, the only "crime" they could have committed before they were captured was trespassing. Of course, now they had attacked some guards and broken another prisoner out. If the blue men weren't already thinking of doing unspeakable things to them before, they definitely were now.

Ibarra must have sensed their hesitation. He shrugged and said, "You don't have to answer that. They're known to take slaves and orphans, too. Sorry your bad luck got you here."

Everyone glanced at one another nervously, but none of the Bui'dus tried to correct him.

"What are you in here for?" Samael asked. It seemed as though he had calmed down a touch. His breathing had slowed, and his eyes scanned the room with renewed attentiveness.

Ibarra smiled that coy smile, his silver tooth flashing in the light. "Captain's not my only title. Smuggler works, too."

Smuggler, Angela thought. *Of course. He looks the type.*

Reminds me of Donny. Thank goodness he isn't here, tied up in all of this.

He continued, spinning around in his chair to face the buttons once more as he spoke. "So now we just have to find where your gear is and we'll be out of here. Easy-peasy. By just referencing your guys' case number, I can find the storage room… Right there." Ibarra pointed at a new blinking dot on the map. Retrieving their equipment would be quick; it wasn't too far from Angela's cell.

"Shouldn't be too hard," Gabe said with a smile. "Things may still turn out all right, it seems."

Jezreal stepped forward, pointed at an image behind him, and said, "Except for that. More guards are just outside the door."

Sure enough, through the window, Angela watched the strange blue men fumble about the double door they were now hiding behind. The biggest giveaway was the black panels that had been taken apart and now dangled by a mess of cords. One of the guards had bent a knee to examine Ibarra's work.

"Is that a concern?" Angela asked.

"I think we're going to have to fight our way out," Jezreal said. She put a fist to her palm, smiling. "Nothing we can't handle." As she explained to the others that Ibarra wouldn't survive a trip through the veils, a smell like eggs hit Angela's nose.

One by one, the others crinkled their noses and guffawed at the rank air. At first, there were chuckles and incredulous looks. Then there were accusations.

"Was that you, Gabe?" Jezreal asked as she held her nose between two fingers.

"What? No! I didn't do it," he said.

"I think you did," Angela chimed in with a smile.

Gabe's face contorted at the betrayal. "I did not! If anything, it was Ibarra. He's been eating prison food for who knows how long."

Ibarra coughed and gagged, waved his hand in front of his face. "Damn, that's foul. I hate to say it, kid, but prison food blocks you up like a dam. Wasn't me."

Gabe shook his head, distraught. "Why do you guys always pick on me?"

"You make yourself an easy target," Sam said.

"He who smelt it dealt it," Jez poked.

"Hey," Ibarra said. "Anyone else feel a little funny?"

The room went quiet as everyone checked themselves. There was a bit of numbness tingling in Angela's toes and hands. Her skin was crawling, and a rush of fatigue made her limbs feel like jelly. She felt heavy, like she was oozing toward the floor. Things flickered in and out. Sound grew quieter and quieter as she felt the ground move underneath her. In a matter of moments, she was on the floor.

THE AIR SHOOK, THE GROUND RUMBLED, AND SOMETHING sharp cut into Angela's wrists. There was so much yelling she could barely make anything out. The smell of dirt and pine replaced the egg she'd smelled just moments before sleep took her. The smell must have been a kind of gas that put them under, and without opening her eyes, she knew she was not in the prison block any longer. The air was warmer and blowing. Her head throbbed, and she was ready to get out of this stupid world.

Rays of light gleamed against the red rock around her. At first, all she could manage was brief glimpses at her surroundings as her eyes adjusted. She was surrounded by cliffs reaching up hundreds of yards into the sky. Pushing herself up from the sandy ground, she noticed that the manacles on her wrists were a kind of steel marbled with some other metal, and a chain connected her to a pillar three times her size. Jezreal, Samael, Ibarra, and Gabe all lay crumpled and chained to their own pillars. But what were they all doing there? And where was *there*? Angela's confusion only lasted for a moment or two more. They were in a fighting pit.

The arena was three hundred yards across with a metal gate set into the surrounding wall every ninety degrees. Rows and rows of benched seating had been carved into the red stone around them. The seats were filled with strange-looking people. Some were the robe-wearing blue people. Others had extra appendages and other features too strange to even comprehend or put words to. Far fewer people looked humanoid than those that did not.

Gods, what have I stumbled into? I never imagined life like this existed. It was always three worlds: Dingir, Kur, and Earth. I never bothered to question the premise or think about the possibility of more being out there beyond the veils. Seeing it firsthand is just like a slap to the face.

Angela laughed at herself. *Why am I so surprised when I've faced down Nephilim and now an ancient goddess? I've seen visions of other worlds more magnificent than this one, and yet the people here still leave me dumbfounded.*

A sound like rattling cranks and rock scraping against rock came from behind. Luckily, her chain was long enough to let her walk three feet around the pillar and see the far gate rising into the air. From the darkness of the cave's mouth came a pack of snarling dogs, pushed and prodded by blue men with staves until they were clear of the portcullis and it dropped behind them.

By the time Angela realized their oddities, it was too late. The creatures had spotted them in the center of the pit and began to fan out to surround what they assumed would be their prey. Unlike other canines, these had greasy, spotted, and furless skin. Thin and sickly, they were certainly starved and hungry. The nostrils were more akin to blowholes, and as they began to growl, their snouts separated into four quadrants with row after row of hooked teeth meant for tearing and pulling flesh off the bone. A snake's tongue danced in the middle of their mouths.

Angela turned to her chains, shook, and pulled. A scream tore out from her lips as she tried to wake the others, but they did not respond. In her frenzy, memories of the shi sticks and the spells Toth had trained her with returned to her.

Focus, she told herself and took a deep breath. She hovered a hand over the chain between her manacles and the other over the chain to the pillar. The dogs were coming closer; she could not wait. The souls inside her whirred. Udug's would work, but she chose her own just for the speed of it. The Anunnaki soul bent to her will easily, its energy forming in a vibrant flash around the skin of her palms. The chains fell free, ends oozing onto the ground in droplets of molten metal.

As quickly as it was done, the strength the spell robbed from her was not small and left her dizzy. There was no time to conserve energy and ramp up slowly, only to open the floodgates and give it more than necessary. The fact that she was still waking from the poisonous gas did not help, either. Even though she was free, she'd still been too slow; one of the beasts loomed over Jezreal, its slobbering tongue dripping as it flicked her hair.

Angela clenched and pulled on her soul with no regard

for herself. She would not lose another soldier. Another friend. Not here, not anywhere. And never again because of her. The veils shuddered, split open, and dumped a tsunami on the dog. The crowd roared. Water crashed in every direction and swept the hound away, foaming and filling the air with the smell of salt. The other monsters backed up a bit, giving Angela time to rush to Jezreal and lift her out of the dissipating water.

Soon, she was coughing and choking. Her eyes blinked, and Angela sighed in relief. The water had touched the other Bui'dus and Ibarra as well, stirring them to life, too.

"The hell?" Ibarra choked. He glanced at the crowds and the dogs with them in the pit, then cussed again. "Get us out of here, little bird!"

Angela groaned and rose to her feet, remembering that she would have to get the smuggler out of here the old-fashioned way. As she ran to him, the dogs got over their fear and resumed their hungry growls. On cautious steps, they moved to circle them. Only then did Angela take the time to count them; there were nine, and the one she'd just hit was up on its feet again.

Placing her hands over Ibarra's chains, she wrestled with Udug's soul and purged its energy. It resisted, but his binds still dissolved. He nodded in thanks, rubbing his wrists as he moved to the center of the pillars. The dogs were not farther than ten yards in any direction. Gabe and Samael pulled on their chains, held out their wrists, and begged to be next.

Angela staggered, out of breath. Stopped where she stood and shook her head. "I can't keep doing this. They're getting closer. I won't be able to keep them off if I release you both."

The disappointment in their eyes pulled on her heart.

She felt weak, but she was glad she held off when a hound snarled and surged. A jaunt through the void caught it off guard, and a soul-fueled blow to its head stunned it. Her knuckles ached, but it had not been enough. Slowly, the thing regained its senses and focused on her. It yipped a warbling sound and the others in the pack shifted their attention to Angela as well, ignoring the Bui'dus as they passed.

They are not as animal as they seem... They take out the strongest, most threatening target first.

Without time to find more lethal tools, there was no choice but to expend her energy further. With will, she calmed herself and removed emotion. Fear and anger washed away, like Toth had taught her and she had discovered for herself in Dingir. Only then, when things inside her were calm, would her souls give her their all. As tired as they were, she pulled and they gave.

A rush filled her veins, soaked her muscles. Refilled and reinvigorated, she shaped the energy with her mind. In an open hand above her shoulder, a javelin of yellow light glittered into existence. At her will, it flew like a dart, pierced the hound's skull, and killed it. Angela took a half step back and covered her nose. The energy the spear radiated burned and sizzled its brain as it flopped.

The other beasts moved, snapping at the air, not one by one but all at once. The spear zipped through the air with every flick of her wrist, slamming through beast after beast, but it wasn't enough. No matter how quickly she moved, teeth and claw found their way into her flesh. She could not concentrate on commanding her spear and moving herself out of harm's way at the same time. The hounds riddled her with cuts and gashes of minimal severity until the last one dropped.

The beasts lay scattered around her, flesh smoldering. Angela let her light fade, and only then did the wall of fatigue slam into her. On her knees, she threw her head back and worked to catch her breath. The crowd was roaring, and they were not pleasant cheers. The people were disappointed that she had not been torn to shreds.

With a groan, Angela pushed herself to her feet. The world began to spin. Ibarra's words were muddled like he was speaking into a can. She didn't understand and carried on past him to Gabe. She placed her hands over his chains, grunting as she exerted herself, and the chains melted free. He rubbed his wrists, said something, but between the thrumming crowd and the buzzing in her ears, Angela couldn't make sense of anything.

Still, she carried on, freeing Samael with the last drop of her strength. Hunger gripped her belly as her limbs turned to liquid. She slumped to the ground, eyelids heavy, and someone came to pull her up to her feet. Although her mind was willing, her body was not. She had to get the others out of here, the Bui'dus home to Dingir and Ibarra to his ship—wherever that was—but she didn't have it in her to even stand on her own.

Her companions were dragging her toward the edge of the pit, but she didn't know why. Something was happening, but she couldn't force the fog from her mind. The portcullis on the far end of the pit was opening, and stumbling out from the tunnel was a fuzzy figure she could not make out but for its massive size.

Jezreal and Gabe gasped simultaneously. The ground was shaking like the footsteps of a Nephilim were bearing down on them, and terror struck. Her heart was racing, but no matter how hard she tried to concentrate and clear her vision, she could not overpower the fatigue gripping her body.

A tiny voice, almost like a whisper, spoke into her mind. Feminine and quiet yet strong and taut. *I sense your distress, the weakness in your soul. What are you doing?*

The voice was smaller than the crowds and the Bui'dus chattering around her but easier to hear. It was not emanating from her soul or her own conscience, but a place far darker: the black rot in her soul.

Call on me, Ti'amat suggested. *You cannot defeat me, cannot save your friends if you die.*

Every part of Angela's still-conscious mind did not want anything Ti'amat had to offer, but she knew this would be the end if she did not take what she could. Hazily, she remembered what the goddess had said when last they spoke and asked, *What is the cost?*

The goddess's chuckling reached her mind. *Yes... I did say there would be a cost, didn't I? But first, the boon. We will discuss the price later, when you are safe. Delve into me and you will receive.*

The hulking figure was drawing nearer. There was no time to debate cost at the risk of her companions' lives. Harrowingly, Angela plunged her mind into the black spot of rot inside her soul. The gap was bridged, the connection formed, the seal broken. Like an underwater spring uncovered in a well, energy flooded Angela's senses. Her mind sharpened, her muscles tensed, fueled by the energy of a goddess.

It was such a sudden snap back into reality that Angela shook the soldiers off her violently, mistaking them and their touch as something hostile. Gabe and Sam staggered back, fear in their eyes and confusion on their faces when they seemed to notice the color of her eyes. Time slowed, and it took strength and concentration to keep herself from springing, to not run and strike at everything around her. She could barely contain her desire to just *move*, to break free in reckless rage.

Jezreal was shaking. She placed an open palm on Angela's cheek as though she was trying to reach her. Tears welled as she said, "Your eyes. They're black."

It took Angela every ounce of restraint not to slap her hand away, to explain that this was more than just a simple connection between her and Ti'amat; this was a stream with ebb and flow, and she had carved its path with her mind. It was nothing more than a distributary in a delta, funneling a tiny portion of Ti'amat's vast river of power to her, yet even this small sampling was intoxicating.

Angela was reminded just how small she really was compared to the goddess, and that was all the spark it took to set her anger ablaze and out of control. All she wanted, for once, was to be in control of her own destiny.

With a flick of her arm, she sent Jezreal flying, skidding across the red sand before coming to a stop. While she would be bruised, she would survive, but Angela could not say the same for the massive figure now barreling across the pit toward her.

This new creature was humanoid in shape, with two legs and two arms, and was toweringly tall. But that was where the similarities ended. A single eye rested in the center of its face. Lower incisors jutted from between its mouth, rubbing its lips raw and bloody. Flaps of excess skin on the sides of its head vibrated as the thing exhaled, snorting like a horse. Its center mass was folded and flabby, with thighs as thick as Angela's whole body. Her hazy vision had not lied to her; its size *was* comparable to that of a Nephilim.

The cyclops howled, filling the arena with its cry. Gripping a club the size of a tree, it lifted its hands above its head to bring it down on her. Avoiding it would have been easy, but Ti'amat's voice spoke to her.

You need not move but your arm.

Angela heeded, raising her arm and catching the club in her hand. Brought it to a stop with such little effort the thing felt weightless. The giant grumbled, gnashed its teeth, and shifted its weight down to push on her. The load increased, but Angela withstood it, a smile stretching across her face. A surge of glee ran through her. She was enjoying the rush, the invigoration of holding so much strength.

The goddess chuckled and said, *Power unrivaled... Feels wonderful, does it not?*

Yes, Angela admitted.

With both hands, she grabbed the club and ripped it away from the giant, sent it stumbling like a clumsy toddler. The thing shook the ground when it landed.

Again, Ti'amat spoke to her. *Finish it.* The goddess's voice was firm and demanding, yet Angela knew that she could make the decision. She was still in control, although Ti'amat could take over her body if she wanted to. Still, some small and curious part of her, some carnal, power-hungry bloodlust, took hold. She gave in. She wanted to know just how deep this black river was.

With an open palm, she funneled that black energy and let its power flow through her. Energy as black as night sprouted from her palm, streaked through the air with the scent of ozone. The beast held up its hands, tried to shield itself as the beam melted its arms before plowing into its torso. Angela gave it more, and the energy blazed through the giant quickly, tearing and disintegrating the flabby flesh until all that was left was a mound of scorched limbs.

The Mother of Serpents was proud. She could sense the faint emotion behind a smile as the goddess withdrew her hand and broke their connection, dammed the stream between them. Angela dropped her hand to her side, feeling the power slip away. Almost immediately, she missed it. She clenched her fists to stay her shaking hands. The high that faded left her with nothing but her own dismal abilities, reminding her that she did not compare to Ti'amat.

Calling upon the goddess brought her there; time froze as it had in her previous visits, solidifying Jezreal, Gabe, and the others in stasis and silencing the sounds of the wind and the crowds. In an instant, the goddess was standing here in a black dress with her hands on her hips. Golden armlets just before her elbows glimmered in the bright desert sunlight. She was smiling.

Angela sighed. "Now the cost?"

Ti'amat nodded. "Now the cost. The power that coursed through you is a strength acquired through eons and countless worlds. The souls I command feed me. They are my food, and I am yet hungry. Before Antum is free and our mights do clash one final time, I will require what is mine. I told you before: let go of what you cherish or it will only hurt more. So choose. Look upon your companions and tell me who you value the least, whose soul might return to me."

Angela gasped. "You can't. No, I won't choose."

The goddess raised a delicate finger to her lips. "You must, Angela, or else I will choose for you. Should it be Gabe? The handsome young man who so early in his life has devoted himself to such a noble cause. Certainly he would have many years of service cut short if we took his soul. Or what about Jezreal? The woman has guile, strength not unlike your own. She would make a good leader someday. I know you feel that way, too. And Samael. Such a crass attitude. So untrusting of you. Perhaps the party would be stronger without him. Look them over, Angela. Choose."

With sluggish feet, Angela did. She walked to each of them, examined their faces frozen in time, and weighed them. The fact that she was casting judgment on each of them felt like the most crushing defeat she had ever experienced. How could she willingly choose who to desert, who to leave behind? It was wrong. A decision she could not make lightly, but was it a decision she *had* to make? Would it be more moral for her to allow Ti'amat to choose? Would she feel less guilty? Angela was not sure.

Her fists were clenched. A tear streaked down her cheek. This was not right. She needed them all. Curling her lip, she turned back to the goddess and muttered, "You heartless wretch, I'll kill you. I swear it. Whatever it takes. Whatever I have to give."

Ti'amat was unaffected. She smirked. "You will give me what I want in the end, Angela. So let go. Choose now or I will for you."

Angela swallowed, wiped the tears from her face. For fear of her choosing Gabe or Jezreal, she had to choose. Gnashing her teeth, she said, "Donny. I choose Donny."

The goddess raised her black eyebrows, surprised. "Oh, really? I did not expect that, but I suppose if it is your choice, then I will honor it. It will be done, but I wonder, why him?"

Angela's gaze dropped to her feet as the disappointment in herself took hold. How could she be so weak? How could she have chosen? She muttered, "Because I don't want him involved in this. He's the last real friend I have, and I can keep him safe if he stays in Dingir."

"That seems a bit selfish of you, Angela, especially with how you kicked him to the side like a dog in your way. And now this? Oh, I wonder what he'll think of you now."

"I'll make it right," Angela swore. "When I'm finished with you, I'll give it back to him and fix the damage you've done."

"Keep dreaming, sweetheart," the goddess said. "I'll see you soon."

Like the flip of a switch, Ti'amat was gone. The breeze blew Angela's hair, and the crowd was full of whispers and murmurs. Jezreal, Sam, and Gabe were not where they had been seconds ago. With the illusion dispelled, they stood around her with cautious looks on their faces.

Gabe ran a hand down his face, sighed. "She's back."

"Are you all right?" Jezreal asked. "You're crying."

Angela swallowed, wiped at her eyes. "Yeah. The cost is just more than I can bear."

"The cost?" Samael asked, arms crossed. "What cost?"

Angela shook her head and sniffed. "Never mind. You'll find out soon enough. Let's go."

She turned away to hide her face, her defeat, her regret. Considering they were the only ones in the arena and the far iron gate was still raised in the air, she assumed they were being let free. Who in their right mind would try to contain a woman who could defeat a giant as she did? Certainly, the people of this world had likely never seen such a feat.

As they approached the open tunnel, guards in flowing robes appeared from the darkness and stood to the side like a royal procession. They shied away from her as she passed, seemed to shrink in fear of her every movement.

"It seems you scared the shit out of them," Ibarra said.

"Scared the shit out of me, too, little bird. What was all that?"

Angela did not answer. Words could not describe how she felt. She had lost integrity and all her sense of pride by submitting to Ti'amat, felt ashamed that she had to rely on a power other than her own to see them through the fight in the pit.

If I had known the cost, I wouldn't have asked her for help, Angela thought. *Never again.*

If she could not handle herself now, how could she handle herself in the final fight? Would Antum take over her body and see her through it? Move her like a puppet? Angela didn't want to think about that. Not yet.

In the widening chamber, a blue-skinned man with a strange headdress, golden and set with jewels, stepped forward and bowed slowly. His robes matched his head-piece's luster with golden buttons and a gold-trimmed red sash across his chest. He tried to speak with her, but it sounded like nothing but a mess of grunts and clicks. Even Ibarra couldn't help translate.

Assuming that this person was responsible for the whole arena operation, Angela had half a mind to give him what for and slug him. Part of her blamed this person in front of her for what now happened to Donny, but as much as she wanted someone else to blame for her choice, she knew it was ill-placed. This weight was hers alone.

The royalty-looking man and a handful of guards walked them back to the prison block. No one spoke much as they traversed the long gray halls, passing through door-ways large and small in the maze. By pressing the palm of his hand on a black panel, the silver door to the storage room slid open. Motioning her and the Bui'dus inside,

Angela found their gear hanging from hooks and piled on a bench.

She muttered to herself in frustration as she slipped on her armor and strapped Teshub's sword to her back. She nearly lost her leg to a bucket when she tried to teleport into a room earlier; all she had needed was one of the unconscious guard's hands. It was yet another grain of salt in her wounded pride. This, assuredly, was not her day. More than anything, she wanted to break down and sleep away the guilt, but the need to compose herself in front of the others helped her swallow it for now. Exhaling slowly through her nose, she holstered her tether gun and slipped its battery into its pouch on her belt, knowing she should feel grateful she was alive to fight another day.

Ibarra's gear was strange and foreign. He attached a half-foot blocky-looking thing to his wrist. It reminded her of the black panels out in the hallway. The gun at his side was a silver metal with pointed angles and sharp edges. It looked confusing but deadly. More importantly, Angela was jealous that he didn't have to deal with batteries or cables that ran throughout his long coat. She almost asked him to let her try it out.

He caught her gaze and smiled. "Little bird has an eye for shiny things, doesn't she?"

Angela shook her head, and as gently as she could, she said, "Little bird might remind you how hard she can punch."

As thick-headed as Ibarra was, he sensed her irritability and only shrugged, remaining quiet as he turned to search through his bag. But in only a matter of seconds, he was speaking again. "You been thinking about what I offered you? It still stands. You and your friends here can come with me however far you'd like." He flashed a silver smile.

"Maybe find a nice quiet bed to lie down in and recover your spirits."

"You don't learn, do you?"

"Only when my life's on the line."

"Trust me, it is," Angela said. She was not in the mood for flirtation or joking.

He sighed, looked away. It was clear that he wanted Angela and her companions to go with him. He wanted something more than the short partnership they had formed. He was intrigued and disappointed, and Angela felt a little bad for him. She was angry at Ti'amat and herself, not him.

Trying to rectify the situation, Angela said, "As much as I would love to spend more time with you and that ugly yet somehow charming face of yours, I can't. Setting out and exploring a whole new world sounds incredible, but my friends and I are going after something that's just as important to our world as it is to yours. Besides, I've got my own smuggler back home. Two would be more bad company than I could handle." She placed a hand on his shoulder.

"It's all right," Ibarra said. "I understand that little birds fly wherever they please. Just know you can find me around Tiphus. I'd normally advise someone watch their back there, but it's clear you don't have a problem with that."

"If only you knew," Angela murmured.

Once fully fitted with their guns, batteries, and shocking knuckles on their hips, they slung their bags on their backs and stepped out into the prison corridors. The blue guards were careful to give them all plenty of space as they were escorted down the halls again. A few held their staves tightly and seemed on edge for the entire fifteen-minute walk to their destination. They paused before a set of silver double doors that whooshed open and bathed them in dry, hot air.

Outside, they walked into another alcove of red rock and sand. The sky opened up, and they found themselves standing on a wide metal platform. Painted blue lines on the silver floor segregated the areas where some hulking, technologically advanced machines sat.

People of all shapes and sizes worked in and out of these things, which must have been their ships. Angela almost laughed aloud at her amazement. She had been expecting ships meant for traversing water in a world where she hadn't even seen a drop. No, these things were meant for the air, and this hangar was full of foreign life.

There were so many languages around her that she could barely hear herself think. Some people loaded freight aboard one crate at a time, and others pushed slaves in shackles up ramps and ladders, beating them with saps.

A subconscious will to free them must have urged her to drift toward them; Ibarra grabbed her arm tightly, pulled her back into the group, and looked into her eyes solemnly. Angela knew what those eyes said. She could do nothing to save them that wouldn't get her into trouble, and there was nowhere she could take them, anyway. It hurt, but she bit her lip and carried on.

Near the end of the ship bay, Ibarra turned to the right and toward what must have been his ship. Behind a massive hunk of gray and brown metal was a much smaller, more angular, and colorful craft. Yellow lines on red paint were scuffed and marred. A few panels were even warped from heat. Both were evidence of either a scuffle or bad driving.

Ibarra pressed a combination of buttons, and a small ramp dropped behind him. It was a wonder how he figured all five of them would fit inside. He must have seen her hesitation and said, "She's small, and not much of a freighter, either, but she'll move fast enough and the vacuum cargo hold has plenty of space if passengers wear a suit. Makes it easier for hiding stuff, too."

Angela feigned a smile, stepped up to him. "I'll take your word on that, Captain. I hope we meet again in better circumstances."

They shook hands. He said, "Same, little bird," then turned to board his ship. As he began climbing the ramp, a thought came to Angela.

"Say, what was that blue light we saw coming down from the sky?"

Ibarra glanced over his shoulder with a look of surprise. "It's a mining operation south of town. You need to get out of the house more often."

Angela shrugged, not knowing what to say. Ibarra gleamed one last silver-toothed smile, brushed dirt off his leather duster, and waved goodbye before disappearing inside the ship.

She returned to the Bui'dus, each of them dirty with red sand and a coating of sweat. They were nervous; she could see it in their eyes. It was exciting and terrifying to think that just a short time ago, they were strangers to this world, being chased down by insectoid creatures only to be taken captive and forced to fight for their freedom. This visit had not turned out, in any way, to be what she had expected. And it had cost her so much more.

While she was upset there was no sign that a fragment of Antum's soul was hiding in this world, she was sure she would walk away with something else: a greater under-standing of her place in all of existence. There were worlds that she could not fathom, could not try to comprehend, and she had to accept that. She had to walk away, understand that even though she did not know how or why they operated, they deserved their freedom from a power far greater than anything any of them had ever met before. Angela could not let Ti'amat win, and she had to right the wrong she had done, no matter the cost.

CHAPTER SEVEN

From the gray-white void, they staggered into darkness. The others were fumbling around, trying to find the lantern in one of their bags, when Angela realized how calm her breathing was. Usually, when she pulled herself and all four Bui'dus through the veils, she had to catch her breath. But not now. Not in the slightest had the trip disturbed her breathing.

That's unusual, she thought. *But what happened back there wasn't usual, either. The strength she gave me, still feeds me... It is and was not worth it.*

The thought of Ti'amat's power pumping through her veins sent shivers down her spine and filled her with guilt. Since she had formed that connection with the goddess, it seemed like their bond had strengthened somehow. Like an infection, Ti'amat's black rot had grown and spread. And now her presence seemed constant, like the pressure of a persistent thought in the back of her mind.

From here on out, I will resist any temptation to call on her again, Angela swore.

The spark of a match blinded her temporarily. A few

gasps slipped from her partners' lips, but in moments, their eyes had adjusted. Jezreal put the torch to the lantern wick and they watched the flame grow together.

"Why are we here again?" Gabe asked.

"To look, think, and plan," Angela said.

And to hide... she thought.

Jezreal held the lantern above her head, casting the light as far as she could to pierce the darkness. The world's boundary was not far; Angela had brought them in close to the edge, and she led the way to it. As they approached, the shimmering glass fragments twinkled to life until mesmerizing images of distant worlds shifted in front of them. Some were as small as coins, others as large as broken plates, but none of them stayed long enough to offer more than a glance into the other worlds.

Samael stepped to Angela's side and faced her, completely ignoring the windows next to him. His arms were crossed. Something was bothering him. He asked, "What's the point in looking at these again? I thought you said you couldn't link these images with the pockets of dimensions out there."

Angela released a long sigh through her nostrils. She could feel the tension in him and in herself. She was a light breeze away from tumbling off the cliff of keeping it all together, and an eerie feeling crept into her bones; she feared this conversation would lead them into another argument. "You're right," she finally said. "I can't. But I need time to think and plan. Maybe catch a glimpse of something useful in these windows. Besides, there's nothing better we can do right now, and I think we all need to digest what happened."

"There's not much to digest and think about."

Angela scoffed. "Maybe for you."

"It seems pretty obvious the next world is going to be another stab in the dark, isn't it? But wait, you know all about the dark, now don't you? Silly me."

"What are you aiming at?"

Samael's jaw tensed. "A little reassurance, maybe? A little comfort? 'No, Samael, I know exactly what we're doing. This next world won't be a completely pointless risk of our lives. This evil goddess that lives inside me and threatens all of existence has no control over me.' Anything like that will do, really."

Angela turned her cold gaze to him. "She doesn't live inside me. I'm a conduit. A gateway. Any person she's touched forges the bond between their soul and her. But to be honest, I don't think it will be long before she can dig her claws into someone's soul and possess them without needing to touch them first. I can feel her getting stronger. Ti'amat is pulling the crystal pieces of herself together and amassing more souls by the hour. But trust me, I am still in control of myself."

"Thanks for the reassurance," Samael said sarcastically. "To think, I remember all those years ago hearing about the Etlu who returned from Earth with a wound in her belly and a bad case of post-trauma. No one ever thought it would lead to anything more, yet here we are. We've fought to keep our city alive twice because of you already. Now thrice. I've seen the goddess's darkness in your eyes, and you want us to trust you? After everything you've subjected us to for *years*?"

Angela clenched her fists as anger lit her blood afire. "Yes. I've made mistakes, but you forget I've *owned* them, and still I stand here fighting for a city that turned its back on me."

Samael was so mad his hands were shaking. His eyes

glistened in the lantern's light. "All you've bred is trouble. Violence. Eighteen years ago, the end of Dingir started with you, and now it's coming up to its finale, brought on by no hands but your own. I wonder if Ti'amat would still be sleeping, had Michael put you down."

Angela swung, smashed her knuckles against his cheek. Samael's head jerked to the side. He wobbled, fell on his back. In an instant, she was on top of him as wicked rage coursed through her. She knotted her fingers together above her head and brought them down onto his chest. He coughed, gasped for air, but not enough to satisfy her. The others were shouting. She couldn't hear them. Didn't want to. Once again, she smashed her fists against his chest, this time with a bit of soul-energy behind the blow. That did it; blood splattered onto her face as he coughed. Gods, the fear in his eyes. The power she had at her disposal. She wanted more.

The others tried to grab her arms as she cocked them back for another punch, but she shook them off easily, sent them reeling back. Samael's eyelids were flickering as his consciousness escaped him. He was fighting to reach the knife at his waist but couldn't get at it.

One more blow, Angela told herself.

She raised the fist above her shoulder, began to throw it down with all her weight when Jezreal's head appeared. The woman had weaseled herself between Angela's fists and Samael's chest. Angela paused.

"Stop," Jezreal begged. Her eyes were wet. "Get a hold of yourself, Angela. Please. Don't let this define you."

Angela's lip curled. She scooped Jezreal's shoulder and tossed her away, grabbed Samael by his bloody jaw, and channeled energy from Ti'amat's rot and sent it into him. His body took it and consumed it quickly, using it to repair his broken ribs and punctured lungs. Grunts and wails of pain flew from his mouth as his body healed. The others stayed back, uneasy and quiet as his health was restored.

This bridge she had made with her mind, from her soul to his, showed her something she did not expect. Deep in the cosmos of Samael's blue Anunnaki soul were sparks of light twinkling brighter than others and of their own volition. She touched one, then reeled back and broke contact as a rush of images came flying into her mind. There were so many all at once that she was dizzy at first, until she realized what she'd witnessed. Images of a whole different life as a whole different person than Samael. Memories from the person who had this soul before him.

Angela staggered to her feet, rubbed her temples, and stepped away from Samael. He was mostly healed other than his need to catch his breath. She realized that her breathing was labored as well, then pointed down at him and said, "Keep his name out of your fucking mouth."

He swallowed heavily, nodded, then laid his head back down to rest.

Angela turned, walked ten paces, and sat cross-legged, facing away from the others. The energy-high she'd had was fading, as was her temper. Her limbs tingled. She wiped the cold sweat from her forehead. Jezreal came up behind her, touched her shoulder, and tried to say something, but Angela shooed her away. "I need time alone. I think I know where I can find a hint. What world to look in next."

Jezreal huffed. "You're not going to apologize for nearly beating him to death?"

Angela faced her, looked up into her green eyes, and said, "He doesn't deserve it."

Jezreal's jaw dropped. "She's getting to you, Angela. Don't give in."

Angela scoffed, turned her focus away and inward. Deep within herself, within the fragment of Antum's soul, she found a dull twinkling light and touched it. Like water from a faucet, images came pouring out of it and into her mind's eye, and she knew what she was looking at.

It was strange to think that she wasn't the only owner of her soul. A part of her still didn't want to believe it was ever someone else's, but the images that came to her were proof that other Anunnaki after Antum and before her had lived a life with this soul. They weren't quite distinct memories, more like echoes of images, emotions, and intent. Some were clearer than others, and there were so many.

The echoes of the Anunnaki before her were more complete and easier to view. She pegged that down to the fact that they were more recent. In those, she recognized glimpses of Dingir and the Ascendancy, but the older ones were unintelligible, garbled, and confusing. They seemed to be missing pieces. But one by one she searched through her soul and filtered through the echoes of the people before her until she came to one that had been inscribed by Antum so clearly she could make sense of it. This echo was so locked in and engrained in her soul that it was as clear as the day it had happened. This memory was a window to the past.

THE SKIES ABOVE THE MOUNTAIN THAT DAY WERE A DULL gray, full of clouds and scarce of sun. All the flowers were closed, the wind chilly, yet still Antum felt the need to attend to her home. Someone else would do it if she asked, and it wouldn't hurt if she waited another day, but she was determined not to let the gloom hold her back.

She trimmed the hedge path that weaved its way to the gazebo behind her home, walked down the mountainside path to draw water from the river below, then carried the buckets back to the top. She used the wind to blow out the leaves, broke the soil where she planned to grow another white-barked tree, and called upon the rain to drizzle over her lot. To many, the labor would have been hard and taken most of the day, but for a goddess, the work only took a few hours.

As well as these tasks were going that day, a dread gnawed at the back of her mind like termites to wood. She tried to convince herself it was just the cloudy gloom of the day, but in truth, she knew not all was right. And it was not just the weather that had brought her down.

Antum took a deep breath and rose from her kneel. At the edge of her parapet that lined the cliffside facing south, she overlooked the grounds below. Wooded hills rose and fell, like the waves of an ocean frozen in time. The trees were redwoods, tall and hardy, but the thin horizon line was where her land ended and Ti'amat's began. Her grounds were scarcer of trees and plants, more of them torn down by the creatures she housed there. It wasn't the creatures' fault they had eaten nearly all there was to eat; it was their goddess's for providing neither food nor balance.

Antum trembled in the cold wind. There was a darkness growing down there, one she had feared for a long time. It had only recently reared its ugly head when Ti'amat discovered that some of her own were breaking the souls given to them to bestow permanent magical effects to material things. The goddess's rage reached levels not seen since ancient times, pushing her to kill and slaughter some of her own creations.

Other gods even reported that Ti'amat had begun encroaching on their lands. Once, Antum had tried to calm her, but that only made the Mother of Serpents suspicious of her. For three days, she had Antum punished at the end of a Nephilim's tail. The scars on her back had healed, but her heart had hardened. There was no saving Ti'amat from the madness that plagued her mind and clouded her judgment. Antum had tried to play mediator and friend for too long; it was now simply the time to rid Vi'dinor of Ti'amat's poison and free her subjects. But to do that, Antum needed help, and she waited four more days before it arrived.

She was in the garden, examining her budding saplings, when the sound of rushing wind under wings and deep breaths came from behind her. The sun was bright that day, and its light glinted off golden scales as they neared. Coming down to greet her was a beast that was not her own, but one that she was quite familiar with. Though carnal, the Nephilim were full of strong passion and emotion. Rage was no stranger to them, but for some, their desire for freedom and justice was stronger than that of any other creature. Antum would not admit to stoking those rebellious fires to anyone until the battle was done.

The golden Nephilim Basmu landed before her with the thud of each great paw and folded his black wings onto his back. Even for his young age, he was large compared to the others. His claws tore ravines in the garden soil, but Antum held her tongue. His gait was feline-like, other than the slight limp to his front left leg. As he approached, tail flicking behind him, he dipped his massive head low to the ground as a sign of respect.

There was dirt crammed between his golden scales, and a few were even scuffed or cracked like a broken mirror, barely clinging to the skin underneath. Worse yet, a recent wound beneath his neck had crusted over with a nasty red and black scab. Nephilim were usually particular about keeping themselves clean, but this close up, it was clear that he was in rougher shape than usual.

His voice permeated Antum's mind. *My grace, I came to you as soon as I could.*

Antum returned the bow and said, "I would not assume the delay was intentional, Basmu, but you are late by the better portion of a week. What happened?"

The beast grumbled and shook his long neck. *Ti'amat is watching me always. I think she suspects I desire to be free of her but does not know of my intentions to kill her. This is the soonest opportunity I've had to come to you. Her gaze is yet affixed to mine own brothers in their attempts to steal her attention. Mother's sickness is growing, and I fear for them if they are found.*

Antum nodded. "I've felt her darkness stretching and growing for some time now. The more souls she amasses, the more power she gains and the more fragile her mind becomes. She cannot contain herself and cannot stand those who do not bend their knee to her. It was like this once before, long ago, and now there are fewer of us willing to fight against her."

In your world?

"Aye. These events are reminiscent of what happened in our home world, Mulki." Antum cast her eyes to the shade in the south. She sighed. "I'm afraid the time has really come, and while I am trembling with fear and thoughts about the outcome of failure, I know that something must be done. I will not allow this world, or our children, to suffer the same as we did. This world must live on."

So the weapon is done then?

"It is. Formed from the purest crystal I could muster and woven with more magical intent than I have ever willed before, the phylactery has been finished. I have not tried it, for my own disappearance would make her suspicious, but I believe it will hide your soul well enough."

Basmu seemed uneasy, shifting his weight on his legs and breaking eye contact. In moments, the gaze of his black eyes returned to her. *You are braver than the other gods. I knew we could depend on you.*

Antum lifted her chin and laughed. It took the beast by surprise. "I am not brave. I sneak about behind my sister's back and seek to use her sons to plant the dagger."

Basmu grumbled. *Be that as it may, I do not see the others aiding us, only you. I did not want it to come to this, as I know you feel. But no god or mortal can withstand the power of all those souls. Eventually, power corrupts, as all living things are prone to its temptations. This must be done.*

She bowed her head and weakly agreed. "It must be done."

They turned from the garden and followed the stone paths out. In the colonnade on the front of the manor, Basmu tried to apologize for the damage his talons did to her grounds, but she hushed him. "The grass will grow again, and the scuffs are signs that friends have visited me." She smiled. "No one will think I am alone anymore."

Through the front double doors made of dark ironbark trees and golden hinges and knockers, the foreroom's open space welcomed them. All throughout, the floors were marble tiles, and the rest of the doors and furniture were made from the same wood. Her home was extravagant but not stuffy. Though mortals rarely visited, she wanted her underlings to experience a balance of sophistication and relaxation, to feel welcomed and not ruled. Yet the gods and goddesses who did stop by would feel at home, or else she'd be too much of an outcast in their eyes. And that was Antum's game. She was the quiet one, the one who kept to the dark on the outer edges, always looking in and making quiet moves when she could get away with them. She was the sneak and she knew it.

When Basmu and Antum passed through the final doorway and into the chamber that housed her essence, she sighed. Something about seeing herself as the centerpiece of this room was embarrassing. All the gods had rooms like these, for up a small flight of stairs to the apse, an altar with her crystalline heart rested. Guarded by spells and seven feet tall, four feet at its widest, the crystal was clear and prismatic in the light. Like the other gods, fleshy bodies were now merely extensions of themselves formed to their own desire. Their true source of strength resided in their crystals, as did their weaknesses. The crystal heart of Ti'amat would shatter to pieces, and Antum would take up the responsibility of imprisoning the pieces of her soul until the end of time.

"The weapon I made for you is in here," Antum said. She walked toward the left side of the crystal's platform, where a smaller door lay waiting in the corner. It seemed mundane and plain, as had been her goal. As she placed her hand on the golden knob and began to turn, the images, sounds, and smells washed away from Angela's mind. The twinkling light inside her soul, the small echo of Antum, faded into nothingness.

ANGELA WAS COLD. ALMOST NUMB. THE SMELL OF SMOKE filled her nose, and her shadow was cast out in front of her. The others had formed a small camp behind her, huddling around a small fire that seemed to illuminate that dark place no more than the tiny flame of the lantern. The Bui'dus did not say a word when they realized Angela was back in her own body. They glanced at her, then turned their gazes away. Angela just stood, walked over to the fire, and sat cross-legged next to them.

For a time, they all thought in silence. There was an uneasy fear in the atmosphere between them now. Samael's chest rose and fell like normal; he was seemingly breathing fine. There were no bruises from the beating she gave him, except for maybe a few on his ego, but the way the others looked at her made her feel guilty. She wanted to apologize, but her pride did not want her to. Samael should have known better than to bring up Michael. His words were meant to cut her down, sow distrust between her and the Bui'dus, and she would not have it any longer.

Yet this uncomfortable aura that swallowed them whole could not continue. They could not function as a team like this, and as much as she didn't want to admit it, Angela still needed them. Together, they had defended against the insectoid creatures in the world of red sand, and they were extra sets of eyes that had monitored cameras and watched her back. They gave useful insight, and they were nearly the closest thing she had left to friends. With so little left to fight for, it made the need for fighting that much greater.

She sighed. "Look, I'm sorry. I lost it, but don't you ever say his name again. Not like that."

Samael looked her up and down for a moment and only

nodded. It wasn't forgiveness, but acknowledgment, and it would have to do.

"We understand you're going through something we can't even comprehend," Gabe said. He leaned back, ran his fingers through his hair. "But you have to remember who you are. If you lose yourself, even if you defeat Ti'amat in the end, is it really a victory?"

Angela swallowed. She did not know. "Ti'amat wants us to do as she commands, and if I do that, I don't know if I'll still be me anyways. All I know is I want a third option. My *own* option, and I think I now know how. That vision wasn't from Ti'amat. It was a memory buried deep in my soul. Antum had made some kind of weapon to break Ti'amat's crystal and defeat her, and I'm hoping I can find it."

She chuckled to herself. "Turns out Basmu was involved. But now that I think about it, I'm not so surprised. When I first met the golden Nephilim, he mentioned how I seemed familiar somehow. Something about my aura. It makes sense that he was feeling the part of Antum I carry with me. He killed Maulkatu for suggesting they rebuild what we thought was just the Anchor Crystal at the time but was really Ti'amat's shell. Basmu must have thought Maulkatu was only drawing his power from the weylines, not from Ti'amat herself. But..." She sighed.

"The last thing Basmu said to me was, 'The key lies in the deepest memories.' On his dying breath, he not only realized that Ti'amat was back, but he recognized my aura and what was ahead of me. What I would face. In that fraction of a second, he gave me a hint that went completely over my head. Maybe Basmu wasn't so terrible..."

"No," Jezreal said. She tossed a chunk of bark into the fire, her gaze shimmering like steel daggers. "He was still terrible. He destroyed and killed for power and freedom, on a promise Maulkatu made him. He might have had honorable times, but he was still made of flesh. And flesh is susceptible to infection. Of the mind or the body, what difference does it make?"

Jez looked back to the fire, her expression glum and depressed. Angela could sense the pain and knew that she had caused it. Anything she tried to say now would only be met with bitterness and arguments. Maybe they all needed a break. Not just from the task at hand, but from her.

Angela rose to her feet and said, "You still have blue crystals, right?"

Each of the Bui'dus looked into the leather pouches at their waists and nodded.

"Good. Return to Dingir without me. I'll be there soon."

Before they could say a single word of either rebuttal or agreement, Angela slipped into the veil and disappeared. They could find their way home, and between worlds, Angela had all the time she needed. Time to search her soul and time to map the barriers of worlds. One by one, she gauged and examined the aura inside her, picking apart the tunes of the orchestra and comparing them to the hum of the worlds around her until she struck a close comparison.

It was a small world, no bigger than the sand world's fighting arena, with jagged and rough veils that felt unusual. Focusing her mind to a point, she cut the barrier and pushed herself through. Dry and cold atmosphere slapped together around her, creating the resonate boom of her arrival. She felt around in the darkness, found something hard, but couldn't tell what it was. From her bag, she lit a lantern and held it above her head.

Everywhere, the crumbled remains of Antum's manor

lay silent. Pillars of pretty marble had broken into chunks of average stone that had cracked floor tiles and snapped dark wooden tables and benches in half. The ceiling was decaying in places. Ahead, a doorway was open.

Over the remains of what was once a goddess's home, she weaved through the great hall and into what would have been the crystal chamber she'd seen in the echo. But when she entered, she came to realize that half of this manor was not here.

There was a jagged line where the right side of the room had torn away from this pocket dimension, forming a cliff-like edge that stared out into a blackness her light could not penetrate. The other half of the manor was most likely lost somewhere out there in the great expanse of the worlds.

As Angela crossed the room, headed toward the door to the left, she wondered if this room was still protected by the spells Antum had left. There was an aura of energy in the room, but not one that she could identify, and it was so small and quiet it seemed to be sleeping. She held her breath and turned the knob.

It opened harmlessly. A set of stairs stretched downward into a dark corridor. She descended quietly, even though she doubted anyone or anything still lived in this tomb of the ancient goddess. The hall was short and opened into a small chamber with little style or flair compared to the rooms above. It was bare. Even the altar against the far wall was simple and bereft of anything atop it. She narrowed her eyes, stepped closer, and searched its smooth surfaces for any secret drawers or buttons but found nothing. That was it. An empty altar with no weapon. But if it wasn't here, where would the phylactery be?

Angela sighed in disappointment. She should have

known better than to expect it to be here. Antum hadn't expected Vi'dinor to break apart when they crushed Ti'amat's crystal; that much she could derive from history and the vision she'd seen. Perhaps the phylactery was still out there somewhere, in some other world.

Gods, it could be anywhere, she thought. *But it could be the key to defeating Ti'amat a second time. If the phylactery isn't here, then what is the lingering energy I feel in this place?* she wondered. *If not a spell and not the weapon... could it be her?*

Angela climbed up the steps with haste, returning to the main floor to rummage through debris with one hand until she found the steps to the chamber's apse beneath the rubble. Placing the lantern down, she heaved marble chunks and wooden beams with the aid of her soul's energy. When the glimmer of rainbow light caught her eye, she worked harder to uncover it as anticipation built inside her. She wanted to see it with her own eyes.

Antum's crystal was cloudy white and resting on its side, unlike how she had seen it in her vision. When she cleared the debris from the top of it, she noticed its misshaped form. There were several pieces here. One large, a bear-hug wide, and another chunk no bigger than a basketball lay a foot away. But what was most concerning was the edge of the chamber that faded into nothingness. The shattered crystal sat on the edge, and a large piece was missing.

She's not all here... Angela thought. *There's more of her out there somewhere, too.*

Angela climbed atop the crystal shard of the goddess that still retained half of her soul, straddling it. She removed her glove, brushed the dust from it, felt its cool, smooth surface. It didn't react to the touch of her skin like she had expected it to, so she closed her eyes and touched it with her mind.

This was the source of the dull hum of energy that filled the manor, but what it emitted was weak, little more than a whisper, or breathing, that declared its presence and the life inside it. This fractured piece of Antum's soul was asleep.

What is going to happen? Angela wondered. *Will I still be me?*

She took a deep breath. Her arms were trembling, but she did her best to ignore the fear bubbling in her gut and bit her lip before pouring energy into the crystal. At once, it vibrated like an engine. A light sparked inside it, casting prisms of color throughout the ruined manor's dusty corpse. A subconscious nature took hold of her, and with her mind, she pulled the fractured soul from the crystal. Like glass reformed, the soul inside her melded with it easily, as though it was meant to be a part of her. Only now did she realize how much she lacked before and what was yet to be fulfilled. Deep inside her, the thrumming lived.

There was one more crystal piece to find, for Antum yet stirred on the edge of wake and sleep.

CHAPTER EIGHT

The space between worlds was cold, but nothing was colder than the sight of Dingir's frozen carcass. For hours she had delayed returning there, dreaded facing the cost of her choice. The skies were grayish white. The snow had piled on while she was away; drifts that had been at her knees now reached her waist. The added weight to the city's foundation made the platforms bob in the wind, turning buildings into groaning giants. The path to the Ascendancy's buried steps had grown narrower. They needed a wind-blocking wall to guard the footpaths through the city, but as much of an impedance as it was to march through the snow, Angela was certain those still around were more worried about the decay and risk of falling. That, and newfound hunger.

There was only one Uri Gallu on guard inside the dark lobby. He leaned back against the wall, pulled his clothes tighter against his skin.

"Sarosha?" Angela asked.

He motioned down a hallway. "Storage. In the back. Watch your tongue. She's on fire today."

Angela thanked him and carried on. The missing guard standing just outside an open oak door was her sign she'd found the right room. Scraping and banging sounds like crates being tossed around came from inside. Unlike the other soldier, this one eyed her cautiously and kept quiet. He seemed to stiffen as she passed through the fog of his breath.

Everyone must know what happened between me and Samael, Angela thought. *But hopefully not my relation to Donny's new condition.* She was not looking forward to this encounter.

Sarosha was dirty. Sweat clumped her hair against her cheeks. Her jacket and overalls were tossed into the corner. The room was a mess, and when the Grand Ensi realized that Angela had entered, she paused, thought long and hard about what to say.

Under her gaze, Angela grew uncomfortable and filled the dead air by asking, "What are you looking for?"

Sarosha's big brown eyes almost rolled out of her skull. She crossed her arms, shook her head. "Food. Rations. Do you have any notion of the trust you've broken? How you've damaged things?"

"How *I've* broken trust? Things between Samael and I have been *untrustworthy* ever since I woke up. Did he mention how he drew a knife on me shortly after we left? How he threatened me? Did he even tell you why I snapped?"

Sarosha's eyes softened. "No."

"I thought not. He mentioned Michael just to infuriate me, saying if my husband had killed me, Ti'amat would still be sleeping. I will not tolerate him digging up my past to throw it in my face. He will not sully who Michael truly was."

Sarosha glanced down at her hands, uncertain. In a calmer voice, she asked, "Do you think that could be true? That Ti'amat wouldn't have come back if you hadn't stirred up Maulkatu and the Nephilim?"

Ignoring the growing spark of anger in her chest, Angela contained herself and her tone. "No. I think she would have woken up anyway. Ti'amat would have wiped out everything we know already if I was dead. With me alive and holding on to the fraction of Antum's soul I have, we're stuck playing this game of hers. The power she's letting me borrow is proof she wants me alive."

The Grand pursed her lips. "That power scares me, Angela. Scares the living sweat out of the others, too. No one should have it, let alone a friend I've known for years." Sarosha's eyes were flickering, blinking away tears of fear. She sighed. "The Bui'dus told me you dove too deep, that your eyes turned black. And afterward they said you changed. You were quiet, distant, and concerned about something of which you would not divulge. A team does not operate on secrets and thrashings, Angela. I'm worried about what this power is doing to your mind."

It irked Angela that Sarosha doubted her resolve, her inner strength to combat the temptation. The Grand did not know what it had cost her and why she would never again rely on a boon from the goddess, but she could not say that. Couldn't admit what had happened. She said, "Ti'amat's power is poison, yes, but it hasn't done anything to my mind, just amplified my emotion, I'll admit. There's no need to worry that she'll take hold of me or the others. I trust her to keep her word in that regard."

Sarosha shook her head, sighed like Angela was missing the point. "It's not Ti'amat I'm worried about right now. It's you. Always stubborn, always the first to a fight and the only one to walk away from it. You know as well as I do that you have a history filled with fury. You jump the gun and lay down swaths of those that get in your way." Sarosha stepped forward, placed a hand on Angela's shoulder, and said, "This power is getting to your head, and the cost is too much. I worked it out, Angela. At about the same time as your fight in the arena, Donny suffered a bout of chest pains. He dropped to the ground. A chill took hold of him. And then the hunger."

Angela swallowed as Sarosha spoke, glaring at her with piercing eyes. What could she say?

Sarosha knows, she thought. *She's put the pieces together.*

Angela could not find the words to speak. The Grand sighed, ducked away to scoop up her jacket and overalls into her arms. "Don't worry. I won't tell him or the others. That's your job, if you so choose to explain his sudden soullessness to him. But I have to say, it will be very selfish of you if you continue to use Ti'amat's power at the cost of your friends' souls."

Angela looked away, too abashed to make eye contact as she said, "If there was a different choice, I would have taken it, and I didn't know what it would cost me until afterward, but it won't happen again. I swear it."

Sarosha pressed her lips together, considering it. "I believe you," she said. "Come. Other things have happened since you were last here."

IN AN HOUR, THE LAST FIGHTERS OF DINGIR TRICKLED INTO the record room and sat at the round table, every one of them grim and sour. Sarosha had assumed the task of gathering everyone, figuring it better to have Angela wait and give the Bui'dus time to think before they saw her again. Angela could not argue. She broke down wooden crates and stoked the coals in the fireplace to pass the time.

Donny settled into the room last, picking the seat closest to the fireplace, his whole frame shaking from the cold. Angela hadn't expected him to come to this meeting, and all the guilt inside her bubbled to the surface again. He no longer carried the gait of a friend and did not greet her. Kicking him and leaving him behind was the least of her offenses. The way his hard eyes looked at her made her wonder if he knew that she was the reason his soul was now gone.

Angela bit her lip, moved to her own seat a few spaces away from him. She swore to herself she'd stand by her choice to keep him out of this fight by all means necessary, but it would be hard not to admit her uneasy guilt.

"Now that we're all here," Sarosha began, "let's get the big things out of the way." She motioned to Angela, as if to indicate that it was her time to say her apologies.

At the sight of Donny, freezing and miserable, the guilt overwhelmed her. He deserved to know the truth. "I know what each of you wants me to say, but I'm not one to lie to you for your own comfort. Donny, your suspicions are correct. In the last world we visited, we were captured, imprisoned, and put to trial by combat in an arena against creatures unlike anything we've ever seen before. I was wearing thin, growing tired. I could barely walk. I called on Ti'amat, and that cost us something I wasn't expecting. It's true: Ti'amat has taken your soul as payment. She made me choose one person. One soul."

Donny's face smashed together in anger. His fists clenched on the wooden table as he spat, tried to come up with something as his temper rose. "W-Well, I don't know what's gotten into you, Angela, but you've taken the word 'bitch' to a whole new meaning. How could you choose me? Kick me to the side like I don't have a right to fight for what I love?"

He rose to his feet, shook his arms as he said, "Don't think I can't see it, Angela. You picked me because you want to keep me here, imprisoned like a useless toddler when it's my life on the line, too. My success is yours. I have every right to risk myself if that's my choice. It's selfish, what you've done. Selfish. Your attempt to cling to the last piece of your old life, me, is selfish."

Angela's jaw clenched, tipped up into the air. How could he not understand that she was fighting *for* him? Her choices were far from selfish. Her neck was the first on the chopping block, and she meant to be the last, too. But it was a bitter pill she would have to swallow; no matter what she said, he would not understand why she pushed him away, and he would hate her for it. So be it. In the end, what mattered was keeping her last semblance of a normal relationship as far away from this as possible.

Donny sat back down, cheeks red, knuckles white as his fingertips clamped down on the table and the cold sweat on his forehead shone in the firelight. He moped, then calmly said, "All I want to do is help you. Help the city. Fight for it, maybe even die for it. And I get pushed aside like I don't have a right to be here."

"I wish it was that simple," she said, "but you need to keep your distance. Why do you think I do not call on Sarosha to join us? Combat is not either of your expertise. Do you hear me? Trust me? Donny, if there was any other option, I would have taken it. I'm sorry for what I did and what this has cost you, but I'll make it right."

Donny did not have anything to say. He just huffed in his seat, pulled his clothes tighter, and kept his eyes off of her. An eerie silence took over the room, one that Angela could not tolerate for long.

"I know what we have to do now," she said. "How we can beat Ti'amat before this game of hers reaches the end. Before she's finished pulling herself together."

Three out of the five people in the room crossed their arms and leaned back in their chairs, looking like they either didn't believe her or were too surprised to speak.

With her eyes settling on Samael, Angela said, "When we were fighting, I reached out and touched your soul. I think it has to do with the awareness Ti'amat granted me, but I found fragments of the people who had your soul before you. Entire lives like flashing memories before my eyes, distant yet resounding. An echo.

"I hadn't put the pieces together before, but it makes sense. Every soul we have inside us came from the weyline, and when we die, they return to those etherical streams. It's a cycle of reincarnation of a sort. We aren't the first people with these souls None of us. Hazy recollections of different worlds live on inside us, and I dug through mine and found the answer. I know how Antum destroyed Ti'amat."

Angela let a long moment of silence pass as the others worked through the theory themselves. They looked to one another for confirmation but only got shrugs signaling nothing more than plausibility. It seemed the others did not know if it was possible or not.

Sarosha was the first to speak, her voice weak and wavering with uncertainty. "S-So how did she do it?"

"Antum made a weapon for that Nephilim we all knew —and hated—Basmu. She called it the phylactery. It was made of crystal, though I haven't seen it, and she imbued it with spells that somehow made it possible for a person to conceal the aura of their own soul. To make them as mortal as a human."

Jezreal leaned back, plucking her bottom lip with her finger as she thought. "A way to sneak up on Ti'amat's crystal…"

Angela nodded. "I think so. But I don't have the whole story. What I found was just a fragment of Antum. There's more of her soul and her echoes still out there in some other world. But I think we can assume two things. Every god and goddess that was alive in Vi'dinor constructed their own temple to house their crystal hearts. Even Antum. Secondly, Basmu took the phylactery to Ti'amat's temple to destroy her, and we might be able to find it if it's still there."

Sarosha furrowed her brow. "But wouldn't that take us right to Ti'amat's crystal now?"

"No, I don't think so. When her crystal heart in Vi'dinor was destroyed, she shattered across innumerable dimensions. She fell asleep from the damage, and most of her shards slowly became attuned to the dimensions they landed in over the eons. We've been using these pieces of her crystals to travel between dimensions for who knows how long.

"But back to the point. I highly doubt that the crystal shard her soul clung to stayed inside her temple. So Ti'amat's heart could theoretically be anywhere. In any dimension. I imagine she's able to move around, too, so why would she stay in the place where she was defeated before? Especially since she knows that Antum was the one who dealt the blow. When we find the phylactery, I can use it to sneak up on Ti'amat and defeat her again."

Sam groaned, rubbed his eyes and his face in disdain, settled his distrustful gaze on Angela, and said, "It is presumptuous of you to assume that *we* will be leaving at all. You lost it back there. Why would I trust you more than the goddess herself? Or risk my life traveling with you again? I'll admit, my tongue slipped. I should not have wished such ill on you, but that does not excuse you for nearly beating me to death."

A sigh escaped her. It was clear that she, too, needed to apologize for what she had done to convince him to join her again. As much as she did not want to admit her need for help, she would have to. She simply said, "If you want to get rid of Ti'amat, you'll come. Plain as that. I still need extra sets of eyes. People with combat experience to watch my back. I let my anger control my actions, and for that, I apologize, Sam. We're closer than we were before, but we still have a little further to go."

"So," Gabe said, running his fingers through his hair, "find the phylactery, hide your soul, sneak up on Ti'a-mat's heart, and smash it to pieces." He smiled a boyish smile. "Sounds like we actually have a plan now. About time."

As much as she wanted to withhold the smile of hope that stretched across her face, she couldn't help it. The small tug of optimism was enough, even though she was afraid of expecting something good to happen for once. So much hinged on her. The well-being of worlds and their people was a crushing weight that tested her confidence in everything.

How could I be facing an ancient goddess? It seems too unreal to be true. Out of all the souls in the weyline that I could have been born with, why did I get Antum's?

An uneasy sensation stirred inside her. Her soul shifted

at the mention of her name, like Antum had rolled over in her sleep. Angela swallowed.

Another person is living inside me, growing stronger as I feed it like it's a babe. The thought made her sick.

"Angela?" a woman's voice said. Jezreal looked concerned, brushed the hair out of her eyes. "You all right?"

"Y-Yeah," she said. "Just lost in thought. I don't think smashing her crystal is going to be enough. That's what happened last time, and Ti'amat survived. But if it's all we can do, it will at least take her out of the picture for a while. Hopefully a few more eons."

Sarosha sat forward, weaved her fingers together, and broke her silence. "So the crystal is just a house for her soul. She won't truly be gone, even if we grind it to dust?"

Angela nodded. "When we destroy the crystal, she'll lose her grasp on the countless souls she controls and fall asleep from the damage. The only one here with the spiritual strength to kill her soul is me. I'm not sure how, but I'll do it. Smother her, trap her if I have to. It really won't matter so long as we get her soul away from all the others she's poisoned. We'll be safe then."

Donny was leaning back in his chair, hands resting across his stomach. It was still so strange to see the transformation he had gone through. Once, he had been fat, happy, weird, and goofy all at the same time. But now all Angela saw was a stiff stranger. He was a thin man, almost to the point of being gaunt. While he still kept his hair as short as he could, his face and head were no longer completely shaved. His blue eyes were always ice hard now. He looked like a man stuck between a rock and a hard place.

Gabe lurched to his feet, sprier than the moment called

for, stretched his arms above his head, and smiled. "Well, I'll go repack our supplies." He glanced to Samael and Jezreal, silently asking if they were coming as well. Jezreal was quick to nod, but Samael thought hard for a moment before giving his consent.

They both would come, though for Samael, it was clearly out of necessity, not desire.

Sarosha held up a finger, stopping Angela from rising. "I forgot to mention something to you. Toth came to Dingir. Twice. He said he needed to see you."

Angela was surprised. "Councilman Toth? What did he want?"

Sarosha shrugged. "The first time he came to check up on you. He usually does about once a month, but you had already left. The second time he returned, he seemed different. Worried. But he didn't have much time, didn't say much other than it was important he saw you. He made it sound like something was happening in Kur."

"I don't know what could be happening in Kur that would be more important than this, but I'll jump over there and see if I can't find him." Angela locked eyes with the Bui'dus. "I'll be back in a few hours. Should give you plenty of time to get ready."

They nodded and made their way to the doorway. Donny didn't move an inch, not even his eyes. He sat there watching her, waiting for her to say something. She buckled under his gaze and said, "I'm sorry," before leaving him behind.

THE MAIN CAVERN OF KUR WAS DARKER THAN SHE remembered it being. The green and white moss that clung to the stalactites above glowed dully, and the public firepits and lanterns that usually lit the market square were few and far between. There were hardly any stands or people, and only a handful of Dalkhu were disturbed by the blast of her arrival enough to look at her. The rest did not seem to care.

Angela turned to the long marble stairway veined with white and gold. Ahead, the Kissum loomed, its pentagonal walls thick and carved with symbolic meaning she had never deciphered. The closest dome beyond the massive black doors appeared to have been repaired after the destruction that the late-councilman Ruchin had wrought upon it. In that first confrontation with the Nephilim, he had brought spears of stone from beyond the veils and smashed the dome to pieces.

The sword on her back jostled and rattled as she climbed. The commoners she passed were suspicious of her, weary, cautious, and downtrodden like their will to live had been defeated. Underneath the oppressive presence of the Kissum, Angela was not surprised. She wondered what had changed here since she had fallen asleep.

Her boots clomped loudly as she passed through the doors and eyed the newer stones. The Council had made progress repairing its beloved building. In some places, the stone that replaced the damaged spots was a completely different shade of a black too close to gray. The veins of marble that spiderwebbed across the floor and up the pillars were broken or heavily scuffed from traffic and no longer formed a single path. The Kissum's grand front foyer was now a patchwork place of shame.

Within moments, a councilman dressed in black robes and red cord came from an arched hallway and spotted her. Before she could make out who it was underneath that hood, he spun around and took off toward where he had come from. Angela did not have to wait long before he returned with a second member. They removed their hoods and stopped in the center of the room.

Melech and Kanu, the two remaining councilmen whom Angela disliked most. Both had played a part in Maulkatu's attack on Dingir with the Nephilim, but only Kanu had shown signs of ever being in touch with Ti'amat. Luckily, his eyes were normal today.

"What are you doing here, Kanu?" Angela asked. "Last we met, you had stains of your own stool on your robes. Ti'amat was riding in your skin for quite some time, barely tending to your needs. I'm surprised she let you go. I'm also just as surprised that your brethren let you return and retain your status as councilman."

Pushing his angled black bangs from his eyes, he sneered at the insult. In a smooth tone, he said, "It is more interesting why you are here. Did you enjoy your long nap?"

Angela furrowed her brow. He spoke as though he had not been there when Angela visited Gor, like he did not remember flying on Lahmu the Red, landing atop that mountain, and giving her Ti'amat's gift of awareness. Perhaps he had been so smothered by Ti'amat's presence that he had no memory of their encounter. The uncertainty of his relationship with the goddess was a cause for concern. However, at least the Mother of Serpents was not with him now, and he spoke freely. She said, "It was not a restful sleep. And you, Melech. I see Toth must have let you live."

The scar on the councilman's forehead flexed when he raised his brow. If she remembered correctly, Melech had only involved himself with Maulkatu's attack in order to protect his people. He had not been pushed by rage or revenge. However misguided he had been, he would certainly be more agreeable.

"That he did. And I am grateful, but it was not an entirely selfless move of brotherly love. He was protecting himself, securing his own admittance to live in Kur. He spared my life, so we allow him his home. There is little more to the arrangement than that."

"How generous of you," Angela said sarcastically. "Toth did more for the Dalkhu than you two will ever do." She shifted her gaze to Kanu. "And your relationship with Ti'amat is tolerated by your peers?"

The councilman dipped his head. "It is. No longer am I the Lawkeeper. Now I bear the title of Arbiter, like Ruchin once bore. I stand between the Council and the Mother to broker peace and promises."

Angela laughed, incredulous. "You think you can barter with her? For peace? You really think you can guarantee her word to leave Kur out of this?"

"It is yet a pact in the making, but yes, I believe so. Things between her and I are amiable, unlike your relationship. It seems you are tied to a certain destiny, born with a fragment of a goddess's soul inside you. Fate is cruel, isn't it?" He bared his rotting teeth in a wide smile.

Anger bubbled inside her. She did not believe in fate, just luck or the lack thereof. The people who looked for destiny were idle, staring at stars and signs, projecting inner hopes onto the outer world in search of an intangible dream, but will and strength were certain.

"Fight it all you can," he said. "By any means necessary. That is your way, isn't it? You may not realize it now, but you are not in control here."

Angela waved her hand, dismissed him. "I've had enough of this."

With her mind, she reached out and sliced a path through the veils, vanishing from sight. As she traveled the void, she hoped that the crash of air had startled the councilmen and knocked them on their asses.

Kanu might think he knows what he's dealing with, but he hasn't seen what I have. Ti'amat does not barter.

She found Toth's chambers by memory, not by sight. The red drapes that usually hung over the entryway had been replaced with a thin black sheet through which she could see candlelight. The change in the cloth's color was not a good sign.

She called for him, and the sound of sandaled footsteps came closer until a hand parted the drape.

"Angela," he said, beaming. Despite his smile, he was worse for wear. Heavy lines of fatigue had settled under his vibrantly green eyes, and his red hair was disheveled and frizzy. What concerned her more was the grayness of his robes and the thin twine that had replaced his red cord.

Angela stepped inside. A broken chair sat in the corner, half covered by crumpled wads of paper tossed to the side. The desk was disorganized and messy with scraps of food and empty cups. It stank like sweat, and he seemed to sense her discomfort.

"Sorry. If I had known you were coming, I would have cleaned."

"It's fine." She dropped her gaze to his robes without thinking about it. "How have you been?"

He seemed self-conscious about his new attire. "Things could be better. As you can tell, I'm no longer the Council's Virtuoso. I had to part with many of my things." His voice wavered like he was defeated. He paused, regained himself, and in a more chipper tone, he said, "But I am still doing what I can for my people, most often in the form of gathering supplies and trading on Earth for those who can't make the journey. I take it Sarosha told you I came looking for you?"

"She made it seem like something was amiss."

He went to his desk and sat with a sigh. "Aye, something serious, I believe. The Council won't grant me a meeting about it. I think they are afraid to acknowledge what it might mean. Afraid to acknowledge there is a bigger problem than they predicted."

"What problem?"

His eyes glimmered in the light as his sorrow gripped him. "There's a boy, newly born in Kur like any other, but with no soul. I have searched and searched, scanned every book, yet I cannot find a reason he is human."

A grim feeling washed over Angela. Immediately, she knew the cause.

"Something has changed," Toth said, "and the Council will not hear me or investigate. Kanu, the scum. I think he knows what is happening but can't defend his precious Mother's actions, so he stays silent. It's her doing. I know it. That's why I came looking for you."

"Give me a minute," Angela said. She sat cross-legged against the cold wall. Hands in her lap, she closed her eyes and focused. With the point of her mind, she burrowed into the veil until she was through. It had been some time since she disconnected from her body, and the slow drain of physical sensation into numbness and nothingness was jarring. Remembering the time she had found a weyline, she called out for the only soul she knew for certain was there.

Michael!

Projecting her inner thoughts into the vast expanse felt like yelling into a deep well. Her voice carried on, and eventually, he answered with a rush of emotion. Happiness, sorrow, and love washed over her. She tried not to think about it, tried to keep herself together when she found him tethered to the darkness that was Ti'amat's weyline.

Thousands upon thousands of souls bound in a great black river of cumulative energy cried out in different tunes. The weyline pulsed, oozed like a tentacle under the control of a single mind. Michael was in there with countless others, buried and smothered in Ti'amat's grasp. She was little more than a parasite. A consumer of souls.

The river was moving, flowing further and further from Kur. Angela steeled herself and prodded it with her mind, gently at first. The weyline flexed, grew more rigid. This was not like it was before.

So many souls crying for freedom, Angela thought. She wondered if Ti'amat could feel her poking around. Before all those souls, she swore, *I will free you*, and turned away.

In her skin once more, she found things as she had left them; the room was cluttered, and Toth stared at her eagerly and intently, seemingly noticing her return and hoping that she had good news. She let him down as gently as she could.

"How is this possible?" Toth's frustration was obvious. He was no longer the calm and collected councilman she had known. His neck was devoid of the chained emerald medallion he usually wore, and Angela wondered if the Council had taken that from him, too. He buried his face in his palms. The events that had transpired since she fell asleep had taken their toll on him.

Angela shrugged. "Take me to the boy. I want to see him."

Toth raised his head. He was crying. "To do what? With no weyline in Kur, he is just a bad omen, just the first of countless children born human. I know three other women that still bear children. All of them will need to be fed like a human. The older they get, the more they'll need. We don't have the stores or the means to survive." He was beginning to break down, his voice cracking. "Why doesn't Ti'amat just save us the suffering? I don't want to fester in this damned cave, working futile hands to the bone for something that is going to end in blood and agony."

Placing a hand on his shoulder, she drew his emerald eyes to look into hers. "I know what it's like to lose hope. To push against something that is unfathomably bigger than myself. I have little faith to offer you, but I can show you that you are not alone. Just because I'm not here, struggling beside you, does not mean that we do not fight the same fight. Take solace. Fight on. The day draws near."

Toth collected himself, wiped the tears from his cheeks, and gave her the best smile he could muster.

An idea struck her, one that might wipe away her guilt and restore her hope in a single blow.

Why should I wait until after my battle with Ti'amat to try and rectify these situations? she wondered. *Both Donny and this Dalkhu boy have no soul, so what if I could give them souls now? Slowly pry it from the weylines... It'll be like taking a single grain of rice from a field. There's no way Ti'amat would notice. On top of that, Antum was a goddess. Nearly all of her power is sleeping inside me. Perhaps I could unlock it and use it to give them one.*

There was only one way to know, and that was to try. A fluttering nervous feeling coursed through her. She put a hand on Toth's shoulder and said, "Take me to the boy. I will give him a soul even if it means I must wrestle with Ti'amat today."

And, Angela thought, *if I can get one for the boy, I can certainly steal back Donny's.*

The ex-councilman's eyes widened. He nodded, rose to his feet, and locked his trembling hand with hers. They were away in seconds and appearing on the rocky thoroughfares of Kur thereafter. When the boom of their arrival deadened, the only sounds were the crackling of a firepit and the coughing of an elderly woman holding her hands over it. They flowed down the street with a quick pace, headed to a battered and crumbling home of mortarless stone slabs and thatch roof.

A haggard middle-aged man answered the door, greeted Toth, and gave Angela a scornful look. They argued. Toth tried to convince him that she meant no harm. He laughed. Angela shouldn't have been as surprised as she was. The last time she was in Kur, the city paid dearly for the fight that ensued.

"She wants to see your son," Toth said. "Please. You can trust me, and you can trust her." He avoided making promises or telling the man why they were on his doorstep, which was for the better. Angela didn't know if she really could do it.

Eventually, the man allowed them inside. It was cold and smelled of dirt. All around the home, patchwork blankets were cast on the backs of chairs and in piles on the floor. A small bucket of souring milk sat on the table with half a loaf of bread. As desolate as the home was, the presence of food was a sign that they were not so poor. The poorest of poor did not waste their time or wares bartering for food the body did not need.

Inside the single bedroom, the mother was coddling the child in her arms. The boy was only weeks old, small and squealing. When he was calm, Angela asked to hold him.

The father glared at her, suspicious, but his mother smiled and seemed eager to share her newborn source of joy.

The woman rose with a smile and said, "His name is Abi Erim," as she placed the babe in Angela's arms. He fussed, but only for a moment. His tiny fingers wrapped around hers, and her thoughts went back to memories that hurt. Memories of Michael. How he had wanted a child for years and how she had never felt it was the right time. She regretted that now. Michael had been right. There would never be a perfect time, and she'd missed that opportunity.

She pushed those depressing thoughts away, vowing not to become emotional in front of these people, and settled where the mother had sat on the bed. The boy's eyes were big and brown, looking up at her with such interest and attention. He cooed, spread his tiny fingers against her cheek. And it was true; she brushed her mind against the boy and found no spark, no aura, no soul.

"How do we begin?" Toth asked.

Angela bit her lip. This was not something he could help with, and the anxiety was getting to her. In a tone harsher than she had meant, she said, "By being very quiet."

Toth apologized and took a step away.

Separating her mind from her body was easier and less frightening the second time, as was finding the weyline. Filled with the sparks of souls as numerous as stars in the night sky, the great black stream of energy pulsed before her. She swore to herself she would pluck one from the stream. The only question that remained was which one to choose. Out of the thousands before her, would it be easier to remove the brightest and strongest soul, the closest soul, or the one that she knew? The latter, while buried deep beneath the surface, might be easier. Out of them all, she was the most familiar with Michael's. If she chose it, perhaps there was a way that she could spur Michael's soul to fight Ti'amat's grasp of him.

But then again, she did not feel at ease about it. He was deep underneath the weyline's surface. It was unlikely that Ti'amat would not notice her digging, and a part of her wanted none other than Michael himself to house that soul. Yet she also liked the idea of some small part of Michael out in the world again, even if it was in a Dalkhu babe.

Shit, Angela thought. *I don't think I can. Michael's soul is still attuned to the energies of Dingir. If I place his soul into the boy, he may burn like I did. He might see his own mother riddled in flames. That is no way for anyone to live, much less an acceptable life for a child...*

That solved her dilemma. It had to be a Dalkhu's soul, and any soul was better than no soul. She searched the river's outskirts until she found an aura that matched, and then she examined it. In its deepest parts, she found the echoes imprinted by the people who had it before.

A young Dalkhu had carried it for less than twenty years. Visions of a hard life of squatting in the caverns of Kur, of being cold and afraid, flashed in Angela's mind. There were brief images of scaled creatures that could only be the Nephilim. This soul had been there in the beginning and more recently in a man who had died from old age. Those echoes were calmer, filled with passion for loved ones and the strength to see them safe. The differences in these imprints were curious juxtapositions of how things had changed for the Dalkhu over time. Hoping that the two experiences would balance each other out, Angela decided that this soul would do.

With a sharpened mind, she delicately cut and separated the soul from the black around it as softly as she could manage. Still, the weyline writhed and pulled away. If Ti'amat did not know what she was doing before, she would soon. The possibility of a horrible outcome struck her, filled her with panic. A jet of black reached out and smacked against her, attached itself around her mind, and threatened to swallow her until she slipped away. It seemed there would be no easy way to take the soul.

Back and forth she sliced and feigned, staying one step ahead of the monstrous stream until the soul was almost free. She dove in, grabbed hold of it, and pulled with all she could give. It budged as the sludge that held it began to pull apart. Angela pulled harder, and the weyline doubled its efforts to hold on to the soul. Like the incoming wave of the sea, the black loomed out over her and rushed in, grabbing her and smothering her. Angela slashed and cut at the ooze as she tried to retreat once more, but it would not let her go.

All at once, the weyline darted, plowed forward like a raging river, and dragged her along with it. They raced across the void as Angela struggled to get free until she was cast back into her own flesh like the snap of a finger.

Babe in her arms, she noticed the room was silent but for her rasping breaths. Toth, the mother, and the father stood around her, unblinking. A speck of dust in the candle-light hovered before her eyes, and Angela knew that something was not right. With them in the room was another person who had not been there before.

"Now what do you think you're doing, Angela?" Between Toth and the others, Ti'amat stepped forward from the shadows with a vibrant white smile on her face. The goddess held her head high with power and pride.

Angela tried to move her legs, stand upright, and face her head-on, but her limbs would not obey. In the heart of her soul, the black rot had taken hold. She was only permitted to speak. "Let me give this boy a soul," she pleaded.

"Is that what this disturbance is about? A soulless boy? Such a small thing to worry about, Antum. But I suppose there's more to it than just the boy. You've always been protective of your lessers. Understandable, honorable, but pointless. Especially now. I hope you haven't forgotten your mission."

Ti'amat took pleasure in convoluting things, controlling them, and being helpless once again infuriated Angela to no end. She curled her lip and spat as she said, "My mission to kill you? No, I haven't forgotten. We'll be free of you, trust me. And don't call me Antum again. I have seen the person who had this soul before me, and I am not like her. I am far more wicked when I have to be."

Ti'amat laughed, loud and irreverent. "Yes, you are different. Smarter. Harder. But the both of us appear to be getting closer and closer to our restoration. I can hear the chorus of your soul wherever you travel, and you are very close to restoring her. Oh, don't give me that look. I keep my word. I do not watch you, but you must understand you are like a dog on a leash. I cannot help it if I feel you pulling."

Angela's gaze dropped to the baby in her arms. So small and fragile. But what could she say to protect him, to convince Ti'amat to let her have a soul for him? Nothing came to mind, and Ti'amat seemed to sense her thoughts.

She said, "Don't be so distraught, child." The goddess walked to her, black hair swaying at her waist, and rested her open palm on Angela's cheek. Her fingers, warm and soft, caressed her. Made it seem impossible that she was heartless. "The Dalkhu are nothing. They are unordained by god or goddess, as are the Anunnaki. I told you once, do not grieve for either. We are above them all, and soon they will not exist."

Angela wanted to pull away. She tried, failed, and tried again. With all her strength, she raged against the goddess's control until everything ached, but the result was the same. She was completely at the goddess's whim. Hopelessness took hold. A tear streaked to her lips, and when she went to wipe it, she was only reminded of her weakness.

Ti'amat smiled, not devilishly like she enjoyed Angela's misery, but warmly, like the way she might look at an injured child. Like she pitied her. Like she thought Angela was small, cute, and her pain was nothing compared to what the goddess had been through. Ti'amat ran her thumb up Angela's cheek, drying it, and removed her hand.

The goddess turned away and asked, "Do you know that the Dalkhu think that all matter of the worlds seeps through spaces in the veil, that all matter crosses like strands of linen to create the worlds around us?"

Silence was Angela's answer.

"It's a valiant attempt to understand the nature of things around them, but wrong. I'm sure you're beginning to see that. The world of fire they call upon? A heavenly body of pure fire. Large, but not a dimension of its own. It's just what they can grasp with their limited view. Their dimensions of water, air, and earth are the same."

The goddess sighed and faced her again. "I want you to understand, Angela, I am not trying to hurt you. I am trying to save you from pain. Save you the guilt you place on yourself. It's Antum I want, and I believe I will get her. I know your type. All of your life, you've fought for things bigger than yourself, but I wonder if you are willing to give it all up and give Antum a chance to save what you love. Let go of everything you know. Everything you love. The worlds are shifting. Our link is growing stronger, empowering you." Ti'amat raised a finger and said, "I'll grant this boy a soul to soothe your ache, but no more. Let them go, accept that you are naught but a tool, or you will be miserable through your final hour."

"You bitch," Angela said. She lurched upright, suddenly in control of her own flesh again, but the visit was already over. The world resumed, the goddess gone. Toth and the others swayed in the room, looking at her with concern and confusion.

"I'm sorry?" the mother began.

Angela shook her head. Apologized. "Not you. She's gone."

The parents seemed confused, but Toth swallowed hard, understanding immediately. He must have noticed the color of her eyes, too, judging by the cautious aura around him.

But what mattered was that the boy had a soul, and Angela sighed. The goddess had fulfilled her promise, but what she had said gave her a whole new array of feelings. She should have felt happy for the babe and angry at the goddess since this was the last new soul to ever come to Kur, but all that tugged on her heart was sorrow. Yet again, she failed because she was not enough. And that meant that Donny would not get a soul, no matter how hard she tried.

The mother and father babbled and cried with one another when Angela handed the baby over. They thanked her profusely, but Angela didn't have the heart to tell them it was not by her strength that the boy had a soul. A quick motion with her head told Toth she was leaving. He followed her out.

On the street, she turned and said, "I could use your

help. I'd be lying if I said I have faith I can get rid of Ti'amat."

The ex-councilman fiddled with the twine around his robes, thinking for a moment before he spoke. "But you just got the boy a soul. I don't—"

Angela cut him off and explained what had really happened. And more. She went back to the beginning, told him everything that had happened since she had woken up. It was not a happy story to tell.

When he finally spoke, his tone had deepened. "I see."

"So will you help us? It's not just for me and the Bui'-dus. It's for the Dalkhu, too. I could use someone who can attune themselves to other worlds and teleport without the encumbrance of a shifter."

She could see the grimness in his eyes. It was like she had torn him in two.

"I... I can't, Angela. I understand your need of me, but others need me here, too. If what you say is true and no more souls will leave the weyline, then Kur is in trouble. The city does not have the means to live on its own as humans. Future generations are at stake, and the Council will not help the lowest of castes. Tension has gripped the Dalkhu by their bones. They will not make it to tomorrow without imploding if someone does not help them today. I'm sorry."

The pit in Angela's heart doubled in depth. Perhaps it *was* her fate to carry this burden alone, to let go of everything she loved, and to forget about even her own needs and allow Antum to use her body as she saw fit. If it was the only way... even she wondered if she could do it.

Angela could only manage a nod to Toth before disappearing between the veils, before bursting into tears.

CHAPTER NINE

The flat roof of an apartment building was not the best place for Angela to recover, but it was the only place she could be alone. She braced against the blistering wind, letting it snip and slice at her skin rather than going to her home or the Ascendency, where someone might see her sorry mood. She tolerated the frost and snow for a time, letting it cling to her clothes until she could no longer bear the cold. She sniffed, wiped her cheeks, and jumped through the veils.

The inside of the Ascendency was not much warmer, but staving off the wind was enough by itself. The others were gathered in their makeshift meeting room, waiting for her. Samael was staring into the fire, leaning his shoulder against the red bricks of the mantle. He had barely noticed her presence before his face went sour. Smiles on their faces, the others, particularly Gabe, seemed almost genuinely happy to see her, but Donny was nowhere to be seen. Angela supposed she deserved the silence from him.

"You're back," Gabe said with a grin. "What took you so long?"

"Business," she said without missing a beat. It was the first thing that came to mind.

He paused at that, examined her attempted lack of expression, but didn't pry any further. Gabe could probably read her well enough by now to know that something bad had happened and detect that Angela wanted to leave that undesirable thing unsaid. It seemed the Bui'dus would oblige.

Jezreal stepped forward. She had a shine to her eyes, an eagerness about her movements. "Well, do we have a method to our new madness? Or are we poking around in the dark?"

"I've been thinking about that. Like I said before, I'm changing our course. We're not going after Antum anymore. It's what Ti'amat wants us to do, and I'm not about to give it to her so easily. Something tells me if we do, she'll move things forward toward her so-desired final clash with Antum and we won't have a chance to sneak up on her. I've searched and searched the goddess for new memories that might reveal the phylactery's whereabouts, but nothing substantial or coherent enough came to me. Which means we're on our own."

"You don't have any idea where it could be?"

Angela shrugged. "Ti'amat's old temple is my best guess. It's most likely a fragmentary world, small and isolated, but that's not a guarantee. I'm pretty certain that the phylactery has to give off at least a moderately sized aura. Antum said she put a lot of energy into making it. Then again, even that may not be true. It was made to hide souls and their energy, so it might be entirely invisible."

Samael shook his head in contempt, crossed his arms like a pouting child.

He did not even need to speak to start a fire in Angela.

In anger, she said, "Let's get this out of the way, Sam. If you've got a problem with me, leave it in this room or stay here by yourself. You think I like not knowing where we have to go, what we have to do? I don't. But this is our best chance. *I* am our best chance, whether any of us like it or not. You think I want this power, this pressure? Every time I wake up, I'm greeted by a past that isn't even mine rushing up to drown me. I'm buried by a burden that I don't want to carry. So far, I don't even have the strength to get us through this without pulling on the goddess I want dead. So you had better shut up, come with me, or stay out of my way. I do not have the energy or time to deal with your bullshit."

Everyone stood there, looking at her. Tears had begun to flow again. It was embarrassing. Angela wiped at them, dropped her gaze to her feet.

Gods, this hopelessness is swallowing me whole...

A hand touched her shoulder. Gabe faked a smile. It was more of an attempt to cheer her up than an expression of happiness because he struggled to find the right words at first. He was the most kind-hearted of the Bui'dus. That was probably a product of his young age. "You're at your weakest when you let yourself think you are alone. We'll figure this out. We have a plan. So let's go find that phylactery."

Angela nodded, left the room, and headed out into the cold. The others were kind enough to give her a few moments alone. She was certain that words about her were being exchanged between the Bui'dus, but she did not want to know what they thought of her now. Breathing deeply helped calm her nerves.

This is the beginning of the end...

Samael had decided to come. He kept his gaze away

from her as the party assembled amidst the snowdrifts. Only when they faced one another and locked hands did he look her in the eyes. A bitterness welled inside her. She did not want him to come and wished he would have stayed behind, but it seemed that their love for Dingir was the one shared bond strong enough to keep them working together. No words were spoken before they disappeared in a flurry of snow.

Necessity deemed that Angela evaluate the scale and size of the worlds they traveled. She was smart enough to close her eyes before plunging them into the void to keep herself from getting distracted by the others' faces throughout the journey. Still, it felt like the better part of a month came and went in solitude, but her efforts were not without reward.

One discovery led to another; a seemingly infinite number of small, fragmentary worlds had nestled themselves between larger ones. The more she searched, the more she found, and each one made her reconsider the plausibility of the last one.

How long should I search? she wondered. *Will I find a finite end to existence or another veil that surrounds all of these? Mayhap the worlds are just drawn to one another by their weight and size and eventually I will find that beyond them is an endless expanse of nothingness.*

She was getting distracted again. The mind could not help but wander. That did not surprise her, but what did was how little her soul had been drained. Carrying four people, even for the quickest of trips, was a large task that councilmen would have trouble with.

A sudden spike of energy jolted her like a strike of lightning to the head. A million bells seemed to be tolling in her mind all at once, ringing and giving her a headache. She was awake now, though, paying full attention to everything around them. *What was that?* she wondered. For a split second, it was like she had made contact with a beehive. There was so much energy and fury that she had to know what world her mind had brushed against as they passed it. *But which one?* They had been moving quickly. *And did the others feel it?* She would have to ask them when they arrived. With the will of her mind and the push of her soul, she turned the group around and began retracing their path, intent on finding the source.

And she did find it. The veil around it was hearty and resiliently strong, but it hummed from the inside out with the strength of a chorus of a hundred thousand voices. At first, she wondered if she had found Ti'amat's crystal heart and the source of her power, but the more she studied the vibration, the more she came to think that this was something—or someone—entirely different. The black rot in her soul did not give off the same aura as this.

Exploring this world was not something she would ask permission for. Sharpening her mind, she cut them a path through the veil and stitched it closed behind them.

Their arrival was quieter than it should have been, and the state of the world was not what Angela had expected at all. Cobblestone cottages with timber framings lined both sides of a brick thoroughfare. The atmosphere was thick enough to put weight on her shoulders. It was humid, smelled rank, and smothered them in deafening silence.

"Something's not right with the air here," Angela said. She brought her hand to her mouth, shocked. Somehow, her voice was barely a whisper.

Gabe turned around, brow furrowed. He mouthed words Angela couldn't even hear from five feet away. Then his hand reached for his lips as he, too, seemed to realize the strangeness they had stumbled into.

Angela tried shouting. "There's something wrong with the air. Can you hear me?"

He got that message and returned his own. For as strained as his expression was, his voice was quiet. "Yeah, I hear you now. Is this where the phylactery is?"

She shook her head. It was easier than yelling. This place seemed to rob her of the satisfaction of breathing; she never felt she had enough air.

Samael stepped between them so he didn't have to be so loud. "If you know it's not here, why are we?"

"Didn't you guys feel it? That surge of pinpricking energy?"

The Bui'dus shook their heads. It must have had to do with Ti'amat's awareness. She explained what she had felt rumbling in the veil. "I've never felt anything like it before," she shouted. "I think there is a god living here."

Jezreal held up her hands. "What? A god? I don't know about you, but we have reasons to be wary around those kinds of people. We should leave."

Samael agreed, but Angela was not as easily convinced.

"Think about it. If there's a god or a goddess who has evaded Ti'amat's grasp for this long, he must be either strong or cunning. Maybe we could convince him to help us."

Samael had begun to sweat, a sign he did not like this place. "What if this is Ti'amat herself? What if we're right outside the door of her crystal heart?"

Angela told him why she didn't think this feeling was her. He was about to start arguing again but stopped himself short. He must have taken her advice and decided to trust her.

Gabe seemed to see the logic. A sparkle of curiosity glimmered in his eye. "Shit, let's find 'em. It can't get any worse than it already is." He laughed, but Angela was not in the mood to make jokes.

"Let's scout the area for signs of life," she said. "I haven't seen anyone yet, but that doesn't mean no one is here. Meet back in this square in five minutes. You see anything at all, you run back here. Stay on your road or the buildings just off it. Don't wander too far."

Faintly, she heard Samael grumble. Angela played deaf. "What was that?"

"N-Nothing." He turned down his street and began to walk.

The others did the same. Angela had no clue what direction she was facing, and the road that stretched out in front of her was not straight. It weaved and bent at a covered bridge a few hundred yards away. As eerie as it was to walk in this strange place and in complete silence, there were things that Angela was grateful for. The homes looked relatively human in construction and size. Most were made from cobbled stones and rough-cut lumber. A few had wooden signs hanging on black iron chains, but the writing was completely foreign.

Fifty paces down, there was still no sign of anyone on the street or movement in any windows. Dark lanterns hung on porches, as motionless as everything around them. There was more wrong to this place than the air. A green rot clung to the wood in places, shingles were broken and missing, and some houses had begun to sag and cave in, all suggesting that this place had been empty for years.

Angela moved to prove it; she climbed her way up croaking wooden steps and stood before a red door, contemplating the risk and reward of entering. Eventually, she justified it, reached for the brass handle, and cracked the door ever so slightly. Peering in, she saw a glass-faced cabinet with goblets and plates on the far side of a dining room. The small portion of the table she could see was clean and tidy except for the thick layer of dust on its surface.

On light feet, she entered. The door retaliated with a groan. It was quiet but still disturbed the complete silence inside. Slowly, she stalked toward the next doorway. Beyond it was the kitchen. Block countertops and hanging utensils. She searched a few cupboards and found nothing out of the ordinary but the lack of food. The other rooms on the main level, an office and living area, were just as empty.

Where could all these people have gone?

Ascending to the second level on old, rotting steps made Angela grit her teeth nervously. She felt like she was disturbing the peace, but when she reached the top and stood motionless for a moment and heard no sounds from any of the doors, she relaxed and walked to the closest one.

At least there are no—

Angela thought too soon. There by the bed lay the hunched skeletal remains of a person. It had long since rotted. Kneeling before it, she examined it closely. There was no smell, skin, or flesh. Not a single bone had been broken, and the only sign of conflict in the room was a tipped-over chair. But resting on the *inside* of the ribcage was a conical stone about four inches long, thicker on one end and pointed on the other. She picked it up, rolled it in her hands. The surface was rough, lumpy, and certainly did not belong inside the remains. She began to wonder if it was a part of the deceased person's anatomy. She had seen strange creatures in Ibarra's world. Maybe this world was different, too.

Or maybe it's what killed him…

She put the rock in a leather pouch on her belt and left the corpse there. Across the room was a desk with a single piece of parchment. She found the quill and inkwell on the floor next to the chair. The black ink had spilled and stained both, but his death had not come before he scrawled three crude symbols on the paper. Unable to decipher the meaning, she exited the room.

In the hall, she realized that she had been gone far longer than the five minutes she had given the others. Knowing that this home—this *world*—was nothing but a graveyard, she teleported to the intersection she and the Bui'dus had departed from. Twenty feet away, the others saw her before they heard her, a sign that even the concussive blast of her arrival did not travel far.

"You're late," Gabe said in a quiet shout. "Had me worried sick."

Angela shrugged. "Sorry. Lost track of time. I found something. A body "

Samael ran a hand over his shaved head as he said grimly, "Me too."

"What the hell happened here?" Jezreal asked. "The skeletons can't be more than thirty years old."

"You think?"

"Yeah. Look at the houses. Sure, there are holes in roofs and rot taking hold, but not a single one is completely ruined."

A sudden bout of fear took hold of Angela. "Did you guys touch anything?"

They looked confused by why that would matter. Only Gabe fessed up to touching bones.

"A plague could have wiped them all out," Angela said.

Gabe swallowed, wiped his hands on his cuirass.

"I did, too. But hopefully it has been thirty years since they died and we'll be all right."

"I found something, too," Jezreal said. She pointed down the street she'd walked, and Angela couldn't believe she didn't notice it before. Jutting over the tops of the homes around them were gray towers and steeples close in color to the backdrop of gray clouds behind them.

"What is it?" Angela asked. The spires were too far apart to be a chapel or monastery with only one building.

Jezreal smiled like she had found a secret treasure. "A castle. But not like any other I've seen before. You can't see it from here, but the drawbridge is down. We can look around inside."

"Alright," Angela said, because who wouldn't want to explore an abandoned castle? "But give me a second. Considering it's the biggest, most blatant thing here, I wonder if it will coincide with the energy I felt before we came here."

The others agreed, gave Angela some space to sit on the ground. Stretching her mind out like she was a catfish feeling a riverbed, she brushed over everything until she reached the castle's wall. From that point onward, a slight tingle of energy grew to a nearly overpowering presence the further she went. That was all the proof she needed to justify investigating the place. She rose.

Even though the likelihood of being heard by anything living was small, they kept their voices low as they walked. Chatted about how they were going to try to convince a god, if there was one, to help them. To Angela, it was simple. Maybe too simple, she admitted. Whoever it was would likely despise Ti'amat for what she did to Mulki and

Vi'dinor. The god would have likely been there for the destruction of both or at least one; she only hoped that gods were better at holding grudges than men. A hunch told her that they were.

The brick road came to a T, and they followed it to the right. Houses were growing more immaculate the farther they went, but the overwhelming silence never faded. Another intersection. To the left, the castle walls loomed over a ditch. Just as Jezreal had said, the drawbridge was down to allow them access, but after the first few steps, the old wood snapped beneath Samael's feet. The others had to help him pull his foot out of the hole. It was then that they noticed the spikes lining the bottom of the pit below. The Bui'dus grew pale, uncomfortable with trusting the old bridge to hold their weight, so Angela teleported them past the barbican and into the bailey.

There, the blast of their appearance did resound against the curtain walls some. It must have had something to do with the aura that surrounded the castle, Angela presumed. The static energy in the air affected the way sound traveled in the atmosphere.

A well sat to their left, in front of what used to be a barracks and stables. Those had been in better shape. A fire had raged in the yard, leaving little more than a third of both buildings and staining the gray walls behind them with black soot.

This was not the only bailey, she realized. An interior wall ran parallel to the front outer wall, and nestled in the middle of it was the castle's main building. By its irregular shape, she assumed it housed a multitude of rooms. The only way to get through the interior wall, and to the keep beyond, appeared to be there.

The iron-banded doors had been rammed and broken

open, the inside destroyed and torched. Ash and bones littered the colonnades of the feast hall. There were no tables left standing and surprisingly no throne to be found; it did not look like this place had even been set up to house one. On the left wing, an immaculate chapel had been desecrated, its colored glass windows smashed with stones that littered the ground. Some books in the library had survived the flames, but none were legible. Servant quarters and the kitchen comprised most of the right wing, and not a single room had been left untouched, but despite the damage, the stone structure itself still stood strong.

There was not a door to the rear bailey, but an iron portcullis. It was lowered and blocking their path. Instead of searching the upper levels for the winch that raised it, Angela took them through the veils again. She doubted the aged winch and pulley system would have raised the metal gate without breaking and dropping it back on them.

The towers of the keep against the far outer wall were taller than all the rest, looming over them and the field of corpses they waded through in that back bailey. Angela saw no movement in the arrow slits but did not feel safe under their gaze.

"What do you think happened here?" Jezreal asked.

"A massacre."

The closer she drew to the doors of the keep, a squarish and stout building of larger blocks than usual, the more the air seemed to buzz with energy. Whoever or whatever she was searching for was inside this unordinary keep. Through the doors was a single dark chamber with pillars and the smell of fire and death. There were no more passages, no stairs, just a wall twenty feet tall and thirty wide. On its upper surface, from waist height and up, petroglyphs seemed to read from left to right.

The first subject was a man, plain but for the sickle in his hand. He created community in the form of homes and houses bunched together, worked the land with animals. In the next segment, a crowd of people pointed up to a sea of stars above, but one seemed larger than all the others. Next came the construction of the castle in perfect representation from just outside the drawbridge. How the last image and this one were linked, Angela was not sure. On the far right, the final carving was of a man on a throne. Behind him were curved stained-glass windows, and his hand was resting on a rock atop an altar to his right. Or at least that was what it looked like.

"I can't make sense out of all this," Angela admitted, nearly stumbling over a few corpses near the wall. The lower half of the wall was nothing but a long stretch of symbols. She didn't even bother looking at those.

"Look at this!" Jezreal exclaimed loudly enough for everyone to hear. They rushed to her. In the center of the wall, below the depiction of people staring at the stars, Jezreal was pointing to the edge where the wall met the floor. Perfectly inscribed in the wall was a semicircle with no symbols inside it but embellished with a massive ruby.

Jezreal crouched. "Look at the way these people died right here. It's like they were reaching for the ruby. A faded handprint in dried blood right next to it, too." She glanced up at Angela, confused. "Do you think they were trying to steal it? Is that what all this was about?"

Angela bit her lip. "No... I don't think so. This many people don't gather and raid a castle for a single jewel of that size."

"Well," Gabe said, crossing his arms, "is there something special about it? I mean, we are looking for an enchanted crystal, after all."

Angela shrugged, closed her eyes, and checked it. "There is a faint glow to the ruby, but the major source of energy is behind the wall. Did you guys see any other doors into the keep when we were outside?"

The Bui'dus all shook their heads.

"This place just gets stranger and stranger," Angela muttered as she kneeled. She drew her curved skinning knife from her belt, tapped the jewel with the hilt. It did not respond or sound unnatural. Using the edge, she tried to pry it free, pushing it up, down, inward, twisting it. Nothing happened, yet she was certain something was special about that ruby. She straightened. "We're missing something."

"Can we just warp to the other side of the wall?" Gabe asked. He put his ear to the wall, pounded it as hard as he could. "Seems thick, but it could just be the stone."

"I'm not willing to bet our lives on it." She looked down at her feet. Jezreal was right; it did seem like a few corpses had one hand stretching out to take the jewel, but the clue they had missed was in the corpse's other hand and the blood on the wall.

"That's it," Angela said, drawing her knife again. She unbuckled the bracer on her left forearm, pulled it back, slid the blade across the back of her wrist. It stung, bad. Blood dribbled. The Bui'dus jolted into action, protested, and tried to grab her. "Just hold on," she commanded. Wetting her right hand in her own blood, she bent and palmed the ruby. It vibrated up her arm. Glowed dully, then flashed. The semicircle of stone was not inscribed into the wall; there was a rumble as it descended into the floor. It was a door.

"A tunnel!" Gabe shouted with glee. Then his face turned sour. "What kind of place uses blood for a key?"

"One we're trying to get into." Angela moved corpses

to the side, got on her knees, and looked down the shaft. "Man, it's a tight fit. And at least twenty feet long. Glad we didn't try to teleport?"

Gabe shrugged. "It was just a suggestion. Who could've known it's that long?"

Angela smiled, turned her attention back to the passage before them. It was dark the whole way through, but beyond the opening on the other side, a dim green light flickered, washing the chamber beyond in an eerie glow. It was hard to tell, but Angela swore she was looking at the legs of a suit of armor before a stone throne.

"Uh, I think I see feet," she said, a touch quiet.

"Feet?" Gabe asked.

"Yeah. We've got company."

"I think you mean whoever is in there has company. Us. We're the company."

Angela rolled her eyes, stuck her head in the tunnel, and began to crawl. The tunnel was even tighter than she first thought. The others whispered loudly at her from the entrance for a moment, begging she come back until they gave in and began to follow her.

From behind, she heard Gabe ask, "Since we're seeking an audience with a kingly god in his keep, do you think there'll be crepes? Tasty treats to welcome us? A whole royal procession with bards and women?"

Samael grunted as he pulled himself forward. "Shut up, Gabe."

"If there are any women," Jezreal said, "you keep your distance. We don't need you mucking this up. This is business."

Gabe moaned his displeasure. "Well, at least on the strictest diets I can still read the menu..."

Angela chuckled, shook her head, and carried on. It was

not comfortable crawling on hands and knees; the ceiling was not quite high enough. She did not want to slide on her belly, but that was the only way. Inch by inch, she pulled herself through the dirt and dust, staring forward as the full picture of the throne-seated figure became clearer.

A bad thought came to her. *If a god demands that his audience pay blood and come to him crawling, he is not a good god.*

If the air outside the keep had been buzzing with energy, it was a full-blown furnace in its deepest chamber. The source of the light was strange green-flamed torches that seemed to run on nothing but the aura in the air. Four spiraling pillars, helixes covered in symbols, surrounded the armored man on the throne. His eyes were open, white, and without pupils, but the god seemed motionless and unaware that she had entered his domain.

The others began shuffling in behind her. Bringing her finger to her lips, she silently told them to remain quiet as she moved closer to examine the body. Garbed in sleeveless robes, vambraces, and plate leggings, this man still had his skin, but it was stretched thin over his bones. And just like in the depiction on the wall on the other side of the tunnel, his right hand was resting on a porous stone held up on an altar next to him, a gemmed ring on every sickly finger. Anxiety gripped her gut. This god was sleeping now, but not for long.

With the handle of her dagger, she poked the flesh of his arm. The others winced, nervous themselves, but they were not close enough to see that a muscle moved beneath the sleeping god's pale skin. It did not seem right.

The atmosphere kicked up, humming almost audibly as one wheezing breath escaped the waking god. There was a groan, a rumble. The lights flickered, but there was no wind. Angela jaunted down the steps and returned to the others' sides, afraid she'd just made a fatal mistake.

Jezreal had her hand on her gun. Angela slapped it away as she took a spot next to her. If the god moved on his seat, she did not see it. A great crackle of lightning leapt from one helix pillar to the other, then crashed into the throne. A presence jammed itself into her mind like a hot poker, digging through her like a cabinet, pulling out the files and examining each of them with such rapidity it hurt. She fell to her knees, as did the Bui'dus. All they could do was clutch their heads and hope it would be over soon. The sensation was paralyzing. The ground beneath her seemed to move and distort until the god had seemingly gotten his fill.

Somehow irradiating light, the god's mouth did not move as he spoke in a gravelly voice. "Who? Who before our own feet comes crawling?" His laugh boomed through the chamber, but Angela had barely seen him take a breath. She was so stricken with fear that a long moment passed. The god seemed to be thinking until his haggard voice came again from the darkness in every corner of the room. "Thou far from home... yet so close. How? Who kneels on weary knees before us?"

Angela sucked in a deep breath and said, "I am Angela Ma'at, and we are far from home. We've come here—" She pushed off the ground, began to rise to her feet.

The room shuddered. "*Kneel!*" A force slammed Angela back down, pinned her there. "We did not command thee to rise. 'Tis our house you befoul with thy transgressions. One does not act without the permission of the many. Now, speak." He laughed again, rumbling the stone and the air.

Angela glanced at the Bui'dus around her, tried to

convey a sense of warning to them without the use of words. This would not end well, she was afraid. The force pushing against her was too strong for her to overcome, but she would not rely on Ti'amat unless she absolutely had to save her own life. Angela swallowed as she realized that meant she might not be able to save the others.

Staying low, she said, "We have come from Dingir, a city not of this world. We sensed your strength passing by and came through the barriers of this village in search of aid. If your godship is willing, we plead for your help ridding all worlds of the goddess Ti'amat. She threatens everything. Even you."

"There is no threat to us, even here in our own chambers. Thou speak of gods and goddesses. Ha! There are none, mayhap except how we are to you, cowering, shaking one. Anywise, we are unenlightened of thine threat."

"You have not heard of Ti'amat? The Mother of Serpents?"

"Nay, says we."

"How is that possible? Were you not there in the beginning? In Mulki, when the All-Father split himself to create the first gods?"

"You speak of a beginning that I am unawares of, for we were already here." The god raised his right hand, old bones creaking, and patted the porous stone at his side with slow falls of his palm. "From the heavens, we fell. Before mortal life had taken to root, our seed awaited the day that man came to harbor us. To worship us." His chuckle was deep and grim.

Something about the way he spoke made Angela believe that this god was somehow unrelated to any of the other gods. He did not come into being like the others had. He knew nothing of Mulki. But what event could have sparked the creation of a new god? The world's destruction? Or did another god create him and leave him here to his own means?

"What do you call yourself?" Angela asked.

"This one is Gasgon, the first, but we do not have a name."

How could he not have a name when he just told it to me? Maybe dementia comes with being an ancient god.

"Now," the old god said, "thou must answer our questions. This Dingir, is it brooding?"

Angela wasn't sure if he was asking if Dingir was in a sad state or if it was growing. She assumed the former and hesitantly answered, "Yes."

He grumbled like that was not the answer he wanted. "Full of thine own? Brothers, sisters. Life?"

"… Yes."

"Thou wish for protection for thine own, from this Ti'amat?"

"Yes."

A wicked smile crept across the god's pale lips. In his mouth, there were no teeth. He said, "Then rise. Come to us. Take our seed. Your admittance to our chamber tells us thou is prepared to bleed. Life's water nourishes the seed. Awakens it."

Something felt wrong. She wasn't sure what it was; she could not sense it exactly. The pressure that had been holding her down faded. She stood, managed one step forward before Gabe grabbed her wrist. They locked eyes. He could sense it, too.

He said, "My godship, might I first ask what happened here? There are fields of innumerable corpses outside your keep and throughout your village. We have not seen a single soul but yours."

Gasgon moaned like he was in pain. He began to untie the cord around his robe with his deathly hands. "The men that lie yet live, free of flesh and pain in our presence. Gasgon was the first. The Finder. From him, we spread across the land. And now, across *worlds*."

Opening his robe, he exposed his chest. From beneath his ribs hung three gray masses as hard as stone. He wrapped thin fingers around the first, shoved it deeper into the cavity of his chest, and cried in pain. Blood flowed, spilling out over the stone and his hand before he pulled it free of his body. His hand shook and glistened as he bore it before himself and said, "Take us to your Ti'amat."

A wheezing laugh rumbled through the chamber as the seed began to pulse like a beating heart. In moments, the blood had soaked in, replaced by a snotty mucus of a thing now alive in the palm of his hand. Beady eyes flickered. It shuddered, rolled out of Gasgon's hand, hit his leg and then the floor with a splat. The thing slugged closer, slowly at first, until it seemed to focus on Gabe. It squealed, bared a mouth and teeth beneath its small pointed nose, which was still as hard as stone. A nose made for burrowing.

Gabe jerked Angela's arm as the thing grew close. "Don't let that thing touch me," he begged.

Gasgon's mental presence had returned, pushing her back down to her knees. She fought. She raged, tapping into the reserves of her own soul for the extra energy. Her hand reached the hilt of the sword over her shoulder before Gasgon's force doubled, freezing her arm in place.

The god laughed. "Ere long you will see. You will know. We will relieve you of your burden. Your Ti'amat. Foremost, we require an offering. A taste to nourish us."

Angela cursed. She should have known that Gasgon would be no better than the Mother of Serpents herself. He could hold her body still, but not her mind. She struck at the veil above the throne like a viper, puncturing hole after hole. Sprouting jets of orange and red flame burst upon him, and at once the power that bound Angela lifted free. The fires roared, carved a hole through his chest, and began to melt through his stone chair in a matter of seconds. The rest of his flesh was smoldering quickly, filling the chamber with his dying stench. Gabe screamed.

"Where did it go?" Angela asked. No matter where she looked, it was not on the floor.

The Bui'du swallowed, sweat beading on his forehead. His face was pale. Tears were welling in his eyes. Too terrified to speak, he removed his trembling hand from his neck to show her the bloody hole where the creature had burrowed. He whimpered, "Angela?"

Gabe bent over, threw up. Almost fell into it when a fit of seizure-like jerks and moans of pain overtook him.

The others rushed to him first. Too mortified to do anything, Angela just could not will herself to move. Gasgon gave one last wheezing shriek before the chamber rumbled out of control. Another lightning storm showed its full strength, exploding chunks out of the floor, walls, and pillars. The god's energy, unrestrained and loosening, was going to bring the keep down with him.

"We have to get him out of here," Jezreal said.

"I... I thought that if I killed Gasgon, his... his *thing* would die with him. I... I couldn't move!" she justified.

"Well, it didn't," Samael barked. "Grab his fucking arms and get us out of here, Angela."

The emotions washed away, replaced by a soldier's numbness just long enough to get a hold of Gabe. The room was getting hot. Gabe, shaking and seizing, was hard to grab. But as she went to push them through the veils to safety, a lacking detail gave her pause. She checked again. Doubled-checked and triple-checked. Only three of them had souls now. Gasgon's slimy thing had somehow eaten Gabe's. It was gone.

Angela staggered back, wanted to fall onto the ground and give up. "That's how he was so strong... Gasgon was a god of leeches. Leeches that eat the soul..." She muttered, "Gabe is doomed."

The others understood soon enough. They were skilled enough with their minds and souls to feel auras and energies if they searched for them. One by one, the color left their faces, too. Gabe could not go home.

Jezreal recovered first. She pointed toward the tunnel and said, "Move. Pull him through."

Weakly, they pulled and pushed and struggled to get Gabe started into the cramped passage. Angela led the way, going backward and pulling him forward by his arms as Samael pushed from behind. The stones above them cracked, dropping dust into her eyes. It was a bitter, tormenting thing to be stuck facing Gabe's shrieks and shudders for the whole twenty feet of the tunnel. He did not want to move, only clutch his chest and lose himself to hysteria. Angela left her own trail of tears, but if he kept it up, he would pass out.

Pulling Gabe through became a blur. Clear of the cramped shaft, she lifted him and dragged him over the corpses and out into the clearing in the bailey. Even outside, under the gray skies where the air was dense and muting, she could hear the keep rumbling as it caved in on itself. She had not bothered closing the holes she'd made, preferring to allow the veils to continue to rip open as time stretched on. Gasgon, the castle, this whole world with every horror he had created would burn forever. He deserved no less.

"Wh-What—" Jezreal choked. Bent over, she tried to catch her breath with her hands on her knees. "What are we going to do with him?" A part of her must have already known the answer, but she was not ready to hear the truth.

There was no easy way to put it, so Angela said it plainly, "We have to leave him behind." The words that came from her mouth were poison, polluting the atmosphere between her and the Bui'dus. They would not recover from this, nor would she allow it. This would be the end of more than just Gabe.

Samael was tense. He clenched his fists like he was about to swing. Angela wished he would. He said, "We can't just leave him here. Not with that thing inside him. He'll need food, and in case you haven't noticed, this place is a bone-dry graveyard."

Angela was ticked off. She did not want to argue with him. Not now, or ever. "I don't want this any more than you, but what choice do we have?"

"Can you do anything for him?" Jezreal asked.

Angela shook her head. Gabe's moans had reduced to whimpers as he tried to listen to the conversation happening around him. She said, "I can't. Go ahead and try to rip the thing from his chest if you want, try to take him back to Dingir, but you'll kill him either way."

"But where did his soul go? Back to a weyline? Can you get it?"

She wondered if Jezreal somehow knew about the Dalkhu boy who was born without a soul. She couldn't do anything for him, had no hope she could get one for Donny, and she would not be able to save Gabe. She pointed to the rumbling keep. The buzz of energy inside was kicking and screaming as Gasgon went down, but it was growing steadily weaker. "Souls are food to these things. It's been broken down. Digested. Even though that energy is dispersing now, there's no getting it back. No way to reform it into a soul. And we may have hurt Gasgon good, but he is not exterminated. The way he was talking, Gasgon will carry on through Gabe. The seed is planted. It will spread. Grow. Keep him alive just enough to serve as a breeding ground for leeches."

Angela felt sick just thinking about living with a parasite like that. Images of the sickly god and the growths under his ribs returned to her. In time, that would be Gabe. There was no hope here, only misery and defeat.

"It's all my fault…"

The Bui'dus had no sympathy to give her. They knew it was true, just the same as her. She sniffed and wiped tears as grief and sorrow clung to every fiber of her being.

Jezreal broke the silence. "Well, let's at least get him inside. Find him a bed until we figure out what to do."

"N-No!" It was the first thing Gabe had said in a while. He was in a ball on the ground, grimacing every time the leech moved inside him. "Just k-kill me. I don't w-w-want to live like this."

The unsung song they'd been afraid to acknowledge had hit its chorus, and it was not received well.

"No," Jezreal argued. "We'll find a way to get that thing out of you. Shit, I'll come back and feed you with a damned baby spoon if I have to."

"Y-You heard the same thing I d-did, Jez. Being around me is going to expose you to the l-leech god, too." Gritting his teeth, Gabe lifted his head to gaze at each of them. "P-Promise me y-you'll keep fighting. Together. It-It's the only way we'll beat Ti'amat."

"Not gonna happen," Jezreal said, her voice wavering as though she was close to breaking down. "No way. We took oaths together to uphold our city by any means necessary, and we're going to *keep* those oaths."

Samael stepped forward, placed a hand on Jezreal's shoulder. He had not said much in words, but his eyes spoke volumes. "Let him go. It's his choice."

Betrayal streaked across Jez's face. "How could you say that?" She shoved him, sending his stocky figure stumbling back. "We can't give up on him. He's our brother."

"And our brother does not deserve to live like this. You can—"

"S-Stop it," Gabe croaked. "Don't fight over m-me. Just do it. Please."

Jez shook her head, fighting back tears. "No." She bent, grabbed him by the arms, and began to pull, dragging him over corpses and toward the castle's entrance. Gabe shrieked in pain. It was a sorry sight to see them reduced to this because of Angela's choice. She should have stayed on their path, stuck to their plan, and found the phylactery and the last piece of Antum, but the desire for an easy, fanciful out had been stronger.

Something took over Angela. She became automaton, walked to Gabe, pressed the barrel of her tether gun to his head, and fired. It was a quiet, hushed pop of steam. Gabe was throbbing, and it was over.

The others gasped. Jezreal let go of Gabe, stormed closer, threatened, backed off, and sobbed. For once, Samael did nothing. These were bad times; she was finding him more agreeable by the minute. When the dust settled, Angela holstered her gun. A pool of red formed at her feet, and she could see herself in it, staring down at her proof of guilt.

194 | AUSTEN RODGERS

Maybe I can't win this, she thought. *If Ti'amat is splitting her strength with me, with Antum, helping me reach a potential I can't even fathom or control, can I really find a way to get an advantage? Do I have to give up everything I am, everything I've fought for in order to win?*

A slow breeze pushed Angela's bangs into her eyes. There had not been wind since they arrived. She took it as a sign that Gasgon's grip on this world was fading. She took in a deep breath. Looking to Jezreal and Samael, she said, "We're over. Done. Go back to Dingir. I fight alone now."

CHAPTER TEN

Three days of searching came and went. While she was no nearer to finding the phylactery, roaming the quiet corners of small worlds did give her time to think and assess, to swallow pain and guilt and turn it into numbness. She did not want to go back to Dingir and face those she'd disappointed. She'd disappointed herself more, she was certain, but swore that she would not return without the phylactery in her hands. That powerful crystal was turning from myth to fable the more she looked for it.

Occasionally, she would return to the world of windows, as she called it, and stand in that dark place for hours at a time to gaze through the shimmering panels at distant places, only to come to the bitter realization that there were so many she could not hope to search them all in time.

There was a shift in Ti'amat's presence as the days went by. The black rot in her soul was like the string on a harp; Angela could feel the goddess's tension building. Sometimes it seemed to vibrate in fits of anger, and she only hoped her rage was not aimed at her. But either way, she feared that Ti'amat's patience would not last long.

Who am I kidding? she thought as she sat before the shifting images. *I think it's true. I think the phylactery, given its nature, is invisible to any sense but touch and sight. How am I going to find it? Antum's—no,* my*—soul holds no echoes I have not delved into and examined. There's no lead for me to follow.*

She began to retrace the artifact's history from its first inception and creation to the present. Recalled everything she knew and dissected it again. The phylactery was made by the spiritual will of a goddess, given the sole purpose of hiding souls and their auras. Antum had been working in the shadows when she made it, keeping her back turned to Ti'amat and using a handful of her own Nephilim against her. As far as Angela knew, Basmu was the Nephilim who last had the phylactery, but he might not have been the one who used it. It could have changed hands, but the fact remained that it had been used in Ti'amat's temple. That was the last place it was known to be, but there was no one saying that it could not have left there.

It could be a waste of time trying to find her temple, she thought. *If only Basmu was still around, I would ask him what happened to it.*

But other Nephilim were still around. Lahmu the Red and Gor the Keeper of Fey would not help her. In fact, asking them about the phylactery would be a warning signal to Ti'amat. The goddess would know that Angela was looking for it.

A grin stretched across her face. When Vi'dinor shattered, creating the great expanse of worlds pictured before her, many surviving Nephilim found safety inside a cavern system that would become known as Kur. Basmu had been one of them, hidden in the deep tunnels beneath the Kissum and Eld Kur. And there had been other Nephilim that refused to surface and heed Maulkatu's call to destroy her four years ago.

A few old beasts may still be down there.

Angela had not been down that low before, and as far as she knew, neither had any other living person. But she suspected that there was one ex-councilman who might have had an inkling of where the remaining Nephilim yet dwelled. She rose, stretched, and set off for Kur. This time, she would not waste her time visiting the Kissum first and set her mind's eye for the tunnel that led to Toth's chambers.

At his doorway, she called his name, pulled the curtain aside, and found the rooms empty and unlit. It was eerie how dark it was in there. Thoughts of rummaging through his papers to find what she could and pass the time came to her, but she would not intrude on him like that. Besides, the Council had probably stripped him clean of anything secretive or important when they booted him from their ranks.

Angela set her sights on the market square in town and teleported there. Little had changed except for the smell of meat and onions sautéing on a nearby cookfire. The place was still as empty as it had been on her last visit, but with fewer people out and about, it was easier to search unnoticed. Toth was not in the markets, so she began perusing the streets of the poorest parts of town and found him with a pack of young boys kicking a ball in the road.

It took the ex-councilman several minutes to notice her. She did not rush him. When he was finished, she led him into an alleyway between homes, out of sight and earshot of everyone.

"You're back," Toth said. The boys had him working up

a sweat. Angela nodded, and a curious expression came to him as he looked her up and down. "You look different."

"How's that?"

"Your eyes. The way you carry yourself. Something happen?"

"I was scared before. More afraid of what I might lose than determined to snuff out Ti'amat. Now I've already lost it, and I'm just pissed."

"Sounds like you've been thinking."

"Three days alone will do that to you."

Toth raised his brows, amused.

Angela said, "I'll be honest with you, I came to ask you for help, but it's not like before. This takes place a bit closer to home. You know Eld Kur and the Scratched Hall, but have you ever been deeper?"

A sense of wariness came over him. He must have suspected something. "Once, when I was younger and new to the role of Virtuoso. I made a pilgrimage of sorts to the collapsed system of caverns where legends claim the Nephilim were yet shut in. At the time, I did not believe they could still be alive. How wrong was I?" He chuckled.

"Wonderful. I need you to take me there. You can leave after that. I won't ask for you to help me deal with them."

"And by dealing with them, you mean…?"

"Prying for information. Killing, if necessary."

His skin grew pale. "I would advise you to be more cautious. If any of the creatures are still down there, they will not be accustomed to dealing with what they view as lesser beings. They are older than the Kissum, hardened by savagery and potent in spiritual strength. The last contact they had with anyone but their own was with Maulkatu, and I cannot imagine that he left a great impression."

Angela crossed her arms. "I'm running out of time,

Toth. I have to do something before it's too late. Take me there or draw me a map."

He scratched his head. "It has been decades. I would not trust my own memory to scribe it, but I will take you as far as I can manage." Putting her hands together, she bowed slightly and thanked him, but curiosity seemed to continue to gnaw at the back of his mind. He asked, "So you think the phylactery will be down there?"

Angela had forgotten she had told him about it. The fact that he had put the pieces together himself was a testament to his cleverness. "It might not be, but it's somewhere to look. At the least, I may be able to learn what happened in the last moments of Vi'dinor and where it could have gone."

"Makes sense. Our path is set, it seems." He sighed. "Give me an hour or so to prepare. I may have some old notes of some use stashed away somewhere."

Angela nodded. "Thanks again, Toth. I will repay you."

He smiled. "If you can get me my necklace back, we'll be more than even."

"Let's not get ahead of ourselves here. We may not live past today."

"THIS PLACE IS NOT LIKE HOW I REMEMBER IT," ANGELA said. "It's darker. And stinks like brimstone."

Toth raised his glow stone higher. Moisture on the stalactites shimmered green. They provided less light than torches but lasted indefinitely and could be easily hidden under their leather wrappings or clothes if necessary. Hopefully, though, they would not get into a situation that would require them to hide.

"I think you're right," he said. "Something's happened to the moss. This way."

They veered to the right, off the beaten path and into the field of pointed stone. When they came to the entrance of the Hall and the cliffside it bore into, Toth stopped to consider something. He closed his eyes for a moment, then came back, confused. "The illusion is gone. Not a trace of it remains."

He was right. The entrance used to be hidden with a wall of stone. She asked, "Did the spell just wear out?"

"Unlikely. Look." The ground was scratched and scuffed in places. Only claws would do that. "Someone has been coming and going through here. You know what that means?"

Angela groaned. "Maulkatu didn't re-seal the Nephilim off. They have been free to roam for four years." A grim thought came to her. "Do you think they know where Kur is?"

"Eld Kur, yes. We are not far from it. But I do not think they could find the way to our Kur. It's high up, and as far as I'm aware, the passages are too narrow. We should tread lightly."

"Won't matter. They'll see us with these lights before we see them. Besides, the goal is to get their attention anyways."

Toth did not seem to like that. A mumble escaped him before he began walking again, and Angela joined him a pace behind. It took a bit before the scratched symbols on the walls became apparent, while those on the floor seemed to continue for the entire length of the tunnel. Angela read as much of the writings as she could comprehend, secretly hoping that maybe there would be enough information here that they wouldn't need to go any farther down and speak to the Nephilim. By the time they reached the end of the Scratched Hall, which split off in three different directions, Angela knew that it would have been too good to be true.

Toth paused at the triple mouths, looked down the throats of each as he tried to remember which one to let swallow them. The uncertainty of it all got Angela thinking. If the Nephilim were free to come and go as they pleased, they might not even be down where Maulkatu had found them. They could have made their way to Eld Kur or even gone somewhere entirely unknown. The deeper they went, the less they were accustomed to their surroundings, and the less they were familiar with, the more likely it became that one of the beasts would get the jump on them. The Nephilim were natural hunters, and some of the eldest ones might not hesitate to make them their prey.

Angela's mind returned to Gasgon's world and the dead things inside it. She carried a terrible weight with her now. Far more than just the responsibility of Gabe, the Bui'dus, Toth, and killing Ti'amat. The guilt returned to her. Gabe was not the only thing that died that day. The partnership she shared with the Bui'dus had perished as well. She would not allow Toth to share that fate. She touched him on the shoulder, turned him around, and said, "I don't think I made this clear before, so I want to now, Toth. At first sight of a Nephilim, you get out of here. No hesitation and no arguing with me on this. You flee, leave me behind. I'll be all right."

He seemed surprised by her concern for him, raising a brow. "Angela, I'll make that decision when the time comes."

"I said no arguing. Do it for me, if not for yourself."

The ex-councilman considered that for a moment, gauged her mood. He nodded, seemed to understand how important it was to her that he steer clear of danger. "Very well."

The scraps of paper containing Toth's notes were very undescriptive, they found. Words scribbled around small drawings of tunnels were a mess to make sense of, and they could not find where to begin. He had not numbered the pages. Sitting on the ground, he shuffled them about while Angela tried to reach down each tunnel with her mind and feel for any sign of life's energy. There were some dwindling lights in each. Of course, none were large enough to be a Nephilim. The caves went deep, and she never felt sure that she had reached the bottom if there was one.

Toth made a sound, rose to his feet, and said, "I have it figured out." The more she quizzed him, the more he grew confident that he had found the correct passage. He did not seem to like being questioned and took off into the tunnel to the right.

Down they went, curving and twisting like they were walking on a deformed spiral staircase. At places, the incline was so steep they had to sit and slide down the rubble-strewn path. It was not a comfortable ride. The tunnel never leveled out but grew more gradual in its descent. There were several intersections at which Toth had to refer to his notes for direction. He seemed to be getting anxious and frustrated until they stepped out into a cavern that must have rivaled the size of Kur's. As they headed downward, the light of their glow stones could not do much to penetrate the darkness, and the sound of tumbling stones under their feet echoed far and wide.

Toth's feet found the edge of a body of murky water, splashing in it. A curse slipped off his tongue, adding to the noise. Angela joined him by the edge to listen and focus on keeping their eyes peeled. They had disturbed the peace of that deep cavern and waited for it to resume. When nothing happened and the surface of the water stilled to a dull mirror, allowing their light to reach a little farther, they breathed easier. Still, they could not see the far side of what could only be a lake.

"What do your notes say about this?" Angela asked in a whisper.

He crouched over, laid his papers against a rock, and held his glow stone close. In a minute, he said, "We aren't far. There's mention of a lake and following the shore to the right, but I also wrote down a note on a particular type of moss that does not seem to be here any longer. I recall this chamber used to be illuminated."

Angela nodded. That seemed to be the running theme the deeper they went, and there was only one solution. "The Nephilim must have scorched it all to give themselves an edge in the darkness."

Toth's eyes grew wide. Quickly, he collected his papers with a slight tremble in his hands. "They can see in this dark?"

"I assume so. They are probably watching us now."

"To blazes with this." He jolted upright, faced the lake, and closed his eyes. A line of glowing orange and red streaked through the air, over the water from one shore to the far side. Flames jutted downward and kissed the surface of the water, creating bubbles and steam. Light in the cavern flourished, coloring the rock in flickering red. The lake was huge, with a small rocky island jutting through the surface on their left. Toth winked.

"Well," Angela said with a smile, "that's one way to—"

A deep, throaty rumble cut her off. Tumbling stones crashed into the water as something raced behind stalactites on the other side of the lake. Angela could not get a good look at the disturbance but thought she had seen the shimmer of scales. Thankfully, it did not come out, only retreated.

They locked gazes. She raised a brow. "I think that's your cue to go."

"Not yet. Let's go across. Over there." He pointed. "I'll show you the chamber the Nephilim used to be trapped in and leave you there."

She stared him down, hard, but he did not budge. "Very well." There was no point in hiding now. Taking his hand, she skipped them across the lake in the blink of an eye. The thunderclap echoed. The Nephilim knew they were there, anyway.

There was still no sight of the creature, but what could not be seen from afar was now clear; up the shoreline and through the stone spires, a dull red glow emanated from the entrance of a tunnel like a fiery maw.

"I take it that's where we have to go?"

Toth nodded.

"Let's get up there a bit closer, stitch up your big fiery spectacle, and then you have to get out of here."

The ex-councilman frowned, having taken it the wrong way. "I was not going to let us get snuck up on."

"You don't have to defend yourself to me. I approve. Now they know we aren't to be hunted. Come on."

Upward they climbed until they stood at the edge of the cavern in the red glow. Angela watched over Toth as he closed the tear he had made. From one end of the lake to the other, the line of fire disappeared. When the cavern was cast in darkness again, Toth breathed heavily from the exertion. That was a surprise for Angela. He had been her teacher in the basics of spells and had always been very skilled with his soul and mind. Perhaps the amulet meant more to him than he let on. She swore to herself that she would get it back for him if she had the time when all this was over with.

"And so concludes our adventure," he said. "I hope you find what you're looking for."

Angela bowed "I do, too. Thank you."

He wiped his forehead, smiled, and vanished. She wished he'd have given her a head's up; her ears were ringing now. But she chose not to be mad at him for it, considering the help he'd given her. Lifting the glow stone above her head, she eyed the path before her, sighed, and tried to shake the nervousness away. Being alone added a new level of fright to the darkness.

The tunnel was a short S shape, and the farther she went, the more she bathed in the red glow from the other side. At its end, the ground shifted to mounds of cooled magma, black and porous. Angela scoffed. The ancestors of the Dalkhu had used a wall of stone to barricade the Nephilim in, and Maulkatu had melted it away. She had already known, but seeing it now confirmed her suspicions; he had not bothered to close the tunnel again, preferring to allow the Nephilim to roam those lower caves.

Just like Maulkatu to throw a little chaos into the mix, she thought.

The source of the red glow was a ravine not ten paces away, nearly overflowing with lava. The smell of eggs was worse closer to the edge, the heat unbearable. Still, the sight was something else. She had never seen anything like this. As long as she could withstand it, she watched the river slowly flow. There was wind there, perhaps an updraft from the heat, but it was not long before she had her fill and warped to the other side. She stared out into the darkness that the red glow could not penetrate and wondered where in the chamber the Nephilim were and how many there could be.

Something grumbled in the deep. The scratching of claw on stone, yet there was nothing to see. "Come out," she yelled into the cavern. Silence followed. Certainly, they were talking among each other and not including her in their psychic conversation. Angela repeated herself: "Come out!" She did not want to step away from the light from the magma behind her. If she stepped farther out into the darkness, she feared one of them would sink their teeth into her. "You have something I need. Information, or—"

A gravelly voice permeated her mind, left her brain stinging as it said, *A malformed Dalkhu does not demand from us. It begs.*

Hoarse laughter came from several directions, that on her left far closer than she felt comfortable with. Already, they were trying to silently flank her.

"I am not a Dalkhu," Angela corrected. "I haven't come from Kur."

Then where, and what?

"I'm an Anunnaki from Dingir, and I have the displeasure of carrying a fragment of a soul of someone you all will be familiar with."

Who?

"Antum."

That sparked the caves alight with activity. The long strides of talons scratching on stone became clomping paws, picking up in speed and growing louder. Growls and snarls came from every direction but behind her, and all at once, several minds slammed against hers. They groped her like hungry hands, smothering her soul and drinking in her aura. There was a beastly snicker and more grumbling among them. Words like "witch," "traitor," and "die" rushed into her mind. Their pace had quickened. The cave was larger than she first thought, and she drew the sword from her back, more for her own security than to try and scare them. They would not be frightened by a sword.

Before she knew it, seven Nephilim came jogging out from the darkness and stopped closer than Angela liked. She'd seen their teeth in action, and the reach and speed of their necks was snake-like. The color of their scales varied: two brown, one yellow, one almost as black as night, a bright red, one a greenish blue, and the final white like dirty snow.

We think that you will learn your folly, ere long. Several of the beasts made sounds that would pass for laughter if they were human. *This does remind us of a time when two sons of Dalkhu came before us and pleaded for aid against a certain one named Angela. But why does the spiritual successor of Antum come to us, the brood of the Mother?*

Two Dalkhu? Angela had forgotten that Shedim was the first to make contact with these creatures. Maulkatu was just the councilman who followed in his footsteps and warped his plans to fit his own desires once he reached out to Ti'amat. Gods, it never was simple.

Angela had to tread carefully. She could not outright say that she was here to kill their goddess, as it seemed that they would follow her a second time if the opportunity came and they learned that Ti'amat was awake. Especially so if they learned that Antum was really not standing before them. She was still sleeping.

Angela would play them, if she could. She said, "I seek something I created long ago in Vi'dinor. A crystal known as the phylactery. The last I had it, I gave it to Basmu to destroy Ti'amat and have since lost it."

It took the Nephilim a few long moments to conspire

and decide how to answer her. The white one tilted its head to the side, purring in its throat as it asked, *Why would the goddess want that vile thing? That crystal's damage is done. Do you know who you stand among? Those your blow has stricken, cast out, and trapped. We will not give it to you. Even if we had it.*

Angela restrained her smile. That final sentence was tacked on. An afterthought. These creatures knew where the phylactery was, no doubt. She said, "I put a great deal of effort into creating that. I'll have it back. Do *you* know who you stand among?" With the tips of her fingers, she traced the edge of her sword, projecting the energy of her souls and forming a purple glow of energy along it. It had been some time since she had tried that trick, but she pulled it off and its effect was satisfactory. The Nephilim took a few steps back.

But it was a short-lived victory. They recovered their resolve. The yellow one took a step forward, shook in its rage as its voice pierced her mind. *You cannot kill what has died a thousand times. Eons in torment, in pain, and in hunger. Give us your flesh, your bones, or else give us the peace of sleep, traitor. You shall not have the weapon. We would not let you take it, in spite, for all you have wrought.*

There was no doubt that these creatures had suffered down in these caverns. In some way, it was Antum's fault and now Angela's problem. But they had done terrible things to the ancestors of the Dalkhu. That could not just be forgiven. Yet it seemed that no progress would be made unless she was willing to barter for it. "I need the phylactery," she said. "More and more every day that passes. I do not want to spill blood now, nor was it my intention to see Vi'dinor destroyed. You must understand, I did not collapse those veils and I did not trap you here. The Dalkhu did that, and you deserved your sentence here. But to prove it to you that my intention is good, I offer you this: a new world. On two conditions, the first being dependent on you handing the phylactery over."

The Nephilim seemed like they did not know what to think; they glanced at one another, rumbling in their throats as they privately discussed. A brown Nephilim turned away, took to the air, and disappeared into the darkness. Her hopes rose alongside her anxiety. Was the creature retrieving the weapon, or was it a ploy? She thought about trying to butt into their conversation with her mind, but before she had a chance, they asked, *What is the second demand?*

Angela smiled. "I will explain that when we get there."

There was a vibrant flash of bluish light in a distant corner of the cave, briefly illuminating its dimensions. The ceiling was low, but it was long and wide. In moments, the sound of wings in the air grew louder, then ceased before the Nephilim came trotting back into the magma's light. A few feet from her, it dropped its head, opened its mouth, and placed a crystal nearly two feet in length on the ground. It was wet, blue, and a lot bigger than Angela had anticipated. The edges were sharp like they were cut, yet it mirrored a more natural formation and was larger in the middle than on the ends. While there was certainly something special about it, Angela could not verify that this was truly the phylactery. She had never seen it in Antum's echoes, and near as she could tell, there was no discernable aura attached to it.

She wondered, *Perhaps that's a sign the old spell has faded. Or maybe that's just a sign it's still working.* Trying it out was an itch she wanted to scratch, but allowing herself to be soulless around these beasts was not going to happen. Only the time she went to use it would tell if it worked, and that time was not now.

The Nephilim interrupted her thoughts. *Is the bargain struck?*

"It is." Slowly, she started forward, moving in deliberate steps so as to avoid any confusion that she was going to pick it up. The creatures seemed hospitable with her taking it now, even going as far as stepping back to give her space. The phylactery was heavy in her arms, its blue surface shimmering in the red light and reflective enough that she could see her own eyes staring back at her. Gods, she hoped it would work.

She set it back down, stripped off her backpack, and began discarding things to make room for it. It took some fighting, but she got it safely tucked inside and on her back. The crystal had to weigh no less than seventy-five pounds.

The time to deliver on her end of the deal had come. She extended an open hand and said, "I have to touch you."

The first and closest Nephilim nodded. They likely already knew how she was going to take them away. They did not seem to take offense or belittle her caution. She placed her palm on a warm scale on its shoulder, then pushed the two of them through. One by one, she traveled down the line of ancient beasts until all eight of them were standing in an intersection of brick roads and cobblestone houses.

It was night. Behind her, a raging hum from the direction of the castle roared like a great engine. Over the tops of still-silent homes, she could see the stone towers were glowing red. The smell of smoke was strong. The fiery hole she had left open days ago to burn away every last trace of Gasgon's temple and keep had torn larger. She was surprised she could hear it at all and noticed that the air seemed lighter than last time. Perhaps Gasgon's energy really had affected the atmosphere of this place.

She turned to the Nephilim, who were too busy examining their quiet surroundings to pay any attention to her. She had to gain it again, then said to them, "This world has no name that I know of, but there is an evil here far worse than anything you could imagine. Do not take this task I'm about to give you lightly. You will be free to explore, commune, and start a new chapter for your species. There are specks of energy out there I can only assume are animals, so hunt and be happy. But if ever you find a settlement like this, decrepit and abandoned, burn it to ash. The corpses house a plague unlike any other, and if it takes hold of you, I'm afraid that there is no cure but death. I entrust this task to you. Protect the life of this world and do not allow the plague to spread."

Looking at the village around them for a threat they could not perceive, the Nephilim did not seem to know what to think. As wicked as the creatures could be, as she had seen them before, she had hope for them. Hope that they could weave themselves a new tale, one of peace and honorable charge. Coming from who they assumed was a goddess, it might just stick.

Is that all? the red one asked.

"If you could restrain yourselves from wreaking chaos for any speaking people you might find, I imagine things will go better for you."

The white Nephilim flared its nostrils, huffed like it was a horse. She could almost hear its thoughts, its rebuttal. If one thing was certain about them, they did not like being controlled if they had nothing to gain out of conformity. Free-spirited, powerful, and passionate in all their flaws best described the beasts.

"Now go," Angela said. "Free this world of its pestilence and roam it to its edges."

One after the other bowed its head and took to flight. A *thank you* reached her mind, but she was not sure which one had said it. At once, they began their work, opening their maws and retching fires upon the first of the homes.

Satisfied, Angela left them for the castle. A jaunt through the veils and she was standing atop the outer wall, looking down at the melted rubble she had made of Gasgon's keep. The tear had stretched from pinholes to thirty feet across. When it was sealed, the rock and stone glowed hot. The stream of fire had gnawed its way into the earth beneath the bailey to a depth she could not see even from her height. Even with the keep smoldering and left in ruin, she still felt that it was not enough to kill the god. Almost assuredly, he would return.

Her mind worked forward and began to plan her next steps. The Bui'dus had taken Gabe's body home with their shifters to be burned and given a soldier's funeral, as was customary. Angela had missed it intentionally. The event would have been small and unknown to all but those who fought beside him, all those who knew her guilt.

She could not guess how they would react to her reappearance after the last three days of hiding from them, but she would arrive bearing a crystal weapon nonetheless.

CHAPTER ELEVEN

The bitter wind received her like an enemy, and the Uri Gallus inside the Ascendancy were little warmer. They stared and watched her pass without a word of greeting, and their gazes met with condescending looks. Long ago, she walked those halls feeling like a soldier going home, but now she was a stray dog roaming a place no friendlier than an untrustworthy alleyway.

Sarosha and the Bui'dus were sleeping when she found them. She awoke them as gently as she could, and when they began to ask questions, she only answered with the necessities to get them moving. "I have news. Meet me in the record room."

The acting Grand Ensi was bitter and depressed. She did not like being woken in the middle of the night. The others were cold and calculating but quicker to oblige the call. When they came in, Angela was in their makeshift meeting room, stoking a few logs she'd started burning in the fireplace.

Sam took his seat first, crossed his arms, and waited so

quietly she thought he was going to fall back asleep. By the time Jezreal and finally Sarosha had entered, the nerves in Angela's belly began to twang. This was it. It was really going to happen. She could not contain her secrets any longer.

"I've got the phylactery," she said, heaving her bag onto the table and unclasping it. With a jerk, she pulled the bag out from under it and took a step away, letting the others lean in and look a bit closer at the crystal. Maybe it was just her hope and belief that there was some magical potency to it, but even as silent and aura-less as it was, the phylactery did have a sense of power around it.

"I'll be a dirty bird," Jezreal said. "It's huge."

"Yeah. And heavy," Angela added with a smile. They finally had something to show for the weeks of suffering and the costs it took to get this far; it felt incredible to have that crystal lying there in front of her.

Sam took the bait first. He stood, reached out over the table, and dragged it closer to him. The crystal scratched the wood, but no one gave a damn, and after he looked it over three times, he said, "Can this really be it? I mean, I expected something marvelous, but this just seems too good to be true."

Angela shrugged. "Won't know till I try it out, and I'm going to need you guys to confirm that you can't detect my soul. I don't know how being soulless is going to affect my ability to perceive things."

"I can do that," Jezreal said. "I've probably spent the most time meditating and testing myself out of all three—" She stopped herself and the room took on a whole new atmosphere of gloom when she realized her error. "I mean of the two of us."

"Gabe's death won't be in vain," Angela swore. "We

will have revenge I will kill that bitch for all she has taken from us and all she threatens to."

As the words left her lips and no one said anything, Angela realized her folly. It wasn't Ti'amat's fault that Gabe had died; it was hers, and nothing could change that. The thought crossed the others' minds, but she saw it most in Samael's eyes. Luckily, he must not have felt the need to share it. Everyone already knew.

Sarosha took a turn with the crystal but didn't spend as much time on it. With her hand resting atop the phylactery, she met Angela's gaze and asked, "So what now? You have the weapon, but you don't know where Ti'amat's heart is."

Another smile. "I think I do, actually. It dawned on me just a little while ago. Almost twenty years ago this city fell victim to an assault led by the unforgettable Councilman Udug. When he fell from the city, we thought he had died —Kushiel, too—only for the councilman, and Kushiel's equipment, to show up fifteen years later. They survived, and when Udug came back, he had a new soul tainted with the presence of Ti'amat. That means he came into contact with her, or someone else, who had been touched by her. I think her heart is beneath this city."

The Grand Ensi rose to her feet, began to pace back and forth as she tugged at her hair. Certainly, she had realized the same thing Angela already had. "If Udug was tied to Ti'amat, and Kushiel shared his fate and his clothes showed up on Earth, that means that when Ja'noel went searching for him, he found Ti'amat's heart." She began to shudder and cry. Ever since the day Ti'amat came, finding Ja'noel had been paramount and the source of her anguish. To see her like this now was heartbreaking. She muttered, "That's why he never came back."

Angela crossed the room, embraced her in a hug. The

Grand did not have it in her to fight it. To stay strong. She took the shoulder she could get, and when the sobbing calmed, Angela spoke again.

"Councilman Toth once took me to a cavern with unusually weak veils. It's a place where it's easy to reach out and find other people. I hadn't put these pieces together before now, but I think that somewhere below the city and somewhere on Earth there are places where the veil is almost nonexistent. Holes in the worlds where the fabric of different realities coincide. It could be lucky, or unlucky, but it's evident enough that both of our Grands fell prey to the same dimension where Ti'amat's heart resides. Once they were there, she could not let them leave."

She straightened Sarosha but kept her hands on her shoulders. Looking into her eyes, Angela said, "I don't want to give you false hope, but there's a chance they are both still alive. I aim to find out and finish this. Tonight."

"Just hold on," Samael interjected. "I understand you're giddy to get this underway, but this is going too fast. We need to stop. Think. Strategize how you're actually going to do this. Sure, we may be able to sneak up on Ti'amat's heart, but what are you going to do to it? What did the Nephilim do to it the first time?"

Angela let her arms fall to her side, shrugged. "Smash it, I assume."

"Right. And we know that didn't kill her last time. So what are you going to do differently?"

Again, she shrugged. "I guess I don't know. Shatter the crystal to paralyze her, then melt the pieces with fire to make sure that the fragments of her soul tied to them don't have anything left to grasp onto. She'll return to the weylines in a thousand pieces or fade entirely."

Samael grumbled. He did not seem to think it would be

that easy, and he was right. He said, "If Ti'amat is still pulling herself together, there are still crystals out there. We even have some. And if even one remains, what's to say she couldn't survive again?"

"How long was Ti'amat sleeping the last time she suffered a blow like this? Ten thousand years? Maybe even longer. I think that's plenty of time for us to track down the last of them. And even if we do miss some and she does come back, I can't imagine she'd be anywhere near as strong as she is now."

Jezreal ruffled her hair dejectedly. "No crystals mean no moving around the worlds for some of us, Angela."

"Then the Anunnaki will just have to learn how to travel between worlds without them. Listen, I don't know what the future without Ti'amat is going to look like. But it's going to be better than letting her live. This is what we've got, and I'm going to do it."

Sam ran his fingers over his head and down over his eyes, pausing to rub them. He said, "It just feels like we are kicking the can down the road."

"Maybe we are, but we won't know until after."

No one had anything to add or a rebuttal. They just sat there, quiet and thinking.

Jezreal piped up. "So if you're just going to do this, why are we meeting here? What's stopping you from just going?"

Angela was caught off guard. She hesitated. Hadn't really thought why she felt the need to share this with them until now. "I guess I just wanted you all to know. Wanted to say that if things go sour and I never have the chance to say it later, I'm sorry. Sorry I let you down, dragged you all into this and countless other things. But I'm doing my best. I hope you see that. I'll give it my all."

"We know," Samael said. He rose to his feet, shook her hand. It was funny how Gabe's death had served as a catalyst for his growing respect for her. The kid did not want to live with that thing inside him and Angela fulfilled his wish. If only every soldier could choose the time of his death.

Sam pulled his hand away, seeming somewhat embarrassed at his exposure. Even though the tension between them was still there, awkward and rigid, she was grateful it was lighter than it had ever been.

"I suppose if this is the last I'll ever see you," Jezreal began, "I want you to know that I've always looked up to you. Even before all this, I'd heard stories through the ranks about you and Michael. You might drag a lot of shit along with you wherever you go, but the people who have a lot going for them always do have hangers-on."

Angela laughed. Thanked her, even though she didn't feel she deserved the honor.

Sarosha had no kind words. Her mind was wrapped up in one single part of the plan. "You bring Ja'noel back to me, Angela. You promised."

"That was a promise I made a long time ago, but I'll try."

ANGELA BENT OVER, LOOKED DOWN PAST THE EDGE OF THE city and into the gray skies below. The snow didn't drift and pile up as much there, but it was still enough added weight for the weakened platforms to groan and creak as they bobbed. The wind roared out there in the open, and every second the flexing metal threatened to give way and drop her before she was ready. Nervous, she said, "Shit. It's ready to go at any second, isn't it?"

The others were not as brave as her, preferring to stand back ten feet from the edge. They did not hear her. Samael pulled the fur cloak around him tighter and walked in place to keep warm while Jezreal and Sarosha huddled up, trying to use one another to block the wind. Donny had shown up for the occasion, too, shivering in more layers of fur than ever before. He had not said a word to Angela since they departed the Ascendancy. The wound between them was too large to heal now. But widening the gap between them was good for them both, no matter how much it hurt.

Angela retreated through the shin-high snow and found a grim yet eager look in each of their eyes. She felt the same. Nervous. Yet with every inch of her being, she hoped that this was the beginning of the end.

"This may be our only chance to surprise her," Sam said. "Our only chance to have the upper hand."

"I know," Angela said. "I'm counting on this working. My hands can't stop shaking."

He flashed his teeth. "That's just the cold. You got this, but it's going to get a lot colder on the way down. Warm yourself up while you can."

"Right." She closed her eyes, stoked the souls inside her, and coaxed a bit of energy from them. The numbness in her toes faded as an inner warmth spread. Heating her body was simple compared to what was coming.

For the first time in a long while, she wore a wing-pack. With a mess of leather straps and buckles, the phylactery was strapped to the back of it, exposed to the elements. There was no other place to put it, and its weight, so far out from her body, made moving and keeping her balance a constant struggle.

She removed the heavy fur mitt from her left hand and reached back, touched the icy bottom of the crystal. Slowly and carefully, she linked her mind to the hollow rock and the Dalkhu soul inside her and began to pry at it, to wiggle it free from her flesh. It did not want to go, but persistence broke it loose. Concentration steeled her mind, formed an iron grip on the thing as she moved it from her chest and into the crystal on her back. When the soul drew near the phylactery, a sudden rush tugged it from her grip, pulled the soul into it like a magnet.

The others gasped. Something visible must have happened. She looked over her shoulder. The crystal glowed now, but otherwise there was no trace of a soul being trapped inside. No aura, no energy. Yet when she dug hard enough, she could find Udug's soul inside it. Relief washed over her. The crystal was the genuine thing, not a Nephilim trick.

Next, she worked the Anunnaki soul she'd been born with. With a brief check, she determined that Ti'amat was unaware of what was about to happen. The black rot inside her appeared normal. The goddess was relaxed. It was a perfect opportunity to stow the soul away, and it was as easy as the last. Her experience detaching her mind from her body in order to scry was beneficial. She had expected that there would be some loss of sensation when she removed her own souls from their moorings, but not like this.

The wind felt twice as cold as it had, and a deep pit of hunger opened up in her belly. It was done; she was no more than a human now. A fragile human who was about to take a leap of faith.

Her gaze met Jezreal's as she asked, "What do you feel? Anything?"

Jez closed her eyes, wind whipping loose strands of hair around her face. It only took her a few seconds to say, "I don't feel anything." She beamed. "The crystal is silent. Go quickly, and good luck. I doubt Ti'amat will go long before noticing your sudden absence. She'll come here looking for you."

Angela nodded. "Good luck to you, too. And stay hidden."

Donny fidgeted in his pockets, stared at the ground in silence. By the way he looked, heartbroken and defeated, and how she knew this could be the last time she would speak to him, Angela lost every sense of self-censorship. She let her heart spill the truth. "Don't worry so much. You'll find her."

His gaze, sad and confused, rose to meet hers. "What?"

"You'll find the one for you. I'm sorry I can't be her."

He sighed as his expression grew glum. "Yeah, I know."

Jezreal slugged Angela's shoulder playfully. "Stop it. This isn't goodbye. Now get going."

A flock of crows took flight in her chest, the tips of their wings brushing the nerves of her heart and painting them with bittersweet feelings.

Gods, this is it.

She turned, faced the edge, and brought her toes to the drop-off. As fear bubbled, she became mechanical, put her back to the sky beyond, and stepped off backward. If this was her last time in Dingir, she wanted her final sight to be of what remained of her city and the people she fought for. The supports and pipes whizzed past her vision as vertigo made her skin crawl. While the city of light and shining brass grew smaller, the wind took her tumbling.

WITH NO WAY TO KEEP TRACK OF TIME, ANGELA COULD not be certain how long she had been falling. It felt like hours of growing numbness had come and gone. The extra layers she had put on were still not enough to keep the wind out of her clothes and from sapping away what little heat her body could produce on an empty stomach. She missed her souls sorely.

The farther down she went, the more the wind seemed to die. Even the air's resistance against her descent seemed to lessen, allowing her to stabilize herself and keep her front side facing downward. She could not pin it down to any particular reason until she spotted the bottom of Dingir. Tendrils of gray clouds looked like tornadoes spiraling downward and coming together at the same spot. In the center of their meeting, the sky seemed brighter, more vibrant, like some kind of unnatural white light shining through the fog.

Moisture clung to her as she entered the clouds, chilling her to the bone and threatening to freeze her stiff. But it was not long before the white light overtook her. The wind rushing past her ceased unnaturally, and the sensation of falling belly-down faded until she felt something hard underneath her feet. She looked down, saw nothing but her boots and the white beneath them, adjusted her weight, and took a step forward. Bile bubbled as her nausea grew. The shift from horizontal to vertical had been so subtle she had no time to adjust her senses. Standing now, she looked out into the expanse and saw nothing until she turned around.

Beyond the flat white scenery, there was no geography with which to get a sense of scale, and the distance between her and the specks of yellows and browns on the horizon was difficult to gauge. Although she was grateful that she had made it alive, a sense of urgency grew. There was no telling how much time had passed, but certainly by now the goddess would have noticed that she was missing.

She pulled the controller from beneath her wing-pack, took to the air, and worked the mechanical wings hard. The added weight of the phylactery bogged her down immensely, made the pack groan at every stroke, but each second mattered.

Damn near an entire village was clustered together. Wrecked and abandoned sandstone buildings sat atop the clean white expanse, crumbling to time and gravity, becoming mounds of brick and wood. Warped metal platforms curved upward like someone had tried to make a cylindrical can out of them. Most of the ruins appeared to be remnants of Dingir's fallen platforms, but some were alien. Pieces of thatch roofs, ripped and torn apart, were scattered everywhere, along with thick cuts of timber, the bark still clinging to them.

Something moved below her. A man, standing inside the battered shell of a building, looked up at her from a hole in the roof. Angela turned around, angled closer, and made another pass. The stranger waved, rushed from the home, and stepped out onto the blank, nonexistent street of the ramshackle village. Even against the colorless backdrop, Angela could see his long gray hair.

Her heart lurched into her throat. She slowed, letting herself fall to the ground, and landed roughly enough to hurt her feet and knees. Without the vigor of souls, the human form was fragile.

Quick footsteps came up behind her, but she took a deep breath to prepare herself for what she knew she was about to see. Kushiel, grinning ear to ear in nothing but the layers of cotton clothes used to shield skin from hardened armor. He was covered in dirt from head to toe, smelled like sweat and something close to rotting. Perhaps his teeth.

"Angela!" he cried. Moving in, he wrapped his arms around her.

She restrained her revulsion, put a hand on his back until he was satisfied.

"What are you doing here? How did you—"

"I don't have time," she said. "Where is Ti'amat at? Where is Ja'noel?" She shook her head. "No, take me to the goddess first."

Kushiel's wrinkled expression grew stern as he understood the severity and purpose of her presence. There was fear and excitement in his eyes. "Stay on the ground and follow me," he commanded. "There are others here who would not welcome you. They would know you don't belong. Hurry, before she checks in on us and sees you."

Angela raced after him, struggling to leap over mounds of rubble spilling out over the white roads, until he veered off between buildings. They sprinted, clambered up ruins, and tore through decrepit buildings until her heart was pounding, her breath was fleeting, and her legs were threatening to give out on her. Kushiel had to wait for her to catch up twice. Even after all the things she had been through, being a human was the most tedious and resoundingly tiring thing she could think of.

Kushiel stopped before a broken wall, waited for her to catch up to him. He put his back to the crumbling wall, leaning against the yellow sandstone, and motioned for her to do the same. When she was by his side, he whispered, "She's right behind us. I'll go find Ja'noel and bring him here."

It took Angela a moment to get her heavy breaths under

control. "I'm going to rest a moment. Find him fast. I don't know what will happen when it's over."

The old Grand nodded, slipped away behind the rubble on bare feet and without another word.

Her muscles were aching, but she forced them to move just slightly enough to peer through the doorless entryway. At first, all she saw was brick and scrap metal piled in a mound, but up toward the summit loomed the goddess she had come to destroy. Ti'amat's heart was nothing like Antum's. The matte black crystal twirled slowly in place atop the rubble, a stark contrast against the white backdrop of nothingness. Twenty feet tall, it was narrow at the bottom, wider in the middle, and as it began to narrow at the top, it ended abruptly where crystal shards were still missing. Judging by the bottom half of it, the goddess was nearly whole.

Angela pulled back behind the safety of the wall. How was she supposed to destroy something so huge and so potent with energy that the very air around it seemed to shimmer and wiggle around its surface? She could even smell the ozone from this distance, clean and metallic.

The pounding in her chest quickened. There could be no more waiting. Every second that went by added to the chance of failure. She moved, stood in the doorway, and stared at her prey atop the mound, half expecting something to happen when she made herself apparent. But nothing did. The crystal just kept floating and spinning in place. The goddess was unaware that she was there.

One foot after the other, Angela began to climb. Rubble rolled under her feet, tumbled down to the bottom of the pile in a racket. She was so afraid, so tired, and under so much pressure that the climb almost made her faint. If there was one thing in her life that mattered the most, this was it.

To kill a goddess as bent and wicked as Ti'amat was to free untold worlds and save innumerable lives. She would change the history of everything, be remembered and idolized for ages to come. There was no greater destiny than this. Perhaps, for one small moment, she considered that there *was* such a thing as fate, because every fiber of her being screamed that she was born to do just this.

At the pinnacle of the hill, the bottom of the crystal began at her ankles and went upward, expanding as it went. She watched reflections of herself go by as the thing spun, then drew Teshub's sword from its sheath on her back. Ti'amat's crystal was so large she had no idea how she was going to severely damage it. Even if she jumped, she could not touch the thick center of it, and the strength of a human arm would not be enough to put the smallest chip in it.

Angela raised the sword above her head with one hand and touched the phylactery with the other, its surface warm and glowing. There was no other way she could do it. She would have to move quickly. Hard and fast, she yanked both souls from the crystal. The fatigue and aches vanished. With all of her will, she summoned all the strength she could muster, formed a vibrant hammer's head of fluxing light atop her sword's tip, and swung.

It connected. Seared and burrowed into the dark crystal. Cracks spiderwebbed across it, releasing lines of a violet glow. The spinning stopped and the ground shuddered. Black light pulsed, raged against the yellow glow of her weapon. She pushed harder, screaming as she threw everything she had into it. Smoking mist drizzled downward, shrouding her feet and the mound she stood on as she carved and smashed a canyon in the crystal's surface.

The air smacked out of her lungs all at once. She was in the air, launched and spinning backward from a crushing force. Her back hit the crumbling wall, and her head met the rubble on the ground below. Growling, she rose, ripped the blade with both hands and prepared to leap. The black crystal crackled with purple lightning. Looking inward, she saw that the rot in her soul was diminished to a speck and barely hanging on to her. Ti'amat was confused, her attention drawn to her own wounds. She was surprised and burning with hatred and pain.

Angela laughed, reared her sword behind her head, and bellowed. At once, she bounded the distance between them, came falling upon the crystal as she brought her weapon down. An audible clang erupted as she smote it. The hammer head of light sunk in, flashed blindingly bright. Their forces clashed, and the crystal pushed back. Then the rot grew. The light faded. The sword flexed, then shattered, half the blade a thousand splinters spraying in every direction.

An invisible hand grabbed Angela from the air, squeezed, threw her down. Brick and steel rose up to greet her. She skidded, lost control, and tumbled down the heap.

A man's voice shouted from somewhere behind her. "Angela!"

Ja'noel and Kushiel stood at the doorway, seemingly dumbfounded at the power rippling through the air. They did not feel safe, or else they would have come and helped her to her feet, she knew. A sharp metal edge had cut along her cheek and bit into her lip, giving her a foul taste and reminding her that she was still mortal. The ground was trembling, the air shuddering as shock wave after shock wave pounded outward from the crystal. Lightning snapped and arced. The cracks in the crystal began to grow, bathing the world around them in violet light.

The goddess was hurting badly. To seal her fate, Angela

opened up the veils to bathe the crystal in flame and fire, then turned to the others. "We need to get out of here. Ti'amat is unstable and trying to keep herself together. I don't know what will happen to this world when she goes." She scrambled to their sides, grabbed their hands, and took them home.

CHAPTER TWELVE

There was a short fall and a face full of snow.
Angela freed her arms and rolled onto her back,
then lay there just watching the puffs of her
breathing drift away on the wind. It was cold, but she was
tired and more relieved than she had felt in a long time. The
weight was off her shoulders, and she could breathe.

Ja'noel and Kushiel were groaning as they righted
themselves. The look of shock on their faces reminded her
that they had not seen Dingir in a long time. Not since the
snow and the heaviest of the decay had set in.

She tried to ease their burden. "Don't worry. There are
still some people around."

The Grands seemed to relax a bit, but the obvious work
it would take to rebuild the city was clearly heavy on their
minds.

Over the wind, someone was shouting. The doors to the
Ascendancy were wide open as a crowd came running
down the steps. Jezreal, Samael, the Uri Gallus, Sarosha,
and Donny all cheered and whooped at the sight of their
missing leaders. The snowdrifts did not hold them back.

They lurched through them, put hands on each other with brilliant smiles. Angela was still struggling to muster the will to stand, so Jezreal found it for her.

Pulling her up, Jez said, "For a while there, I didn't think you were going to make it."

"Me either," Angela groaned. "Fucking cold fall, though."

Jez laughed. "I bet. Look at them."

Sarosha was crying as she held Ja'noel. Resting his chin on her head, he tried his best to console her, but nothing would stop the tears of joy from flowing. When she locked her gaze on Angela, Sarosha mouthed words with quivering lips. She said, *Thank you.*

Angela smiled and nodded. She'd never felt this good or this proud of herself before. For once, there was hope for the future. It might not be the easiest or the best future, but at least it existed. She'd taken vows, sincerely meant them, and had now upheld her promises. Dingir still stood, she was alive, and it was the beginning of a new era.

Donny was standing to the side of the party, idly keeping to himself. She could see in his eyes that he was happy for the others but not for himself. Angela approached him to see if she could do anything for that. She asked, "Got any good books in the works?"

His eyes grew wide; he was surprised that she had brought that topic up. He said, "No, I haven't touched a pen in a long time." He looked away. Something was brewing in the back of his mind.

"Well, something tells me that you'll have the opportunity to sit down in the near future."

A half smile stretched across his face. The kind of smile that was meant to appease, to show appreciation for the comment, even though he did not believe it. They stood there, side to side, watching the others' reunions in silence until he gained the courage to say what was on his mind. "Did you mean what you said?"

Her mind drew a blank. "What did I say?"

"That I'd find the one for me, and it couldn't be you."

A sigh escaped her. His eyes were searching her face for a single expression that would tell him he should hold out hope, but things had changed for her. "Yeah. I just... I don't know what I'm going to do, but I just get the feeling that maybe I'm better off this way. That's not to say that I don't... don't have feelings for you. I do. It's just that... Ugh, this is embarrassing."

"It's just Michael. Isn't it?"

Angela gave him one of those smiles. "After everything, I don't know if I'll ever feel the same. The older I get, the more that happens. And the more that happens, the more I change. I ask for help when I need it, protect those who are in danger, but I know I still have my fair share of problems. I'm afraid of not mattering, of my sacrifices, the things I've fought for, the things I've learned and who I've become... I'm afraid of it all being in vain, of losing who I am. I get so blisteringly angry that I lash out, and that's nothing new. You know it. I just think that you deserve someone who can focus on actually being with you, not a tired soldier girl who's still trying to sort out her life."

He nodded, distraught, then, out of nowhere, smiled. Somewhere in there he saw a glimmer of hope, an entrance for him to work his way in. He said, "You know I have a twelve-step program for that hot-headedness of yours. Rageaholics Anonymous."

Angela laughed.

"We put a bag on your head and no one knows it's you.

I wrote the program myself. I could help you get through it."

She eyed him with a grin, knew what he was thinking. All she could say was, "We'll see."

A snowball fight broke out between the Grands. Sarosha's tears had dried and her smile returned. It had been a long time since Angela had seen her do that. A thought came to her; with Ja'noel and Kushiel back, Angela was no longer one of the leaders of the Ascendancy, leaving her free to roam and do as she pleased. There would be a lot of thinking to do. A lot of resting, too.

As Sarosha ran to Angela, she yelled with delight and tried to take cover behind her and use her as a shield as clumps of snow flew through the air. The once-again Grand Dubah fell to the ground, laughing. Angela had to help her to her feet. Then the laughter stopped. She stumbled a little more, and when she finally found her footing, her hand was clenched near her chest. At first, Angela thought Sarosha was packing a snowball, planning a sneaky move to nail Angela with it, but Sarosha just stood there, holding herself, looking confused and concerned. She said, "My chest hurts."

A groan escaped Samael. He dropped to his hands and knees, elbows disappearing in the snow. The others staggered like they were about to faint, put their hands to their chests one by one. To all but Donny and Angela, something was happening. The wind picked up, began to roar as it raced between the buildings and kicked up a flurry of blinding snow. Then a woman's voice spoke into her mind.

I warned you, and you do this.

A glance at the soul inside her confirmed the worst; the black mark of Ti'amat had doubled down. Fury emanated. The goddess lived. When she thought the wind couldn't blow any harder, it did. City streets all around them groaned. Buildings jumped in place as ice chunks the size of trees snapped in half and shattered on the ground. Metal screeched as it tore free. The gale shoved Angela harder than she could bear. She dove for the narrow, cleared pathway in front of the Ascendency and shouted, "She's alive. I have to go—"

Sarosha threw her weight on top of Angela, taking cover in the snowbank as debris began to fly. Fear returned to her eyes. "What's happening, Angela?"

Angela didn't take the time to answer. Hoping the others could hear her, she screamed, "Take cover!" It took too long to get out from under Sarosha without pushing her up and into danger. By the time she peered out from the snowbank, buildings were being ripped apart brick by brick as mouths of the hungry void began to feast on Dingir. There were dozens of holes in the veil that she could see and certainly many more she could not. The darkness in her soul throbbed, and the gashes grew larger.

Angela bit down and fought it, tried to reach out and pull the veils back together again with her own strength. It was not enough, only a minor inconvenience. Reaching inward and delving into Ti'amat's ocean of power, she tried to rob what she could, but what the goddess wanted the goddess got. She would not lend Angela the strength of a fly.

"Angela," Sarosha sobbed. "What is happening? Answer me!"

"Ti'amat. The closest world to Dingir is pure air, with winds strong enough to rip limbs from their sockets. She's evaporating the veils somehow. We have to get out of—" Dread overwhelmed her, cut her words short. Her companions had been clutching their chests for a reason. The others could not leave Dingir, for Ti'amat had taken their souls.

A great groan and the shriek of tearing metal filled the air as a building not fifty feet from her began to shred and break apart. A piece of metal panel crashed onto the ground, skittered its way through the snow in front of the Ascendancy. Ja'noel was still out there, trying his best to hunker down, but he was not low enough. The sheet smashed into his face, cut him from jaw to hairline. His face turned red with blood, but he was still moving. Just barely.

Sarosha screamed, tried to get up, but Angela hugged her tightly and kept her down. Gods, that wind was cold. Even when she was buried underneath the Grand, her face felt like it was already frozen from the tears. Sarosha's or her own, she wasn't sure, but she would not let this be the end when she had a soul to give. With all her mental might, she grabbed hold of the Dalkhu soul inside her and moved from her body to Sarosha's. The Grand stopped struggling for a moment, noticing the change inside her, then looked deep into Angela's eyes as if to ask what she was doing to her.

The wind howled, ripped the brass spires off the top of the Ascendancy and turned them into javelins, then began disassembling shingles and the roof itself. All of a sudden, the snow around them began diminishing as a vacuum opened up above them. She could feel the suction beginning to lift them off the ground. It was time to go.

They vanished, raced toward Earth. Angela did not know where else to go and prayed that Earth was not under attack as well. With all of Sarosha's weight crashing into her chest and stomach, they landed on the edge of the jungle that Angela had trudged through so many years ago.

She groaned, shoved the woman off of her. By the time she got to her feet, the Grand was scratching at herself with fervor. Immediately, her skin was raw and red.

"What did you do?" she balled. "What is happening to me?" A flicker of fire burned behind her eyes, flared from her nostrils.

"Shit," Angela murmured. "Soul-flame. My soul is still mostly Anunnaki, so this is going to hurt, but I have to touch you to get that soul back so I can go get the others, alright?"

Sarosha mumbled something to herself, hesitated as Angela lurched forward to grab hold of her. The Grand screamed, instinctually began to hit and fight her. Angela would have been mad at her, but it did not matter now. Like an extra sense, Ti'amat's gift of the awareness of worlds already told her that it was over. Dingir was lost. Ripped apart. Missing.

Angela had to sit down, bury her face in her hands. She did not care about the mud or the bugs or the heat. It was over. There was no anger. No sadness. Just the unrelenting shock and numbness from knowing that the place and the people she had fought the hardest for were gone in a matter of moments. Not even a minute had passed.

Sarosha crept closer, holding out her hand hesitantly, her voice deep and warbled from the soul-flame when she said her name. Angela chose to say nothing. How could she articulate these thoughts, these feelings, in a way that did them justice? She was overloaded. Broken down. And just too damn tired. How could she stay strong? How could she try to help Sarosha carry the load she was about to drop on her when she couldn't bear it herself?

The sorrow did come. It built up slowly. She cried, lay on the ground and curled up, got mud in her hair and on her face as she wept. Everyone but she and Sarosha were dead. No matter how much the Grand tried to reach her, Angela could not speak. The plan—*her* plan—did not work, and now the others had paid the price again.

What did I do to deserve this?

"I tried to tell you before, Angela. It's not what you did. Until now, that is. It's what Antum did."

The goddess Ti'amat was standing straight and proud at Angela's feet, looming over her like a willow tree with her long hair blowing in the breeze. She was not smiling, and her tone was sincere. For a brief moment, Angela forgot that she was insane. She thought that maybe she did deserve this. Maybe there was a certain destiny for her and fighting it would be harder than just letting it happen, than letting go.

Sarosha was standing back, her hands over her mouth. She shuddered as she asked, "This is her?"

That surprised Angela. Sarosha could see the goddess. And the wind was blowing. This was unusual. It meant that Ti'amat was there in a fleshy body and not just in Angela's mind. She was just as beautiful, and just as terrible, in person as she was in visions. Grimly, Angela said, "This is Ti'amat."

Ti'amat smirked, but Sarosha swallowed and said, "She just came out of the earth. Right in front of me. Coming together like a bubbling puddle."

Before Angela had a chance to respond, Ti'amat motioned to the phylactery still strapped to Angela's back. "I told you to let go of everything you cherish before it hurt, to accept that Antum is your only future, and now you went and did this. Just as she did. I should have known better. She has rubbed off on you more than you'd like to admit. Now hand it over."

Angela did, and with both hands the goddess bore the crystal in front of her. The phylactery began to glow. Blue first, then red underneath her fingers before the whole thing was lit up like iron in a forge until it crumbled in her palm and disintegrated into dust on the wind.

Ti'amat wiped her hands when it was done, a sour look on her face. "You may not feel like you're Antum, but here you are, having gone against our understanding behind my back. Same as her. It's time we speed things up. Get on your feet."

Stumbling and sobbing, Angela obliged. The goddess forcefully grabbed her by the arm, took them through the veils faster than she could think. Before she knew it, Ti'amat was shoving her back onto the ground. Instead of mud and heat and bugs, there was stone and cold and dark, dead air.

Angela looked around. This world wasn't even the size of an average room. A small fragment of floor and wall only four by eight feet with jagged edges where this world had been fractured. Where it ended, a sheet of impenetrable shroud hovered.

On her hands and knees before a chunk of crystal, Angela knew why Ti'amat had taken her here. Before her, in the quiet rock on the floor, was the last piece of Antum's soul. Ti'amat had known where the pieces of Antum were the whole time.

Ti'amat pointed as she said, "I wanted you to come to this yourself, Angela. Wanted you to struggle. To earn it. Discover who you really are and fight me with a vengeance that shatters cities and realms, only so I could crush every last dream, every bit of hope, and every last bit of you, Antum."

The goddess shook her fists in rage. Her lips trembled

as she said, "I loved you, Antum. We were sisters. And you betrayed me. Gave my own children the means to kill me. Now here we are. The same place as before. You child. How hard a punishment do I have to give you for you to understand that you have brought about the death of your people yourself? It did not have to go this way, but you are a spitting image of the sister I loathe. How many souls and worlds do I need to swallow for you to feel the heartbreak I did? You are Antum, and she is you. You destroyed everything I created. Vi'dinor was mine. Now do it. Touch the crystal. Restore her now or I will crush every living thing within my reach."

When every great effort put forth fails, the will to be strong dies. Angela had no defiance left in her. She took the crystal and embraced it. Did as she was told. The energy inside it vibrated, jolted from its shattered home, and lit her up like lightning. Attaching to her soul, it melded and healed, became one with her soul.

A great stirring began. Spinning and whirling lights mirrored stars and galaxies and worlds within her. Antum rumbled and moved. Every twinkling echo imprinted on the soul from the life before her own grew brighter. In the darkness of that sliver of world, a blue glow flashed before her eyes; the outline of the goddess stood before her in streaks and lines of whizzing balls of light. It was like she was in that very room. Her wavy hair poured over her shoulders. A circlet of flowers rested on her head, and a flowing dress draped over her. She crossed her arms, rod in hand.

Angela glanced back. Ti'amat did not seem to see the waking goddess as she did. This was a projection of sorts. A spirit showing itself. The more the seconds ticked by, the more she seemed to become real. To think and wake. A pressure began to blossom, expand from the soul inside her, and push on Angela's mind. It felt wrong. The goddess tried to grab hold of her. Antum opened her shining mouth to speak, but Angela shoved her down. Focused on the now and her body's place in it.

Antum craved to come out. Angela could feel it. More than anything, she wanted the freedom to move about, to take control of her fate once more. But that meant that Angela would have to give up everything. Her mind. Her fight. Her body. And Angela could not do that. She was her, no one else. She bit down hard, swallowed the spirit, and pinned it down until the glowing image of that ancient goddess faded. The room darkened. The pressure subsided.

Ti'amat bent over her and snickered, seemingly sensing the change in Angela's soul. She said, "Hello, sister. It's been a while. I hope you recover quickly because I'm only giving you one day. One day for me to scrape together the last shard of myself, and one day for you to prepare. When our final moment comes, it will be fair. I will split everything I have with you, as promised." Ti'amat stood upright, smiling impishly. "Just one more day, sister."

CHAPTER THIRTEEN

The crackling embers of the bonfire did little to warm her bones. Occasionally, a drop of water would fall from the cavern roof and sizzle. She watched those methodically, mesmerized by the beat and lost in her own thoughts. There was no knowing how much time had passed or how much was left, and as much as that should have kept her moving, she could not be stirred.

Sarosha had tried to speak with her many times, but Angela barely listened. She was exhausted and did not have any sympathy for the Grand's plights. Again and again she tried to get Angela to take the Dalkhu soul back from her. Angela knew what it was like to have that soul inside her. It was torture. Veins should not burn at every beat of the heart. Skin should not come alight with scalding flames, but Angela had insisted she keep it for a while longer just in case they needed to flee Kur, too.

But Sarosha did not care. Angela could see it in her eyes: agitation and hopelessness pushing her to the edge of her wits. Constantly, she scratched and picked at her skin.

Pulled on her hair and suffered occasional bouts of wincing and groaning. It was not a good way to live.

One by one, Angela examined the echoes inside the soul buried in her chest. She never would have guessed that her soul, when completed with the Anunnaki and Dalkhu halves, would come alive with the fervor it did. It took great care and focus to keep watch over Antum. Twice, the goddess reached out and touched Angela's mind. It took persistent vigil to keep her down, but eventually, Angela would need to sleep, if she even had the time.

One of the goddess's memory-like echoes Angela took great interest in. She watched the images over and over in her mind. The final moments of the goddess's life. While watching historic events through Antum's eyes could not confirm who had dealt the shattering blow to Ti'amat, she had no reason to believe it wasn't Basmu. When the strike had been dealt and Vi'dinor began to tremble, Antum had sensed that something was wrong and hastened a flight across the continent.

Ti'amat's temple was crumbling in on itself, the foundation falling into a pit in the ground. The mountains that loomed overhead shook, spilling rock and snow on the once-gorgeous structure below. Back and forth, Nephilim and small, pointed-ear people fled, screaming and yelling. Antum genuinely believed that the damage was good enough to kill Ti'amat, but with her final, raspy breath, she tore apart the veils of Vi'dinor in an act of spite, declaring that if she could not reign over that world, no one would.

A hand took hold of Angela's shoulder, pulling her from her spell. Sarosha. Her eyes were soft and watery in the dim glow of the dying fire. Angela could no longer see the soul-flame that plagued her. Since she restored Antum's soul with its Dalkhu half and restored balance inside herself, those visions had ceased.

Sarosha said, "I need to know. Answer me."

Angela rubbed her eyes, cleared the fog from her head. "Need to know what?"

"Why did you choose me?" Sarosha choked out. "Out of everyone in Dingir you could have saved, why me?"

Angela groaned. She knew where this was going, shoved the Grand's hand off her. "You were on top of me. Simple as that."

"You should have saved Ja'noel. He would be far more capable of helping you figure out your shit. He should be alive, not me."

Angela rose to her feet, walked to the other side of the firepit they had made between stalactites. "What would you have me do? Toss you to the wind and run out into the hurricane myself? We escaped by mere *seconds*. I wouldn't have even made it to him in time. Stop feeling sorry for yourself and play with the cards you were dealt."

Sarosha's jaw dropped in astonishment. "Oh, like what you're doing? Hiding in your shell and waiting to die? Michael would be ashamed if he could see you now."

Oh, that got the kettle boiling. Angela whipped around, stepped closer to breach the Grand's space. "Well, I'd rather deal with his disappointment than your whining. Grow up. Take a look at what I'm actually dealing with right now. One goddess wants me dead, and the other wants to use me like a puppet. Every plan I've tried was an attempt to create my own path out of this. All I wanted was a third option that allowed me to break free from destiny, and each one has failed. Blown up in my face. So get off my back. I'm doing my best. But you? Your thoughts of yourself are right. You are weak. And helpless. And so damn self-centered it's a wonder anyone fell in love with you. Take your own advice: swallow that fucking pill and do something about your situation."

Sarosha took a half step back, raised a hand defensively. Angela had not realized her fist was balled and half-cocked. She relaxed, returned her arm to her side, and walked past the Grand, preferring to venture into the stony spires around their camp than apologize.

"Where are you going?" Sarosha asked after a moment.

Angela picked up the pace, motioned with her hand. "Off. To find better company."

Fuming mad, she hoofed it through the stalactites. Sarosha would be fine on her own. If anything, she blended in with the Dalkhu better than Angela did. No one would bother her out there, but if she did run into trouble, Angela couldn't say she cared. The Grand would have to take care of herself for a while.

The longer she walked under the glowing moss above, the more she cooled down. By the time she reached the outer row of shoddy homes, she was calm, even somewhat regretful of her harshness. It could have been handled better, but the mention of Michael like that just stoked a fire inside her she could not control.

She should have known better after what happened with Sam, Angela thought. *I know what it's like to live with the constant threat of soul-flame. It's hard, but at least I wasn't quite so helpless. I took charge and—*

"Angela," a voice said. She stopped where she stood, couldn't tell where the voice was coming from until a man cloaked in dirty gray robes pushed himself to his feet next to the backside of a house. In the dark lighting, his clothes closely matched the color of the stones he had leaned against. He cast down his hood, grinned as a form of greeting. Toth said, "I thought that was you out there. No one else makes a fire that far out. It's actually illegal, not that it would be enforced. And as far as I'm aware, no one else can travel through the veils anymore, so the sound of your arrival, departure, then re-arrival was a bit odd."

That was a pill even Angela hadn't taken yet. Since their arrival in Kur, she had noticed the quiet, both in sound and the aura of souls. It seemed as though Kur was on target to share the same fate as Dingir, although at a much slower pace. Angela had chosen to ignore it for the last few hours, focusing instead on the soul inside her. She had to take one thing at a time or she was going to snap and give up. Stop fighting and let Antum take control.

Sensing her hesitation, he said, "I take it things did not go as well as you thought they would."

Angela could only nod.

"I thought so. But you did get the phylactery, didn't you?"

"Yeah, I did. I just didn't hit her hard enough. I thought I had her. The place was rumbling. She was breaking apart. I was afraid the whole world was going to collapse on us, so I—"

"You don't have to recount it to me. I can see it pains you."

"Thank you." Angela sighed. "Say, if you knew it was me out there, why didn't you come out?"

Toth shrugged. "I figured with all that had changed so suddenly, the souls disappearing one by one, you needed time to think about things. I was getting impatient, though."

"You, running out of patience? Gods, that truly would have been the pinnacle of this Armageddon."

It felt good to make him chuckle, but it did not last long enough. The moment passed, and he grew glum and serious again. "That's not the only thing I'm running out of. Starvation is a real concern. Not just in the future, but right now. Kur has some supplies stored, but not enough to eat like humans for very long."

"Well, is there anything I can do to help?" Angela asked. "I have my soul. I could go and get something from Earth."

Toth's emerald eyes stared her down as he considered something. Certainly, he knew the end was coming. He asked, "Are you sure you don't have anything better to do, Angela?"

"I mean, probably. But nothing's coming to me. I think..." She sighed. "I think I just need to stay busy right now. Keep my head on straight as the clock runs down."

Toth nodded, motioned with his hand toward the road. "Come with me, then. You look like you could use a walk."

They passed between homes and stepped onto the dirt road. People were out and about, running from house to house, bartering for whatever scraps they could find. The market square was equally rambunctious. People shouted at one another, trying to offload whatever they had. None of the talk was positive. Anyone who had food would surely keep it for themselves. For the city to start off with empty stomachs all at once, with so little food around, it was a wonder there was not more chaos. When the poor and hungry felt that they had exhausted all chances of feeding themselves, robbery and worse would begin to plague Kur.

They passed a mob, noticed a group of children hiding underneath a wooden stall. They were trying to chip away at the polished stone floor with hand tools in order to dig up the ornamental gems beneath the clear sealant. To Angela's surprise, Toth did not try to stop them from defacing the square. Others would pick up on their example soon.

The stairway up to the Kissum was packed. To make it through the double doors and into the foyer, they had to follow behind a line of people hungry for more than just food. They shouted and raved, wanted to know what the Council was going to do for them. Only Melech and Daevas appeared to be present for the people, and gauging by the mood in the air, their answers were far from satisfactory. Toth and Angela took care to slip through the crowds and into the archway to the left unnoticed.

They were the only ones walking that hallway, and they garnered the gaze of commoners before they made it to the next open chamber. Toth explained that he wasn't exactly welcome to peruse the Kissum's stores, so they doubled down and picked up their pace rather than inviting any more trouble than they had to.

As they passed the doorway to the central dome, Angela paused. Through it, she spotted a councilman, black robes and red cord, on his knees in the center of the room, his back to her. Sobbing echoed against the cold stone. The hood rested on his shoulders, revealing stylized black hair. It was Kanu. Without a second thought, she crept closer, stepped into the domed chamber despite Toth's whispered warnings.

The councilman was looking up at the mural on the ceiling, something Angela had never noticed before. The level of artistry and detail suggested it was greatly impor-tant. Near the base of the dome, a frothing ocean of rock and waves held snakes, fish, and stranger things yet. People and creatures roamed on forested, grassy, and rocky land above that, but what was most curious was the highest and center point of the vault. Overcasting a single star was the black shadow of what could be none other than a Nephilim.

It had talons and scales. Its neck was too long to be that of a bird.

Kanu crumpled over, whimpered to himself or in prayers to his goddess. It seemed that even he, the great medium between Dalkhu and Ti'amat, was soulless. She thought she heard him mutter something about the Mother but could not be certain.

Angela could not hold her tongue. She said, "I tried to warn you, Kanu. She doesn't care about the Dalkhu."

Tears still fresh on his cheek, he choked on words and could not speak. He had put all his faith in his goddess and was now reaping the fields he sowed, coming to terms with the fact that she had cut him off from her, taken their souls, and left his people to starve—if she didn't destroy Kur first.

Angela left Kanu sniveling, hoping that he would rise out of his despair soon enough to be of some use to his people. She did not want to rub it in his face maliciously. What was done was done. If he did come around soon, she vowed not to let her old grudges get in the way.

Toth led her deep below the Kissum, where the smell of mold and stagnant air was constant. The storeroom they entered was not far from the crypts. Glow stones on the walls revealed the room to be of moderate size, with crates, bins, and baskets of beans, rice, salt, wheat flour, and corn-meal. But it appeared that someone else knew about the storeroom.

Hovering over an open barrel of salted pork, Toth said, "The Council has a special board responsible for keeping a rotating stock of emergency food every few months. It seems a group of enlisted have taken their first pick already." He sighed. "We'll need to take count and come up with a plan for rationing it. Some to be handed out immediately, and some to be held on to."

Angela nodded. "Sounds good. I know a pair of idle hands that can help."

SAROSHA GROANED, HEAVED THE WOODEN BOX UP ONTO A barrel, and dropped it with a thunk. "Why are we wasting our time with this?" the Grand asked. She began to pry the boards and nails loose with a metal bar. "There are better things you should be doing than this."

"Like what?" Angela asked. She counted the bags of rice inside the crate and tallied the number in a journal. Luckily for them, all of the grain foods were divided into smaller five-pound packages that would be easier to distribute to the commoners. "The Dalkhu are people, too. And they need to eat. We need to set them up as best we can, and as far as I'm aware, this is all we can do."

"I know the Dalkhu are people," Sarosha said, rolling her eyes. "But we have bigger things to worry about. Won't it just be a matter of time before Ti'amat swallows this world, too?"

Toth stopped what he was doing, stared at them, perhaps expecting them to explain.

Angela gave Sarosha a dirty look. They didn't need to give the Dalkhu a reason to panic more than they already were. "Don't even start," she said. "I don't want to hear how you think it's pointless. It just might be, but if something happens to me, these Dalkhu are going to be the only people to keep you company for the rest of your life unless you figure out how to use that soul and get out of here."

"She has a soul, too?" Toth interjected. "I thought Ti'amat took them all."

Angela shook her head. "All but the ones I had. I gave

Sarosha Udug's so I could get her out of Dingir. It's been…
a trying time for her."

"Oh," Toth said. He turned back to his work, but the
look on his face betrayed his contemplation on the matter.
He worked faster now, like he was excited or hopeful.

Sarosha moved on to the next crate and cracked it open.
Ground flour was in this one. As Angela counted, the
Grand's tone shifted. Quietly, she asked, "Do you think
something's going to happen to you?"

That was a question Angela was not ready to consider
too deeply. She shrugged and wrote down the number of
bags.

Sarosha grew sour at Angela's lack of a response. She
said, "So you want me to act like Dingir didn't happen? Lie
about how we brought this onto everyone?"

Angela dropped her hands to her side, frustrated that the
topic would not seem to go away. "Yes, Sarosha. For now,
we keep it to ourselves. Everything. Including the phylactery. It was the only chance we had, and using it wasn't a
mistake."

Sarosha put her hands on her hips. "Are you saying we
don't have a chance now?"

"No."

The color washed out of Sarosha. Her expressions
changed from anger to sorrow. "You're lying. We're
doomed, aren't we? You don't know how you're going to
kill Ti'amat, and you're too afraid to say it."

"No, I do, but—"

Sarosha threw up her hands. "But what? What are we
doing here, Angela? If you know what to do, why aren't we
doing it? Is feeding the starving going to kill Ti'amat
somehow?"

Angela clenched her teeth, swallowed hard. She did not

want to think about what it might take to kill the goddess. This woman was going to cause a blood vessel to pop if she kept prying. "Why are you trying to stir up trouble?" Angela asked, shifting the conversation. "You're so miserable you can't help but make everyone else feel miserable?"

Sarosha dropped her crate. It landed on her foot, smashing it and worsening her mood. Her eyes were wet as she pointed and said, "Ja'noel is *dead*. Along with everything else I worked my entire life for. The least you could do is pretend you know what you're doing. Give the rest of us a little hope."

"I have given this fight everything I have, Sarosha. Forgive my meandering with pointless tasks. I have to kill every last part of her or she'll just come back in another era or another world. So when you ask me if I have hope I'll be able to kill her, what I really want to say is not enough to go around. Not enough to pick you up. I don't know what to say to make you feel better. If you want to give up and walk away, fine. But you have to realize that what I'm fighting is bigger than anything you have faced, so cut me some slack."

Sarosha raked her face with her fingers and said, "My skin is *on fire*. Every second of every minute. It hurts so bad even my body is convinced I should be dead by now. Take it back. Do *something*. Anything at all but this."

Angela huffed, irate. "I've lived like that for weeks. Get used to it. Every time I think of Antum's name, I feel her stir inside me, like this soul isn't even mine anymore. It's its own thing, and it wants to come out. If you—"

Sarosha put her hand on her gun. She was trembling as her lips curled. Taken by surprise, Angela cut herself off, tried to read the Grand's expression for hostility but found no signs of it. Sarosha sighed, tears forming. Between choked breaths, she said, "You don't understand. I need this right now. I need your reassurance because I don't think I can go on like this. All you're letting me believe is that I have to wait to die, and I'm not going to do that. I won't be in agony for the rest of my life."

A chill ran down Angela's spine as she realized that yet another life was in her hands. She did not want the responsibility. No more. Her gaze bounced between Sarosha's watering eyes and the gun in her hand. Sarosha would end her life before the worlds came crashing down on her. As much as Angela believed that an individual had a right to choose when they passed on, she did not want the weight of this burden. She did not want to lie, to give false hope, but she refused to allow this to haunt her.

Angela took a deep breath as she formed the words, then said, "These times are hard. They are testing in more ways than any of us can handle alone. I'm sorry you're going through this, and I'm sorry about Ja'noel." She sighed. "You're right. There are better things we could be doing, but you don't see the big picture. When Ti'amat is ready and we collide, there's a pretty big chance I won't come back. You'll be alone unless you find friendship in the Dalkhu. I'm trying to give you all the best start you can have without me, because after this, it's up to you to find something to fight for, whether that's yourself or the Dalkhu." She motioned to Toth, who watched and listened from across the room. "They aren't as bad as Dingir makes them out to be. Trust me. Relax. You'll find a reason to live."

For a time, the only sound was the slow breathing of heavy thought. No one moved. No one spoke. Sarosha sniffled, wiped under her eyes, took a deep breath, and, most importantly, removed the hand from her gun.

Toth stepped out from behind his mound of sorted crates and said, "Bickering isn't going to solve any of these problems." He turned to Angela, emerald eyes gazing into hers. "Give me the soul. My body is attuned to a Dalkhu's soul. It won't hurt me."

Angela hadn't thought of that. It made sense. Toth would be able to use the soul to teleport, lightening the workload, and defend the Dalkhu if an emergency required it. He was also probably the only Dalkhu whose judgment she trusted with that kind of an advantage. She nodded, motioned for him to come closer. To Sarosha, she half smiled and said, "Looks like you've got your wish."

The Grand smiled, too, the tears on her cheeks shifting from ones of terror to ones of joy. Placing a hand on both of them, Angela closed her eyes. Using her own body as a conduit to transfer the soul was easier than she had anticipated. It took less than a minute. Upon completion, she turned her attention inward and checked on the soul inside her. Antum was still at peace for the time being, but the black spot in the center had grown in size, lending her vitality and power. It had been a slow, subtle change that skulked up on her. She chalked up the ease of giving Toth the soul to her connection with Ti'amat.

Toth shuddered, then relaxed on the floor with his back on the wall. He closed his eyes, intent on mastering that soul's characteristics immediately, while Sarosha seemed more relieved than Angela had hoped she would. She traced the skin on her arms and face with her fingers, taking joy in her new flameless existence. The sensation of touch on normal skin. Angela just hoped the Grand could find a new purpose to live for.

CHAPTER FOURTEEN

The cavern breeze carried up the scents of cooking food. Already, the commoners had been given their shares and were hastily throwing meals together, some of which would be the first meals they had ever eaten. There were smells of baking bread, a common dish of rice seasoned with cumin and garlic mixed with strips of salted pork from Earth, and simmering mushroom stews. From above, she watched the people gather around the cookfires and rejoice. They would survive another day.

But what about the day after that? Angela wondered.

She did not have all the answers she needed and had come up to sit upon a buttress of the Kissum to think. She would have been alone if not for the grotesque she sat beside: a small winged creature of carved stone that looked like a cross between a Nephilim and a man. Meditation was something she had not practiced just for the sake of it in some time. It did little to help her plan but did help calm her nerves and put her at peace with the uncertainty that would soon be upon her. When she first became an Etlu, she had sworn vows and sincerely meant them, but at the time, she did not know that the oaths she was taking would eventually evolve beyond just Dingir and apply to every world.

In the green glow of the moss above, the grotesque had no condolences to offer, for what lay in her mind was her burden alone. Like it or not, she knew it. Time was running out, and she meant to leave Kur rather than bring the fight here.

A blast of air and the crack of thunder caught her off guard, nearly sent her tumbling off the edge, but Toth was there to grab hold of her.

"You scared the crap out of me," Angela cursed.

"I hope not literally," he said, sitting down beside her. "I have no intention of changing your diaper."

"Well, you'd better get your practice in now. You're going to outlive all those people down there. Gonna have a lot of asses to wipe in the days to come."

Toth chuckled. "That's why we have the children. Cheap labor."

Angela laughed, but the feeling was gone quickly, and she sighed. "Do you think they will remember us? The things we did and the way it happened? Or will time just convolute everything? Our names and sacrifices? I know what I have to do, but I don't know if I have the strength to do it."

He shrugged. "The flow of time erodes all. We'd be foolish to believe we'll be remembered forever, but it's the hope and dream of everyone to have an impact beyond their own life. Take solace, Angela. You will not be forgotten so long as the Dalkhu live."

She had always respected Toth, especially for his insight. He saw things clearly, things she thought she kept well hidden, and it was hard to believe that when they first met, she had nearly drowned him in the veils. How time had changed their relationship. Angela pushed herself to her feet, careful not to lose her balance, and said, "I mean to do one last thing for the Dalkhu. I may not be able to bring the weylines here and give everyone souls, but I can still manipulate the veils."

Toth rose beside her. "What do you mean to do?"

She held out a hand. "I'll show you."

He took it, and they disappeared from the Kissum's roof. Down below, in the market square, Angela sat and crossed her legs among the murmurs of people and the sizzling of cookfires. For a while, she scanned world after world, searching for some distant corner and safe haven. With her connection to Ti'amat as strong as it was, she could peer into each and examine them for signs of life, discern geography, and learn a great deal about the worlds without setting foot on them.

A long time passed before she chose. With her mind and the power that she had been lent, Angela hooked a world like a fish and pulled. The fabric of veils shifted, and other worlds gave way and cleared a path until the world she wanted rested right next to Kur. Ti'amat would know that she had moved a dimension, but Angela wondered if she could sense what would come next.

With hardened concentration, she ground and dug at the veils until they were weak and pliable, then turned them outward and connected the veils of the two worlds. A shimmer of floating light became rays of sunshine. The cold air of the cavern washed away in a warm, humid breeze, and the gasps of commoners were replaced by the chirping of birds. There in front of them all, a doorway to another world, full of lush forest and the smell of recent rain, awaited the Dalkhu.

Once every strand of fabric had been sewn together and the pathway through the veils was stable, Angela rose and said, "There was a place beneath Dingir where the veils that separated it from Ti'amat's world were nonexistent. Udug, Kushiel, and I fell through it. I've been thinking about it, and I think this may be a safe way for soulless people to bypass punching through the veils entirely."

Toth held out his hand as he moved to the portal, stuck it through without harm. When he turned back to face her, there were tears in his eyes. "Is it Earth?" he asked.

Angela shook her head. "I think it's best not to have all remaining people in the same world, to keep them spaced out. Have the Dalkhu gather their things. There's plenty to eat there, I believe, but be cautious. I don't know what dangers may be in store, but you have a new home."

ONE BY ONE, THE PEOPLE OF KUR WALKED THROUGH. MOST had never seen a jungle or a sun, and they stepped through with eager and anxious expressions. A few thanked Angela and tried to kiss her hands and feet, but she would have none of that. Some Dalkhu had been too stubborn to leave the homes of their ancestors. Those people who could not be convinced were given ample food to last them a week or more. Angela ensured that they understood their decision: when their food ran out, they would be on their own. Toth blamed their false sense of security on their full bellies.

At the end of the line came Sarosha and the ex-councilman, packs on their backs and walking sticks in their hands. Toth bore an amulet on his chest, its copper chain and green emerald shining in the portal's light. Angela pointed at it. "You got it back."

Toth smiled devilishly. He tapped his chest and said, "Kanu and Melech could not say no to the only man with a soul to use it. I'll do my best to keep them in line."

Angela nodded, then turned to Sarosha. There was a glow to her expression. "You look better."

The Grand gave a half smile that seemed genuine. "I feel better."

"I'm counting on you two to lead these people. It won't ever be the same again. They'll need your guidance and experience."

Sarosha seemed taken by surprise. She must not have expected to be given a task like that, but she did not argue. It would take her a while to get fully back on her feet. Toth, on the other hand, had already been a greater leader than his Council. He would fall into the role naturally. Together, Angela hoped that they would remind one another that there was a reason to fight on.

"You're not going to come with?" Sarosha asked.

"No. I'm going to close the door behind you, but I'll be there soon enough."

Toth eyed her suspiciously and did not seem to believe her, but Angela said no more. They hugged and did not say goodbye.

CHAPTER FIFTEEN

The haggard gentleman placed his mug on the wooden countertop and swore. "I warrant I'll be a fish soon if this rain doesn't let up. Water in the crawlspace, mud in my boots. I can't get the wagon three feet down the road before it gets stuck and the horse breaks its ankle."

"How long has it been raining?" Angela asked.

The man beside her looked good for his age; he was thin and athletic, but his hands trembled like leaves in a windstorm when he held up his fingers. "Three whole days and not one minute of sun. I can't help but wonder if we've pissed the gods off. It isn't even the rainy season yet, and it's getting worse. Started off as a drizzle, now this." He motioned to the tavern's open doorway.

Tarsus had always been a wet, muddy city, but now it had become a swamp. The rain pooled in the street and had nowhere to go but into homes and businesses. Even now, the wooden floor near the door was waterlogged.

She took a long draw of her drink, set it back down, and swallowed. "Nah," she said. "I don't think the gods that do this kind of thing give a rat's ass about us. Sometimes we're tools, but we're of no value beyond our use. Do you get mad at an ant?"

The old man bit his lip, considering it as he looked her up and down. He seemed intrigued. "You never said where you're from. Too smart to be a fisherman's wife, and that's all the women we seem to have around here. Tell me, where are you from?"

Angela shrugged. "Around."

"Then what business brings you to Tarsus? You can't even be my daughter's age. I'd guess by your armor you're a battle-maiden or mercenary from the north. Am I right?"

"Nope. I'm just burning time, and I'm certain I'm older than your daughter. I just needed a drink."

"All right, maiden," the older man said with a tone of suspicion. "Whatever you're here for, it must be pretty lucrative. I see you playing with that pouch on your belt. Looks heavy."

Angela paused. She had not realized what her hand was doing and let it go, drained the last of her mug, and scooted it across the countertop. When the barkeep came in to refill it, she waved him off and placed what silver she had next to it. Both men's eyes grew wide at the small pile.

"Well, you must be a sword for hire," the fellow patron said. "That'll pay the 'tender's rent for a month."

"I'm just feeling generous. Thanks." She rose, walked out into the rain without another word.

The storm really was fierce. It was coming down in buckets. The wind howled as the sky roared and flashed. It didn't take but ten seconds of trying to navigate the driest parts of the road before she was soaked and muddy, but the storm did provide a certain kind of cover. She stepped into the alleyway, out of sight, and vanished between worlds.

What should I do now? Angela wondered. *We're so close to the end that I don't have time for much.*

There was no way to be certain exactly how much time had passed. All Angela knew was that a full day was upon her and she'd barely napped for more than a few hours. A small part of her mind nagged at her for not resting enough, but she couldn't have slept more even if she had wanted to. Her nerves were on fire, and the growing black connection to Ti'amat in her soul had begun to stabilize, a sign that it was nearly time.

A thought came to her. She veered off, slipped through a layer of veil, and arrived in a valley surrounded by mountains. Even in the dark of the storm, it felt a little like going home. Not as much as the feeling Dingir gave her, yet undeniably, this place was a treasure in her heart. It symbolized friendships she once could have never imagined forming and the years she had spent free of rules and the chain of command. She did a lot of good those years. And stepped on a lot of toes, too, she supposed.

At the edge of the sinkhole, looking down, she sighed. The flooding was worse than she had thought. All the runoff from the mountains seemed to pool here. The murky water nearly filled the hole in the ground and hid the garden and the trees below in its depths. Somewhere down there were Neti's ashes and Teshub's remains. She kneeled in the mud and said a few words.

Lightning arced throughout the sky, rippling across the clouds like a wave. But that was not going to be the only storm that night. A woman's voice spoke into her mind.

It is time.

A blast of thunder too close and flash-less to be lightning shook the air behind her. With a deep breath, Angela rose to her feet and turned. There she was: Ti'amat, in the flesh. Instead of her usual choice of dresses, the goddess was adorned in armor the rain could not seem to touch. Spiked pauldrons, sleek and black with a shine of oil, rested on her shoulders. The breastplate on her torso and the cuisses on her thighs matched the dark shade, while the clothes underneath were red. So too were the beaded armlets on her biceps. Otherwise, the goddess had chosen to keep her arms bare. She would strike quickly and unhindered, and nothing would have fit the Mother of Serpents better.

"You haven't let her out yet," Ti'amat said. She sounded somewhat disappointed. "You do remember that this is between her and me, don't you, Angela?"

Angela shook her head. "You made this fight between me and you long ago."

The goddess's laugh was throaty and genuine. "I suppose in one way of thinking, yes, I did. But I still don't want to fight you. Tell you what, you let Antum out and I will make you a promise. If she kills this body, I'll go away into my own corner of existence and wallow in my own pity, never again to *terrorize* and *dominate*, as you say."

"Like you would really do that."

Ti'amat clacked her tongue and wagged a finger. "Have I not kept my promises thus far? After all we've been through, Angela, I would think you'd be a bit more trusting of me. Am I not honest?"

"You are," Angela admitted. "But I will not call upon Antum. Your death will be by my hands alone." Reaching over her shoulder, she unsheathed what was left of Teshub's sword and held it before her. The blade, only a foot and a half in length now, was slightly bent and ended abruptly where the rest of it had shattered.

"You're going to kill me with that?"

Angela took a deep breath, focused energy from her soul, and restored the blade's missing edge in shimmering bluish light. Rain sizzled and boiled against it. "This will be the end of you. For all you've threatened and all you've destroyed. I would not want this to be remembered any way but this: a god slain by the hands of a mortal being."

She charged, crossed the distance, and lunged with the tip of her sword. The goddess spun on her feet. The first strike did not connect. Neither did the second or third when she brought the blade back up in frenzied slashes. Ti'amat bubbled in giddy laughter as disappointment washed over Angela.

She wondered why she felt that way. *Did I really think it would be over that easily? I feel that I have to catch her off guard and do her in quickly, or else I'll tire before her. I don't trust her to keep her word when she says that she's splitting her power with me.*

"Come on, Angela. You're a goddess, too, now. If you hold yourself back, you'll never win."

Angela tightened the grip on her sword, jabbed with it and her mind. A semicircle of fire erupted behind the goddess as she stepped back to avoid the light of her blade. Ti'amat stumbled, fell to her knees just before the wall of fire. With a groan, Angela brought her weapon down upon her head, but at the last moment, a shield of black and purple glyphs appeared above the goddess's outstretched palm and knocked the blade to the side.

A force sent Angela skidding across the ground, leaving trenches in the mud. Ti'amat rose and extinguished the fires. "Better!" she said. "But you have so much more available to you. Here, let me show you."

The ground beneath Angela's feet rumbled before lurching up at her. A pillar of earth erupted, pushed her upward several feet before she jumped off. As quickly as the spire had appeared, it was reduced to a mound of mud. A second came at her, then a third. This was not what it appeared to be, Angela realized. These were not the product of holes between worlds. These pillars were reconfigured earth, formed and shaped by Ti'amat's will.

"Now let's try something a bit sharper. Move quickly, Angela."

A spear of violet crystal stabbed upward from the soft ground. The first one had moved so fast it caught her by surprise and nicked her fingers. A dozen more came at her, one after the other, sending her spinning and moving as she tried to predict where the next one would strike. A sick feeling bubbled in her gut. Ti'amat was playing with her. She could end it whenever she pleased.

How do I know the limits of the powers available to me if I've never tried to use them to that extent before?

All Angela knew was that she had to turn the tide. She could not hope to avoid everything that Ti'amat threw at her. There one second, behind the goddess the next, Angela swung with all her might. A strange resistance pushed against her blade the closer it came to her armor. The light reached the sheen black surface but only left behind a wire-thin scratch when it should have opened the goddess's back. A subtle protectionary spell enchanting the armor must have lessened her blow.

Ti'amat did not seem mad; she jaunted forward and put a wall of translucent crystal between them, then smiled. "Sneaky, sneaky," she said. "But I've yet to be impressed. Why don't you let Antum show you how it's done? Let her out. I will see her. You can't hide who you are for long. My punishments will only grow harsher and harsher."

Angela growled. Frustration was mounting. The single

blow she could manage did not seem to hinder the goddess in the slightest. "I'm me. No one else. Antum might have had this soul before me, and she might live on through it, but I'm the one who dictates what happens here."

She tugged at the soul inside her and through her strength of mind withdrew more of its energy. Antum stirred, hesitated, but did not deny her. Golden light formed in her hand. With a flash, she hurled an orb of light through the air like an arrow. It punched through the crystal wall, clipped Ti'amat's pauldron above her shoulder. The goddess was gone and missing before Angela could see the extent of the damage, a sign the hit had been more effective than the last.

A boom rippled through the air from somewhere behind her. Angela spun, scanned the mountainside until she saw Ti'amat looming atop the edge of a cliff. Her voice, unnaturally loud, carried across the valley. She was pissed. "You know, one time I brought all the matter of a world together and compressed it until it was the size of a pea, then removed my hand and watched it explode in a fraction of a second. In another world I replaced the water with magma and killed it slowly with thirst and ash. This world, I will drown."

The skies rumbled and rolled as clouds began to multiply and grow. The heavens opened, spewing a rainstorm like Angela had never seen before. She could barely look up without it flooding her eyes. It seemed to be only a few droplets short of standing in a waterfall. Before she knew it, the water was above her ankles and rising.

I can't fight in this, she thought. *I have to find a way to get this water off me.*

As far as she knew, there were two ways she could go about it. The first method was more in line with using the energy to heat the air around her and boil it off before it touched her. That would be faster but taxing on her mind.

The second method was a spell: splintering her soul and implanting her armor with energy and the will to fulfill the desired effect, like Ti'amat's own armor seemed to do. Then again, Ti'amat had destroyed a lot of Nephilim when she had discovered that her children were chipping pieces off their own souls to create spells some thousands of years ago. She had considered it a perversion of her gift.

How the goddess was able to stay dry must have been some unknown third option, or perhaps when one's soul was anchored to crystal and not limited by the extension of a fleshy mind, the possibilities expanded.

The goddess stretched out her hand before her. The skin of her palm faded to black as energy pooled there. She was growing impatient, and Angela knew she would not have enough time to try to enchant her clothes.

A beam as black as a starless night raced toward Angela. Without thinking, she dove for it, crashed into the murky water that was deep enough to cover her head. Soaking wet, she rose to her feet and shed her belt that held her batteries and Anunnaki weapons. They would be of no use now.

Quickly, she projected her energy outward, letting it blossom around her like a bubble. The air vibrated with life and an electric-like tingling sensation as the temperature rose. Directing the energy into the shape of a hollow sphere around her allowed the inner area to remain a bit cooler and evaporate the water as it fell. The soul inside her gave its energy easily, even now, as she withheld the strain of her sword and the atmosphere around her.

Angela warped and, to Ti'amat's surprise, appeared on the cliffside above, then dropped and swung at her wildly.

The goddess jerked back and leapt, bounding up the cliff-side to the next bluff with inhuman ease. Angela wondered if her body could do the same, given enough energy. Something about tapping into Antum a bit more seemed to give her increased speed. Her muscles reacted faster to her mind's commands, and she felt stronger than she had moments ago. While her sword had missed, she could see that her bolt of energy had hit Ti'amat's shoulder squarely enough to punch through her black pauldron and scar the flesh red beneath. But unfortunately, she had not done suffi-cient damage to inhibit the mobility of her arm.

Ti'amat spoke from above. "The fury in your eyes is chilling, Angela. You are the incarnation of fire, aren't you? You burn so hot you disintegrate those around you and bring ruin down upon yourself. You are fire's soul embod-ied. Wrath and rage. You should lend that anger to Antum before it's too late."

"Enough!" Angela screamed. "Stop running and die!" Raising a hand, she clenched a fist before the sky and brought it down. The atmosphere did her bidding; clouds birthed arcing lightning, slammed down, and smote the mountainside in tumbling earth and smoldering trees. A cacophony of pounding thunder rolled on, lightning striking the area until a bolt crashed into the goddess. She fell to her knees, howling and smoking, but did not stay crippled for long.

She returned the trick, called upon the electric charge in the sky, and cast lightning down upon Angela. Luckily, she had seen it coming and ripped a tear in the veil to sprout a ceiling of stone above her. The shelter proved useful and less taxing than trying to shield herself by negating or deflecting the blow.

The water had risen faster than she had expected and

was already pooling only a dozen feet beneath the cliff she stood on. Angela would have to move higher, but soon they would not have enough mountain for the two of them. Briefly, she grieved for all the people in Tarsus who must have been drowning, then vanished between the worlds.

She appeared thirty feet from Ti'amat. Faintly, the goddess's black armor had lost its sheen, its magical protection, and was warped from the scorching heat of lightning. Ti'amat, slumping from exhaustion, said, "That will not happen again."

Angela smiled and dared to hope that this was not impossible.

That only seemed to piss Ti'amat off even more. She could not stand the trouble that Angela was giving her. She said, "If you will not let Antum free, then try and withstand this by yourself!"

Holding her palms up and stretching out her fingers, she gritted her teeth, and the mountain jumped. Came back down and sent Angela's skin crawling from the vertigo. The crash that followed rumbled the Earth and threw her stumbling down the bluff until her hands found anchor on a shrub. She thought the worst was over as she climbed to her feet and scanned the peaks for Ti'amat, but beyond the battered firs and flooding rock, a tsunami was rolling closer along the water's surface.

The goddess had taken flight, floating well above the danger. There was no hope in the world that Angela could withstand the crushing force of a wave like that, and soon there would be no ground left to stand on. Her only hope was to follow suit and direct herself upward. Despite the energy it took and how long it had been since she last pulled off the feat on her mind, the Earth dropped away beneath her as she rose. It was not as hard to levitate as it had been before.

Frothing in anger, the sea was a monster of its own. The high wave came crashing into the mountains, bucked upward in a spray a hundred feet high before swallowing the rocky peaks entirely.

Searing pain struck her shoulder. Angela bellowed, began to fall. Before she could make sense of what had happened, the goddess was bearing down toward her, a dozen black spears of ultraviolet light following close behind. She stopped and motioned with her wrists, and the weapons heeded. They arced outward, then dove in like striking birds. They would not miss.

A voice warned her that she could not stand firm against them by her strength alone. If it was Antum who spoke to her or her own consciousness, Angela was not sure. She groaned and clutched her wound, dug deep, and delved her mind into the rot in her soul in hopes that the Mother of Serpents could not defeat her own power.

A rippling orb of light-bending black appeared around her. She could feel when the spears sank in, so she gave the protective shell even more concentration and effort until the pressure faded. It seemed to have worked, but Antum stirred angrily in her as though she did not approve of Angela using Ti'amat's energy. She was aware of what was happening around her.

Angela swallowed, pushed the goddess down, and dispersed the shield.

Ti'amat hovered above, glaring down with her arms folded across her stomach. Her hair was soaked, the black makeup around her eyes smearing down her cheeks. She said, "You're running out of chances. My patience wears thin. Let Antum step into your skin so that I may have a word with my sister. I know you can hear me in there, Antum. Do not make me crush you both."

If there was ever a time to strike, it was now. It would be her answer. She pulled all she could from her soul. Shrouding herself in yellow and orange, Angela flew like a bolt from a crossbow. She became a star, a meteor, streaking through the night with a tail of flame stretching out behind her. In the blink of an eye, she was there, slamming her weight and all the strength she could muster into Ti'amat's side. The goddess screamed, went spiraling off until she crashed into the water below.

It took everything Angela had left to keep herself in the air. Slowly, her soul replenished its vigor as she watched the waves below. Ti'amat did not come back up. At least not quickly. It appeared that the goddess hadn't had time to prepare any defenses before Angela struck, so she had taken the impact wholly and unnegated. While it likely hadn't killed her, it would do a number on any fleshly thing.

Angela cursed under her breath. What came broiling out of the water was not what had gone in. Nostrils flared above maws lined with hooked teeth. Two… Three… Five scaled heads rose from the abyss on necks that never seemed to end. Before her eyes, the Nephilim grew shoulders as wide as buildings, breaking the foaming surface of the water. Wings that could darken any sky unfurled, creating sizable waves on their own. And as deep as those turbulent waters were, Angela had no doubt that Ti'amat was standing on the ground below like it was no more than a wading pool.

"You made a promise!" Angela screamed over the storm. "I destroy your flesh and you leave these worlds alone."

Each of Ti'amat's heads seemed to grumble in laughter. She spoke into her mind. *It is the same flesh and truer to my own form.* The goddess began to come closer, her rolling shoulders taking long seconds to move her massive limbs. *It has been too long since I have walked in scales and swam in the salt. Too long since the worlds knew my terror and strength, Antum.*

Rage and desperation took over. "How many times do I have to tell you that I'm not Antum? This is unfair! I will not give you the satisfaction of revenge for something I did not do."

All your life you've fought to be a part of something bigger than yourself, and now you say it is not fair? You are correct. It rarely is fair. Where was fairness the day I was attacked? Where was justice when Mulki was torn apart by a thousand frenzied, selfish gods? I was justice. But it is the natural order of things. Chaos reforms and renews in a cycle of destruction and restoration. Like the sea, chaos cannot be calmed. It is always churning, plotting, smothering, liberating, and I am chaos. Its hand. Its flesh.

Lightning crackled in the clouds, flashes of light illuminating the violet and black scales on the goddess. Taller than any mountain, she loomed, her size oppressive. Every head shifted side to side like a snake's as she waited for a response, but Angela could not rebut. Could not say anything she had not said before.

Ti'amat was right. She was chaos, and it wasn't fair. It never had been.

I extend a final offer to you, the goddess rumbled. *Lay Antum down before me. Give me consumption of her soul and your body as tribute, and I will give you all you long for. Your friends, your loved ones, alive and safe. I will call upon their souls and birth them in new flesh. There will be peace in a world just for your people. Think of those you have lost and what I could do for them.*

Angela could not hide it from herself any longer; she could not win this by her strength alone. Her mind returned to the day she'd been accepted as an Etlu. The time she'd spent training, and the vows she had sworn before the Grands and years later before Teshub. She sincerely meant all the promises she had made, but there was no way to truly prepare for losing everything. It just became a solemn acknowledgment. A sorrow. A regret. A fear. It was not how she wanted it, but that was how it had been for a long time. She knew what she had to do and would pay the price for it.

When she relaxed her mental guard, the invisible field of projected energy that kept her dry dissipated. The rain was pinpricks of ice needles on her skin, the wind furious. A tiny twinkle in her soul reached for her mind, making contact and forming a bridge between her and the goddess inside her. A feminine voice said, *Do not settle for anything less than your own path.*

As quickly as it had come, Antum's presence faded, retreated back into the soul. The goddess seemed to understand the delicate balance they were constrained by. The moment she came out was the moment that Ti'amat would get what she wanted, and it would be over. Antum was there on the edge of her consciousness, aware of what was happening, but did not take control as Angela moved toward the monster before her.

Ti'amat understood, a throaty purr of delight emanating from her throat as she opened her maw. Between the rows of jagged teeth and over the forked tongue, hot breath with the stench of fish washed over Angela. The esophagus widened large enough for her passage, and once she was inside the slickened fleshy walls, the gnawing began. Not on her body, but on her soul. Inside the body of the Mother of Serpents, all things of flesh and spirit were food.

A tear. A sob. It was not how she wanted to go, but she had said the vows and sincerely meant them. She had made promises to more than just herself. As disgusting as it was to destroy one evil and birth another, there was no other option. Angela removed the seed from the pouch at her waist and held it in her hand, considered its rock-like hardness and the thing it would become. *Life's water nourishes the seed*, she remembered. And Antum agreed.

Angela gritted her teeth. Reeled back her arm. Cursed the goddess's name. And she plunged the seed into the soft flesh of her throat, pushed and twisted until the thing was buried. Ti'amat thrashed, her roar pounding against Angela's eardrums. Blood flowed, wetting the stone and painting her hands and armor in red. The pinkish walls flexed and shook violently, bashed against her, but Angela could not feel it. She couldn't feel anything. The seed began to writhe, to burrow deeper. Before long, Angela began to feel it. The gnawing on her soul softened as Ti'amat focused on the thing that now traveled through her muscle and ate away at her essence and everything connected to the goddess. Angela did not have much time.

She turned inward and drew upon herself and the black rot inside her. As Ti'amat fought the seed of Gasgon, was distracted by it, Angela pulled more power than she had ever before, reached across skies and veils, and began her work. Ti'amat seemed to sense the power Angela was stealing from her, knew what she was doing with it and tried to fight it, but the leech proved to be the bigger concern. Soon it would consume everything: the weylines and their souls.

When Angela was done, she tried to free herself from Ti'amat's black hook, to break her connection with her and free herself from the goddess's doom, but Ti'amat writhed, rumbled, and would not let her go. They would share the same fate. As she struggled, the mucus- and blood-coated walls beneath her feet shimmered in a red glow that became a billow of curling fire racing upward.

Angela closed her eyes before the flames overtook her. Pain ate away at every fiber of her skin. She had to turn inward. Block it out and let numbness take her as strength was sapped from her.

And she was standing on a white marble floor. A small room with a domed ceiling of glimmering blue, two chiseled pillars, a small altar with a single potted daisy. Beyond it was a woman on a red seat, a crown of leaves in her auburn hair. She smiled with vibrant white teeth, and Angela knew who the woman was. She was inside her own soul.

"You did well," Antum said. Her voice was soft and warm, befitting her small frame and dainty features.

Angela sighed. She did not know what to say. This did not feel like a victory. It felt like a compromise.

The goddess seemed to sense what was on her mind. "Gasgon is not eternal, Angela. He will fade, and all the energy he has consumed will disperse. It will be as it was so long ago when the All-Father gave himself up so his children could be born. One ocean of energy, untainted and pure. It will bubble and gather again, reform into new souls, and life will begin anew."

A tear streaked down her cheek. "But I want to be *there*. To see it happen. To be in *her* shoes and see him again.

Where's my reward for all I've suffered? I'm not ready for this to be the end."

Antum spoke softly. "We seldom are. But all things live and die. The worlds will be destroyed and reborn again and again. Sometimes one world will encroach on another in acts of violence, and some will go on undisturbed for all eternity, but all are subject to life and death. It is the cycle of chaos. None can break it. Life can only flourish upon that which has been destroyed. The ashes of flame and fire nourish new seeds, Angela. This is not the end. It only marks the beginning of a new rebirth."

Antum smiled weakly. "You have shown your strength and proven that character of soul does not define who you are. It is the choices and sacrifices you make. So come," she said, patting the seat next to her. "Rest."

And Angela did. She took her seat next to Antum and sobbed, recited the words she hoped she would never have to say. The words she had remembered since the day she became an Etlu.

"I hereby fulfill my vow. I've fought in days of strength and times of weakness. I lay down my mistakes and regrets before my brothers and fulfill my final calling. My life for those I cherish. I do not go silently. I am not forgotten."

Antum smiled, leaned in to embrace her. In moments, everything faded.

EPILOGUE

Toth parted the tent's flap and stepped out into the rays of light beaming through the trees. Sucking in air, he savored the smell of cooking fish. Stopped to apprec_ate the warm breeze blowing his hair. It was humid. Birds sang and insects hummed by. Before him lay the center of their camp. Dozens of men and women hurried about their simplified lives with smiles. Children played games in the trees and plucked sweet orange fruit from the grove in the distance while the adults kneaded dough, constructed stick and thatch shacks for those who did not yet have shelter, and gathered around cookfires and told jokes. It had been a long time since Toth had heard a laugh.

The crunching sound of sticks underfoot came from his left. He turned. Sarosha nodded, acknowledging him without a word. The Grand had been doing better these past few days. For long periods of time, her gaze occasionally lingered out at the horizon and at the stars above through the rustling leaves, but she was coming around. Toth suspected the orphan who had taken a child's interest in her was a big reason she had made as much progress as she had. The others, though, when they came, seemed to unsettle her again. She did not know what to think.

"Morning," Toth said. "Did you sleep all right?"

Sarosha scratched her forearms, kept her gaze low. Recent developments were still bothering her. "Okay. I just... I just don't understand."

"Neither do I, but I try not to question it."

Sarosha furrowed her brow. "Am I just supposed to accept it like it never happened? Be okay that... whatever this is isn't the same?"

Toth put a hand on her shoulder, urged her deeper into the camp. "You think too much. Take it one day at a time."

The Grand sighed and departed, leaving him to walk the forest paths by himself. He did not mind. She needed time to heal, and there were other people he wanted to see. Weaving through the trees, he tried to think of any other time he felt so revivified and eager to take on the challenges ahead. Even his first trip to Earth did not compare to the hope, the will, and the energy to fight on in this place. And he was not the only one that felt that way. The Dalkhu would never be the same again.

Toth veered off the path and down to the shoreline, where crystal waters shimmered in the morning sunlight and the fat Anunnaki sat on a rock with a pole in his hand. He hadn't been such a large man when Toth knew him, which made it curiously funny why he was as such now.

There I go again, Toth thought. *Thinking about it too much.* He told himself to accept things at face value. At their simplest. It did not need to be more complicated than that. Almost everyone had a hard time trying to wrap their minds around it, but they would get there together.

Up the bank, he found the tent he was looking for and

rounded it to the front. A thin young man, half bent over and dressed in casual, baggy clothes, was peering through the flap and had not noticed Toth's approach. He tapped him on the shoulder, sending him reeling around in a fit of panic that only lasted until he saw that it was Toth who had touched him. The boy got his nerves back under control with a deep breath.

"What are you doing, Neti?" Toth asked.

Sweat beaded on his tan forehead, clumped his black hair. He whispered, "Hey. Just hold on. Watch." He held up a finger and had a pillow in his other hand.

The boy seemed mischievous, but Toth could not detect the slightest trace of ill will. He straightened. Neti was up to something, and he had every intention to watch. "Be nice," Toth said.

Neti's impish grin stretched from ear to ear. He nodded, crept through the tent's entrance, and waited only a half a second for Toth to follow after him. He shouted, "Welcome to the bastion of pain," then slammed his pillow down on a lump of blankets on the floor.

There were curses and grunts galore from that pile of rags before a pillow came flying up in retaliation and caught Neti on the head, knocking him on his ass. Angela sat upright, blonde hair full of tangles and knots. Green eyes ablaze and hell-bent on revenge. Strength. Passion. There was rage, but also goodwill and the desire to empathize and bring justice. Toth could see it in her. That was Angela. She was there before him, just as real as the one who had led them to that world.

Angela swung again, missed. "You turd," she said. "Quit moving so I can beat you."

Neti bellowed and jolted upright, made his way for the door behind Toth, only to be tripped on a well-timed foot placement on Angela's part. He hit the floor with a grunt, swung once more to try and land the last blow, then rushed out of the tent, laughing the whole way.

"Good luck sleeping tonight, Neti," Angela growled.

The boy could not help but peek his head back inside one last time. "What are you going to do? Wipe your boogers on me?"

"You child!" She threw the pillow and missed again.

He laughed and took off running as Angela began to rub her eyes, moaning. For a moment, there was an awkward feeling bubbling in Toth's gut. He wasn't sure if he should leave her for a while so she could get up on her own terms, but she stretched her arms above her head, yawned the sleep away, and rose to her feet. There was enough headroom for her, but Toth had to stoop. He said, "Sorry about that. If I had known that was what he was up to, I would have—"

"Don't worry about it. He's always pulled stunts like that. I like to think he'll learn some—" Angela cut herself off. Put a hand over her lips and contemplated something. "Is it weird that I talk like this? Like I've always known him like a brother?"

Toth shrugged. "It seems to be typical with all of you. I actually was hoping the rest did you some good. I thought maybe we could talk more about what you remember."

Angela scratched the back of her head, began trying to work out the tangles in her hair with her fingers. "See, it's not really like that. I'm her, but I'm not. I can't remember everything she went through unless I have some other memory to go off of. It's like a great long chain is wrapped around in a big knot in my head, and I have to take it one link at a time as things come up. There are pieces of things that stick out more than others, but it's mostly intuition or ingrained feelings."

"What do you mean by that?" Toth asked.

"Well, like when I look at Neti, I think I feel what she did about him. Like I'm an extension of her, or a copy based on her memories and emotions. The others must be the same, too. All images of their old selves, but different and independent at the same time."

"And Michael? What do you feel about him?"

Angela tried to hide the smile, the blush on her cheeks. "I... Well, I like him." She shrugged. "His presence is comforting."

Toth nodded, ran his fingers over the scruff on his face. If there was to ever be a sign that Angela had completed her mission, this had to be it. A final send-off. A last motion of goodwill and goodbye to those she was leaving behind.

"Did we really come out of the ground?" Angela asked.

"Sort of. A bit more like bubbling and building upward than crawling out of the dirt, but in general, yes."

She bit her lip. "I don't know what else you want to know from me, where you want me to fit into all of this. Is there a spell you could whip up to help me remember more?"

He shook his head. "I don't know if any spell would work on anyone who is soulless. And besides, as quickly as you came around, I would not be surprised if there are limits to your memories. I doubt you could recall everything of hers. The details of those memories may simply not be there."

"So what are we going to do now?"

"For now, we rest and rebuild." Toth reached into a fold in his robe and retrieved a small notebook. Holding it out, he said, "I only ask that as things come to you, you write them down. Angela has given us a fresh start here. We can shape it like the Earth we knew, or something else entirely different. And while things may go out of our control at times, we will do our best to carry on toward a brighter future."

Angela took the notebook. Smiled. "There is one thing I remember. I think it was important."

"What is it?"

She took his hand and pulled him through the doorway and back out into the sunlit forest. Toth had no choice but to be dragged along; her grip was iron and she did not answer his questions. When she found Michael leaning against the bark of a tree, it became clear. She paused, seemed to examine his hazel eyes, his long, athletic form and curly brown hair, then took a deep breath.

Angela approached him and said, "She wanted to be here more than anything."

A LETTER FROM THE AUTHOR

That's a wrap! Five years of dreaming comes to an end in three books, 275,000 words, and about 1,000 pages in print. Man, what a trip. I'm glad you're here and thankful for everyone who has helped out on it. I hope this crazy mash-up of mythological and modern genre fiction ideas satiated your hunger for an original fantasy led by a strong female character. I've wanted to get to this point for so long: my first trilogy complete.

What's the next story? It's already begun. By the time you're reading or listening to this, I've already begun releasing a LitRPG story on the web that I drafted two years ago. It's titled *Dex Warrior*, book one in a series called *Libertas Online*. Inspired by stories and worlds like *Sword Art Online*, this one lets me capitalize on my long-time geekiness. To show it all.

As of the time of this writing, you can find it on popular free-to-read websites like Royal Road, Wattpad, and Inkitt, although I plan on eventually releasing it in e-book format when it's ready.

For now, I'll be further developing that world and story,

fixing mistakes, and growing in a new direction as I let an idea for a different fantasy series mature a bit longer. If you'd like to help me out and get a peek into my creative ways, you can join me and the team on Patreon. I'm so thankful for every single member I have there. Livestreams, polls, and advanced copies are just a few of the perks. I hope to see you there, but if I don't, I'd just be happy knowing you've enjoyed Angela's story.

Onward!

Austen Rodgers

contact@austenrodgers.com

Become a patron

ABOUT THE AUTHOR

Austen Rodgers is a science fiction and fantasy author living his best (and only) life in Waterloo, Iowa. He spends his free time painting miniatures for D&D and other role-playing games and dabbles with fantasy maps of his own creation.

Wait, you're still reading? Cool. This is the paragraph where I tell you about all of my accomplishments. But, to be honest, I hate talking about myself. So, here's the quick and dirty version: In 2015 I published my apocalyptic novel *The Book of a Few*, and earned my BFA in Creative Writing from Full Sail University in 2016. In 2019 I launched the first two books in my fantasy series, *The Flame Seer* and *The Fire's Scar*, and completed the trilogy with *The Fire's Soul* in 2020.

Slaying warlocks isn't an issue, either.

Find my other works on my website:
www.austenrodgers.com